POSEIDON'S TRIDENT

WAR ON THE GODS
BOOK TWO

POSEIDON'S
TRIDENT

For Tory
You were by my side throughout the entire process of writing this book—encouraging me, offering new ideas, and reading the manuscript before anyone else. I'm so grateful for you and everything you do.

For my parents
Not only have you guys been endlessly supportive of me in pursuing my writing career, but you've also helped me in going back to college. You're the best parents in the world.

And for my readers
Every follow, like, share, comment, and review you guys have given me has been pivotal in pushing me forward with this story, and with my writing in general. I consider myself blessed to have your support; I hope to continue to earn it.

P.S.
I wanted to add a special dedication to Zach (Giggles). I may not have used all the information you gave me about forges, but the conversation we had about them pushed me past one of the biggest blocks I had while writing those scenes!

CHAPTER ONE

FATE

Sixteen years before the Storm . . .

January 5th, 2002

Anteros shook as he flew toward the Olympian palace, forcing himself to flap his feathered, butterfly-shaped wings despite the fact they wore heavy on his back from all the travel. He'd used most of his strength flying to Earth and back, so much he wasn't sure he'd ever recover. But he'd done it for the love of his immortal life; he'd done it for Calliope.

Around him, stars of the galaxy twinkled, while colorful planets orbited a blazing sun. The sight was truly one to behold, and usually such a thing would entrance Anteros and leave him giddy. However, today was different.

He gasped for air. Sweat seeped from his skin, the electrifying power which usually coursed through his body nearly frozen in his veins. He balled his fists, rage boiling in his gut. *This is all Zeus's doing*, he thought. *Zeus is the reason she's gone.*

He approached the giant mass of floating rock which now held the pearlescent palace, the same giant mass of floating rock that had held it ever since the gods had been deemed no more than myth by humanity many years ago. For thousands of years they had resided on Earth, but ever since humanity had ceased to worship the gods, most of them were no longer powerful enough to reside permanently on the planet without using an unbelievable amount of strength. So, they took a place among the stars, watching mortals from afar.

The gods, since then, had desperately hoped those on Earth would at least remember their names and all the grand things they'd done in their lives; it was the only way they wouldn't fade away entirely.

Anteros landed at the front of the palace, on the glistening steps leading toward the entryway doors. He wiped the sweat from his brow, then charged inside, ready to confront Zeus about the atrocious crime the King of the Gods had committed.

Anteros's bare feet pounded against the golden tiled floor. A brilliant view of the galaxy beyond was visible through the wide, arched windows, the halls lined with marble statues of deities. Music and chatter resounded from one of the main dining halls. *They must be having a party*, he thought, and raced toward the sounds.

He reached the brightly lit dining hall, full of gods

and goddesses talking, dancing, and feasting. Tall columns supported the chamber's curved marble ceiling, which featured carvings of the Olympians and other powerful deities performing insurmountable tasks: Artemis as she placed Orion's body among the stars, Dionysus as he fought Death to free his mother from the Underworld, Athena as she sent a storm to destroy a fleet of ships in the Trojan War, Zeus as he cast Typhon, the Father of Monsters, into Tartarus.

Anteros glanced around the room, trying to spot Zeus, but the giant bearded god was nowhere to be seen. Anteros spun on his heel and darted toward Zeus's bedchamber. *I have to find him.*

After almost twenty minutes of running through the palace halls, Anteros reached Zeus's bedchamber door. The barrier towered above Anteros, intricate designs of storm clouds, lightning bolts, and peacock feathers carved into the wood. Anteros didn't bother to knock, and instead shoved the door open and stumbled into the room.

The room was grand, almost as large as one of the palace's dining halls, although it was meant for only two: Zeus and his wife, Hera. The columns, walls, and ceiling were white with golden swirls winding up from the floor, the canopied bed and the rest of the room's furniture a deep royal blue.

At the far end of the room, wide steps led into a glowing, bubbling pool of water. There, a woman with long brown hair bathed, stroking what looked like a miniature

Earth, which floated just above the center of the pool.

The woman turned toward Anteros and gave him a piercing glare. "What do you think you're doing in here?"

Anteros fell on one knee. "Hera, Queen of the Gods. I mean you no disrespect." He cleared his throat. "I'm searching for Zeus. It's urgent. I must speak with him immediately."

Hera rolled her eyes. "Zeus is in the garden, no doubt spending his night with some common whore." Her lips curled into a sinister smile, and she turned her attention back to the miniature Earth. "Whoever she is will regret it tomorrow."

Anteros stood and gave Hera a bow, then dashed out of the bedchamber, leapt into the air, and flew toward the back of the palace—in the direction of the Garden of Olympus.

Once Anteros entered the garden, which alone was half the palace's size, he flew overhead, keeping his eyes peeled for Zeus and whatever mistress the god was surely involved with this time. Cypress trees lined the garden's edge, while the rest of the space was a maze of bushes, statues, flowers, and fountains trickling into ponds.

Within minutes he spotted a thicket of rustling bushes. Kissing sounds and girlish giggles wafted up from it. He swooped down toward the thicket, and just as his feet met the dewy grass, Zeus and a pretty Dryad emerged from the bushes. Their cheeks were flushed, their robes and hair a mess. When they saw Anteros, Zeus narrowed his eyes, and the nymph gasped.

Zeus rested a hand on her shoulder. "Run along, my dear. I think Anteros and I have something to discuss privately." She nodded and scurried away.

Once the nymph was out of sight, Anteros squared his shoulders and looked up at Zeus. The King of the Gods was over a foot taller than Anteros, his power greater than any other god's, but still Anteros did not cower. "I know the truth about Calliope," Anteros said. "I know it in full."

They began to circle each other. "Do you, now?" Zeus sneered. "Because if you did, I think you'd be far too terrified to tell me so. Unless you're even more of a fool than I thought."

Anteros let out a cold laugh. "I may be a fool, but at least I have a sense of justice. At least I am no coward." He paused and softened his tone. "The Fates told me that if I faced you now, if I found you as soon as I reached home, you'd agree to reunite me with her. Please, bring her back. Do as I say, and I won't tell anyone what you did to her. Not a single deity. We can leave all of this in the past."

Zeus chortled. "And if I don't agree to your deal?"

"Then I will tell everyone." Anteros flew up, up, up, reaching for the bow and quiver of arrows slung over his back. "And they'll know what kind of king you really are."

"Fine," Zeus replied, jumping into the air. "You shall have your wish. I will reunite you with your beloved Calliope."

Zeus seized Anteros by the throat with one hand and

clutched both his wrists with the other. Anteros cried out, trying to wriggle free, but Zeus tightened his grip.

Sparks of electricity crackled from Zeus's palms. The energy lengthened and twisted, forming a hissing, arcing rope of lightning which bound itself around Anteros's neck and arms, scorching his skin. Smoke curled off his body, his wings folding in on themselves.

Zeus pulled his hands away and glided across the garden, dragging Anteros along by the lightning-rope. "Visiting the Fates and telling me about it was an unwise decision. But you will not have to regret the decision for long."

Anteros opened his mouth to speak, but what came out was barely more than a whisper, his throat raw. "I would do it a million times over if it meant seeing Calliope again." Zeus chuckled at the reply.

Within minutes they reached the end of the garden farthest from the palace, at the edge of the jagged rock which the gods resided on. Zeus pushed past the last of the trees. Earth, far below them, became visible.

"For the last several thousand years," Zeus began, "I believed the only way a god could die was if no one believed in him and he slowly faded away. But now I know that to be false." He grabbed a fistful of Anteros's hair and dangled him over the edge. "Tell Calliope I say hello."

Anteros tried to scream, but he felt as if flames were crawling up his esophagus, and the sound caught in his throat. He tried to flap his wings, tried to break free of the lightning-rope, but he couldn't move.

Zeus reared his arm back and hurled Anteros off the edge of the rock. Anteros shot toward Earth, and the endless galaxy around him morphed into a blur of black-and-white lines.

Only a few seconds passed, and then Anteros slammed through what felt like a stone wall, his bones cracking. Once he'd made it through the first, he shot through a second, then a third, then a fourth, electrifying agony racking his body.

He rammed through a fifth wall, and finally the pain grew unbearable. The sensation was that of dozens of scorpions stinging his skin and, at the same time, of a parasite devouring his insides. It felt as if the molecules making him *him* were being torn apart.

Anteros collided with a sixth wall, but this time he couldn't break through to the other side. For a moment he wished he were dead, that he could die.

And then he did.

* ⁓ * ⁓ * ⁓

Now ...

Summer, Year 500 AS

The lair of the Fates—the deities who controlled every living being's thread of life—was exactly as Zoey remem-

bered it. It was deep inside a cave farther east from where they'd come, with millions of blue strings woven through the vine-and-flower walls and over the grassy floor. In the center of the cavern, candles were scattered around a wooden spinning wheel.

Once the group landed on the floor of the cavern, Zoey and Diana jumped off the back of the pegasus they rode most frequently, Aladdin, while Andy and Darko climbed off Ajax, and Kali hopped off Luna. Zoey glanced around the lair. The three goddesses were nowhere in sight.

Diana tucked her shoulder-length blonde hair behind her ears. "Hello? Please, show yourselves. We need your help again."

Kali sauntered to Diana's side. "Took us long enough to find this place, and now they aren't even home? I hope we didn't come here for nothing." Sarcasm laced her tone, a smirk on her lips.

Diana shot Kali a glare. "First of all, three days is *not* a very long time. And second, the last two times I've visited the Fates, it took them a little bit before they appeared. Be patient."

Kali crossed her arms. "No need to get defensive, Princess."

Diana jabbed a finger at Kali and opened her mouth to come back with what Zoey assumed was a snarky reply, but before she could say a word, Zoey rolled her eyes and stepped between them, throwing her hands in the air.

Well, at least, she threw *one* hand in the air. During

their quest to Hades less than a week ago, her right hand had been cut off and sucked into the pit of Tartarus in a nasty fight against the Queen of the Underworld, Persephone. Diana had healed Zoey's injury as best she could, but Zoey was left with a fleshy stump stopping at her wrist.

Zoey had practically forgotten she was even missing a hand, and she could still feel it there. She could rotate it at the wrist and wiggle its fingers in her mind's eye. But then she'd look down, and with a pang of grief she'd realize it was gone.

It frustrated her and took a lot of effort to get used to; everything was backward now, and she felt ridiculously uncoordinated. Her right hand had been her dominant hand, and anytime she went to grab *anything*, she still reached with it. But when she went to clasp her fingers around an object, she only grabbed air, and then she'd remember to use her left hand instead.

Zoey lowered her arms, glancing between Diana and Kali. "Would you two cut it out already, or at least save it for later? I'm sure the Fates don't care to hear your bickering."

Familiar cackles echoed through the air, and smoke curled up from the grass. "On the contrary," began the disembodied voice of an elderly woman. "The petty squabbles of mortals are most entertaining." The smoke grew until it formed three bony old ladies clothed in long robes, with pupil-less eyes glowing blue. Zoey recognized the old ladies right away. They were the Fates: Lachesis, Clotho, and Atropos.

Lachesis stepped forward. "Welcome. We knew you'd be visiting us again soon."

"What is it that brings you back?" Atropos asked, grinning.

Andy adjusted his glasses. "We figured you already knew. You know, since you 'see everything' and all."

"Oh, we do," Clotho said. "Atropos likes to tease."

Lachesis cleared her throat. "Daughter of Apollo, I will get right to answering your question. I am sorry, but we cannot offer an alternative way into Poseidon's palace for you. You're going to have to use the route you know."

Diana knows a way into Poseidon's palace already? Zoey thought, confused. Diana had said she didn't know how to get there, and that was why they were visiting the Fates now. They needed the Fates' help to reach Poseidon. Stealing his Trident was the next step in their quest.

"Diana, I thought you had no idea how to get there," Andy said. "What do they mean, the route you know?"

Diana ignored his inquiry, staring hard at the Fates. "No, there has to be another way to get in. Going through the Labyrinth—I mean, even if we found our way to the center, we'd still have to kill the Minotaur, and even if we managed to slay him, we still couldn't use the palace's portal."

"Wait, what?" Zoey asked. "There's a portal into Poseidon's palace?"

"You mentioned the Labyrinth," Andy added. "And the Minotaur. I think I read something about that on the internet once. Isn't the Minotaur a monster with the head of a bull and the body of a man? The one who lived in a labyrinth-maze-thing and ate a bunch of kids every once in a while, like a sort of sacrificial ritual?"

Diana nodded. "Yes. In the old days, the ruler of Crete—his name was King Minos—well, his only son had been killed in Athens during the Athenian Games because the Athenians were jealous of the prince's skill. King Minos was ready to go to war with Athens because of this, and to appease the king, the Athenians agreed to send seven boys and seven girls to the Labyrinth once a year, as food for the Minotaur, and as justice for the prince's death."

"Uh, okay, more important than the history surrounding this monster," Zoey interrupted. "You mentioned a portal in the Labyrinth. The *palace's* portal. I'm assuming you meant Poseidon's palace. Why don't we just use that?"

"Because going there is out of the question," Diana answered. "It's in the center of the most complicated labyrinth ever constructed—well, at least, it's in the center of a *replica* of the most complicated labyrinth ever constructed. The portal is also guarded by the Minotaur, which happens to be one of the most feared monsters from the old days. He's said to live in the center of the Labyrinth now, right alongside the portal. Plus, even if we made it through the Labyrinth and killed the Minotaur, it would be for nothing. No one except Poseidon himself can use the portal. If another god tries to use it, they're ejected from it, and if a demigod or regular mortal tries to use it, they're killed."

"What's the point of this portal, anyway?" Andy asked.

"Poseidon uses it any time he needs to make a trip to the mainland as ordered by Zeus," Diana replied. "The Labyrinth is located just beneath his city, so it makes for easy travel. He could use his god-powers to manifest into his city, but without a mortal making a sacrifice to him for the specific purpose of traveling that many thousands of miles, it would more than likely tire him out. It takes a lot of power. Sure, he'd regenerate and be fine, but gods are lazy. They don't like to use much energy if they don't have to. So, as an alternative to making the trip every time Zeus needs Poseidon to do something, Zeus permitted him to construct the portal. Since Poseidon had a part in creating the Minotaur, he decided to rebuild the Labyrinth, and to put the monster back inside it to guard a portal that demigods and men can't even use."

"Hey, that's right," Darko said, snapping his fingers. "Poseidon *did* contribute to creating the Minotaur. It makes sense he'd use that monster to guard his portal. When King Minos was fighting with his brothers over who would rule Crete, Minos prayed to Poseidon to give them a sign that Minos was meant to rule, since no one would question the authority of a god on that sort of stuff. Poseidon sent him a snow-white bull as a sign, and in return for being made king, Minos was supposed to sacrifice the bull to Poseidon.

But by the time Minos became king, he'd grown attached to the bull, and tried to trick Poseidon by sacrificing a different one and hoping the god wouldn't notice.

"Obviously Minos didn't trick Poseidon at all, and Poseidon was super mad. He asked Eros, Aphrodite's son and a god of love, to make Minos's wife, Pasiphae, fall in love with the snow-white bull. Eros did as Poseidon asked, and . . . well, the result of Pasiphae and the bull's, uh, 'union' was the Minotaur."

Zoey grimaced. "Ew."

"That's disgusting," Andy said.

"I'm telling you guys right now we can't risk entering the Labyrinth," Diana said. "There has to be another way to reach the palace. A ship, a spell, a . . ." She trailed off, her gaze falling to the ground.

Atropos frowned and pulled out a pair of scissors from her robes. "You dare question the advice of the Fates?" She kneeled and began cutting the threads closest to her. "Do you forget we are all-powerful, all-knowing?"

"Are you saying we won't die if we use the portal?" Diana said. "Or that you guys are willing to counteract the enchantment on it so we can pass through?"

Atropos laughed. "If you used the portal today, you would die. As for counteracting the enchantment, we will not. We have already helped you enough, Daughter of Apollo. We told you where the Chosen Two of the Prophecy were to be resurrected, explained how the gods can be defeated, and cast a protection spell on you and your allies against the gods. Granted, it cannot stop them from finding you if they physically stumble upon you, but even so you can ask no more from us. We have done all the universe permits."

Zoey creased her brow. "If we can't go through the portal, and if you guys won't cast a counter-spell on it, is there someone else who could?"

Clotho stepped forward. "There may be one."

Atropos shot Clotho a glare. "They must struggle if they are to rise victorious. Tell them no more."

"They have already struggled much, and they will only continue to, even if I give them his name," Clotho replied.

"Who is it?" Zoey asked.

Clotho grinned. "Prometheus."

"The *Titan*?" Darko blurted.

Atropos stood. "Indeed, the Titan."

Andy scratched his head. "Where can we find him?"

Lachesis gestured at Diana with one hand. "The Daughter of Apollo knows the answer to that question."

"Look at that, Princess," Kali said with a wink, nudging Diana with her elbow. "You're about to make yourself useful." Diana's eyebrow twitched.

Zoey bowed to the Fates, and the rest of the group followed her lead. "Thank you so much for your help," she said. "I'm not sure how we can ever repay you."

"Free humanity from the gods," Lachesis replied. "Give them back free will. That is all we have ever wanted from you. But like we said before, other than what we have already done, we can help you no more. You must earn your victory."

"They'll earn it for sure," Darko said. "They slayed Medusa all by themselves. They can do anything." Zoey smiled, and Andy's gaze softened. He put an arm around Darko's shoulders and gave the satyr a squeeze.

Atropos shooed them away with her hands. "Now go, be off with you."

Diana stepped forward, hands clasped behind her back. "Before we go, I had one last question for you, and before you shut me down, it doesn't have anything to do with helping us. It's more of a personal thing. My father—well, he hasn't spoken to us since he healed me when Karter struck me with lightning. I'm afraid for his safety. Can—can you tell me what happened to him? Please?"

Clotho and Lachesis shared a glance, their eyes sad. "Apollo was discovered helping you, child," Clotho said. "Within a day, Zeus and Poseidon annihilated his city. The citizens who refused to flee, remaining loyal to him, were killed in the destruction."

Zoey gasped and shared a look of shock with the rest of the group at this news, while Diana trembled, looking to the ground. "All those people . . . my father's followers . . ." She wrung her hands. "What about my father, then? What has Zeus done with him?"

"There are several potential outcomes for Apollo's current predicament," Lachesis replied. "But for now, Zeus holds him hostage on New Mount Olympus and plans to imprison him in Tartarus for his treachery."

A sense of dread flooded Zoey's senses, and everyone in the Fates' lair went silent. Apollo had helped them so much with their quest, all to ensure his daughter's safety. Now, because of it, his city was gone and he'd be thrown into the most horrible eternal prison Zoey could ever imagine existed: the blue flames of Tartarus.

A lump formed in Zoey's throat. She swallowed it down and dabbed the tears from her eyes before they could trickle down her cheeks.

Kali stepped beside Diana and rested a hand on the Daughter of Apollo's back. The demigod hung her head. "I had a feeling that was what happened to him, but I needed to ask. Thank you for telling me."

With that the group mounted their pegasi, not uttering a word, then flew through and out of the cave into the afternoon sunlight peeking between the hundreds of green pine trees towering above them.

They landed and climbed off the pegasi. Zoey cleared her throat. "So, once we find Prometheus, he'll be able to help us through the portal into Poseidon's palace. Hopefully. But where is he?"

"About a day's travel from Aphrodite City," Diana said, her expression tight, as though she were trying to hold back a dozen emotions at once. Zoey couldn't blame her, considering what the Fates had just told them about her father. "It'll take us about a week to reach him. He's imprisoned there, and every day the Caucasian Eagle comes and eats his liver. He's immortal, obviously, so it just regenerates every night."

"Hey, I think I've heard about him before," Andy said. "Isn't the liver thing a punishment from Zeus for giving man fire, or something like that?"

Diana nodded. "Yes. Prometheus made humans, and he gave them some abilities like the gods', although they're much weaker and, of course, mortal. Eventually Prometheus taught humans how to make fire, which was Zeus's last straw. Zeus imprisoned Prometheus in the Caucasus Mountains with chains forged by Hephaestus, the Blacksmith of the Gods, and sent the Caucasian Eagle to eat his liver every day."

"But didn't someone set him free?" Andy asked. "I thought someone helped him out eventually."

"He was set free by Heracles," Diana replied. "Heracles slayed the Caucasian Eagle, and with their combined strength, the two broke Prometheus's chains. He was free for a while, but nearly a century ago, he fell in love with a regular mortal woman who lived in one of the cities and they had a baby together. Zeus believed it was Prometheus's way of trying to bring the 'Dreaded Prophecy' to fruition, considering Prometheus's track record of helping out humanity, and then decided to re-imprison him the way he had been in the old days to avoid any sort of rebellion."

"Makes sense," Andy remarked. "And freeing him from the eagle should be easy, considering we have Medusa's head."

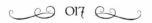

"Exactly," Diana said. "With Medusa's head, we can just turn the bird to stone. It'll be easy and over in no time. Now, let's gather some provisions and head his way."

Working together, the group stuffed their bags full of roots and berries. The pegasi grazed while they worked, and once they were satisfied with their findings, they mounted the pegasi and began their journey east.

They soared over the forest and ruins of old cities for a long while, and as the day passed, the air grew slightly colder. While they flew, the wind bit Zoey's cheeks, sending her into fits of shivers.

When the sun began to set, Diana instructed the group to land and make camp. Just as they were about to descend toward the forest floor, the guttural roar of a bloodthirsty beast sounded from behind.

Zoey's pulse quickened. She whipped her head around to see a flying lioness the size of a truck, leathery dragon wings attached to the creature's back. From the monster's neck arose a second head, but rather than another lioness's, this one was that of a goat's with razor-sharp teeth. Where her tail should have been, a writhing, hissing serpent stemmed from her rear. She roared again, and a line of orange fire blazed from her throat, searing the brisk evening air.

"What the hell is that thing?" Andy cried.

Diana shot the monster a glance. "It's the Chimera. Darko, use Medusa's head. Turn her to stone."

Darko fumbled to retrieve the sweatshirt holding Medusa's head from his pack. As the group sped on, he tipped every which way, coming dangerously close to tumbling off Ajax and into the forest below. Just as he got the bundle out of his bag with shaking hands, the Chimera roared again. Her fiery breath grazed Ajax's back legs.

The pegasus whinnied, halting midair. He kicked and thrashed, his hair sizzling, and Andy and Darko clung to him. The pegasus bucked them again, and the bundle slipped from Darko's grasp.

Zoey's stomach clenched as Medusa's head plummeted toward the trees below.

CHAPTER TWO

NYMPHS

Andy gripped Ajax's neck for dear life, the sulfurous scent of scorched hair filling the air. As the pegasus writhed in the air, Andy knew just one slip of his hands could mean being thrown off.

Darko's arms were wrapped tight around Andy's waist. "Medusa's head—I dropped it!"

"Are you freaking kidding me?" Andy replied through clenched teeth. Without Medusa's head, it was going to be a billion times harder to kill the monster, and they needed to do it before this thing charred them to a crisp.

Ajax bucked again, and Andy did his best to hold on and stroke the pegasus's mane. "Shhhhh, it's okay, Ajax," Andy said. "You're okay."

Diana directed Aladdin to face the Chimera and blasted several golden spheres of light at her. The monster dodged the attacks. Kali veered Luna toward her, spear in hand. Staying by the monster's side, Kali sank the spear into her goat head's throat. Kali wrenched the weapon in her neck, blood gushing from the wound. The lion head roared in distress as the goat head fell limp.

Kali tugged the spear back, and just as Luna began to flap away from the Chimera, she swung her lion head toward them and roared again. A stream of fire shot for them.

"Kali!" Andy cried.

Kali yelped as the flames hit Luna's wing and crept up her arm. Diana tried to direct Aladdin toward Kali and Luna, but the Chimera blocked them with another wave of fire.

Luna whinnied, flapping her unharmed wing frantically as smoke curled around them, but it was no use. Kali and her pegasus tumbled out of the pink sky and disappeared into the trees. Diana and Zoey screamed for them.

Crap, crap, CRAP! Andy thought, beads of sweat forming on his forehead, his muscles tense. "Hold on, Darko," he said, and the satyr tightened his grip on Andy.

Andy squeezed his hands over Ajax's mane, directed the panicked pegasus toward where Kali and Luna had fallen, and kicked his feet against the creature's sides. Ajax heeded the command and they swooped down.

Within moments they reached the forest floor. Andy leapt off Ajax's back, Darko close behind. They stumbled through the trees.

"Kali! Luna! Where are you?" Andy called, heart hammering against his rib cage. No one answered.

Soon they reached the edge of a stream, and Andy's

stomach twisted at what he saw. Kali lay beside the stream, facedown in the dirt, her body turned so that her burnt arm rested in the water. Beside Kali, Luna lay on her side, her injured wing mangled beneath her body. The pack of supplies Luna usually carried on her back had fallen a few yards away from her, the Helm of Darkness and the group's bundle of spears scattered about the ground.

Andy and Darko rushed toward them. Were Kali and the pegasus just injured, or had the fall killed them?

Andy grabbed Kali by the shoulders and turned her onto her back. She was unconscious, covered in grime and bruises, but her chest rose and fell with shallow breaths. Andy let out a sigh of relief.

"Is she okay?" Darko asked.

"She's alive at least," Andy replied. "I don't know about 'okay' though."

"Diana can heal her, I hope," Darko said, glancing back to where they'd come from. "Why don't you stay with her? I have to go find Medusa's head."

Before the satyr could begin his search, a roar sounded from above. Flames rained down, setting several trees ablaze and broiling the air. The Chimera landed before them. She slammed her paws against the forest floor. The impact shook the earth.

Diana and Zoey landed Aladdin alongside Andy and Darko and jumped off his back. The Chimera bounded toward the group.

"How're we supposed to kill that thing?" Darko cried.

The monster stopped and roared, sending a stream of fire toward the group. Diana conjured two spheres of light and chucked them at the attack.

"It'd have been simple if we could turn her to stone," Diana said as the fire and light clashed. Upon collision they burst, sending sparks whizzing over the group's heads. "But that's not possible at the moment, so we'll have to do something else."

Andy darted toward the group's scattered supplies and seized two spears. "Was there someone who killed her in the old days?"

The Chimera roared again and again, sending blasts of fire toward the group. Diana blocked the attacks with spheres of light. "Bellerophon did, yes," she answered in a panicked tone. "He used his spear to lodge a block of lead in her throat. When she breathed fire, the lead melted, and she suffocated. But we don't have any lead!"

"We'll have to find some other way, then," Andy said, tossing a spear in Zoey's direction and keeping the other for himself. She threw her handless arm in the air, trying to catch the spear, but it only clattered to the ground. She pressed her lips into a thin line and kneeled to pick it up awkwardly with her left hand.

Darko readied his bow and arrow while Diana continued blocking the Chimera's attacks. "A little help, please?" she shouted. "Sometime today would be nice!"

Zoey ran toward the Chimera, ducking to avoid the flying sparks, weapon in hand. She brought her spear down on the Chimera's leg, but the attack barely scraped through the monster's fur. The monster snarled and swatted Zoey with a paw. Zoey yelped, tumbling backward, and crashed into a tree.

Andy's nostrils flared. No one, *no one* messed with his friends and got away with it.

From the corner of his eye, Andy could see the Helm of Darkness as it lay on the forest floor, its metal gleaming in the light of the flames. *Let's see how you fare against us when I'm using that*, he thought.

While Diana threw spheres of light and Darko shot arrow after arrow at the Chimera, Andy grabbed the Helm and pulled it over his head. Chills charged through his body. He held up a hand and wiggled his fingers, but they couldn't be seen. He was cloaked with complete invisibility.

He advanced toward the Chimera, steering clear of the projectiles, then leapt onto her neck and pulled himself up by the thick, matted fur. The monster craned her head back and snapped her jaws. Her serpent tail hovered over Andy, hissing all the while. He raised the spear above his head, then, with all his strength, plunged the weapon down the monster's throat.

The Chimera shrieked and coughed, orange flames shooting from her mouth like cannonballs. Fire licked Andy's hands. They erupted with searing pain, and he cried out, throwing himself off the monster's neck.

Andy rolled across the forest floor. His head slammed

against the ground. The Helm came loose and tumbled to the side. The Chimera turned toward him, rage in her eyes, the spear still caught in her throat.

Diana darted in front of Andy as if to guard him from the monster and conjured a final sphere of light. She brought her hand back and chucked the sphere at the Chimera. The attack hit the creature in the side with such intense force she went flying backward into a cluster of trees. As she hit them, several branches impaled her body. Gooey moss-green fluid seeped from her wounds. She roared, her serpent tail shuddering, until finally she fell limp.

Diana gasped for breath and ran to Kali's side. She lit her hands with golden light and placed them on Kali's shoulders. The light expanded through Diana's and Kali's bodies like water after being dumped onto a hardwood floor, and they began to glow.

Andy pulled himself up and trudged toward them, trembling. Small tendrils of smoke curled off his bloodied and blistered hands. The acrid fumes coming from them smelled of charcoal and copper, and they stung as if someone had peeled off his skin and poured salt in the wounds.

Zoey climbed to her feet and made her way toward Andy. When she spotted his injuries, her eyes went wide. "Andy, your hands . . ."

He groaned, wanting to scream out a volley of curses from the pain, but held them back and gritted his teeth. "I'll be okay."

"I'll heal you after these two," Diana said, sweat already

running down her face. She let her light fade, and Kali opened her eyes.

Kali glanced around, her expression morphing from confusion to shock as she spotted Luna beside her. "Oh no." She rested a hand on the pegasus's stomach. "Diana? Can you—"

"Uh, guys?" Zoey interrupted. "I think we need to go."

Andy looked over his shoulder, and his breath caught in his throat. The Chimera's attacks had started several trees on fire during their fight. Now the crackling flames slithered along the grass and onto other trees, spreading like a viral infection through the forest around them.

Ajax and Aladdin galloped toward Diana and Kali, whinnying frantically as though saying, *If we don't get going, we'll be barbecued!*

"Zoey, Darko, and Kali, grab the Helm and as much of our supplies as you can," Diana said, rushing toward the unconscious pegasus. She lit her hands. "I have to heal these guys, and then we need to get out of here."

"What about Medusa's head?" Darko asked. "Should I look for it?"

"It's too late to worry about that now," Diana said, placing her hands on Luna's stomach. The glowing golden light expanded through Diana's and Luna's bodies. "Just grab what you can, and hurry."

Zoey gathered the Helm and tucked it under her arm. Darko ripped arrows out of the monster's body and threw them into the quiver slung over his shoulder, while Kali retrieved their fallen spears and stuffed them into the nearest bag.

Diana pulled away from Luna, and with the demigod's help, the pegasus wearily climbed to her hooves. The wing that had been crushed under her body remained mangled, hanging limp at her side.

"What's wrong with her wing?" Kali asked.

"Because all her weight was on it while I was healing her, it must not have healed properly," Diana said, gasping for breath. "I'll have to try again."

Andy looked over his shoulder. The flames crept closer to them. Blistering heat cooked his skin, smoke choking his lungs. "I don't think we have enough time."

Zoey and Darko joined the rest of the group, and Zoey put the Helm in Kali's pack. "Luna can't fly like this," Kali said.

"And I can't direct Ajax with burnt hands," Andy added, coughing.

A tree behind them split with a loud *crack*. It groaned and crashed to the forest floor, sending the group stumbling back. Sparks and ash rained over their heads. Ajax and Aladdin flapped their wings, bolting into the sky.

"Run!" Diana cried.

The group splashed into the stream, Luna behind them. Cold, fast-moving water tugged on their feet, but they pressed on.

They reached the bank, but still had not escaped the fire. More burning trees collapsed, two toward the stream.

As they fell, the flames engulfing them spread to the vegetation on the other side of the water.

The group dashed through the forest, zigzagging around roots and logs, fire on their heels. Andy's throat grew drier every second. His heart felt as if it might burst.

As the group ran farther, the trees grew sparser, and soon they approached what looked like a clearing stretching for miles. For a moment, relief flooded Andy. Surely once they reached it, they could get a head start on the fire and maybe get some fresh air.

Crippling dread replaced relief as the group entered the clearing and halted at the edge of a jagged cliff. Nearly a hundred feet below, a wide dark lake beckoned them.

Andy clenched his jaw and cursed. He looked over his shoulder. The forest fire roared, closing in on them. "We have to jump." He seized Zoey's arm with one stinging hand, Darko's with the other, then threw himself off the edge of the cliff.

As they fell at lightning speed, questions raced through Andy's mind. What if there were rocks close enough to the top of the lake that they'd be injured or killed after breaking the surface? What if the impact alone was enough to render them unconscious, and they drowned? Or what if, even if they survived the fall, new monsters awaited them in the water's black depths?

We had to get away from the fire, he thought. *This was our only chance.*

They crashed into the lake feet-first, and Andy felt as

if hundreds of icy rubber bands were snapping his skin. Murky water swallowed him, liquid swirling in his ears. His hands stung even worse than before, but he held tight to Zoey and Darko and kicked his feet, tugging them up with him.

He broke the surface and gasped for breath. Next to him, Zoey did the same, then Darko.

Zoey swung her head from side to side, her expression drawn in concern. "Where're Diana and Kali?"

As if to answer the question, Diana burst from the water ten feet to the right, Kali close behind. Kali's eyes were wide with panic. "L-Luna," she sputtered. "We can't pull her up."

Diana lit her hands with golden light as though she were about to heal someone. "C'mon, all of us together can save her." She sucked in a breath and dove back under. The rest of them followed suit.

As the group swam down, fish scattered. Far below, the blurry outlines of sharp rocks and floating algae awaited them.

Diana led them farther down, and finally they spotted Luna. She floated through the water, her legs twisted at odd angles. Her eyes were closed, bubbles floating from her parted lips. Andy stroked and kicked, using all his might to reach the pegasus's side as fast as he could despite the pain in his hands.

Finally, they reached her. Andy, Zoey, and Darko each grabbed her by a leg, while Kali and Diana swam underneath her and pressed their hands against her belly. Together, the group pushed.

Every muscle in Andy's body burned. Within moments he felt as if his lungs were about to shrivel up. *I need to breathe*, he thought, and fought back the urge to gasp. Diana's light seemed to grow dimmer and dimmer. *I need to breathe.*

Andy opened his mouth and sucked in a breath of the lake. His lungs filled with water. He kicked harder, trying to keep hold of Luna, but she slipped from his grasp. He tried to snatch her again, but something wrapped itself around him—something slippery, and even colder than the lake—and pulled him backward.

He shoved against whatever it was, jamming his elbow into it, but it only held onto him tighter. *Shit*, he thought. *It's a lake monster. It's a lake monster, and we're all dead.* He imagined the creature that must have captured him: it was probably large enough to stomach a house and had rows of sharp teeth, with fifty-foot-long tentacles snaking around it . . .

Andy gasped, sucking in another breath of water, and Diana's light went out completely.

* ⁓ * ⁓ * ⁓

Silence. It surrounded Karter, suffocating him with sinister claws. He had no one. Not a soul. No reason to fight. No reason to live.

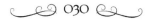

His muscles ached, chills bolting through his veins, but he ran anyway. Ran through pitch-black caverns, unable to see even his hands when he held them up to his face.

"Karter," called the familiar voice of a young man. "Karter, where are you?"

Karter's eyes filled with tears. It sounded like . . . "Spencer?" His knees trembled, his legs burning from the effort of it all. He was in so much pain, but if Spencer was still alive, if Spencer was looking for him, it didn't matter. He would press on.

The walls turned and twisted, his head spinning.

"Karter?"

He kept running, sandals pounding against the rocky floors.

"Where are you?"

White light began flickering far ahead, illuminating the cavern. A short walk forward, a tall young man with deep-brown skin and a beautiful young woman with hazel eyes held their arms wide open, out to him.

Karter's body filled with soothing warmth. It was Spencer and Syrena, his two best friends, both back from the dead.

He had a reason to fight again. Had a reason to live.

He leapt toward them and fell into their arms.

"Spencer—Syrena—you're alive."

"Spencer?" a young man who was not Spencer said.

"Syrena?" a young woman who couldn't be Syrena said.

Karter's heart sank. He looked up to find himself in the arms of two people who were familiar to him, but who certainly weren't his best friends.

The first was a scrawny boy with youthful features and

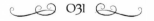

short brown hair. The second, a pretty girl with eyes the color of a clear summer sky and a mess' of long curls hanging from her head.

It was Andy and Zoey. The two mortals Karter had helped in the Underworld in a desperate attempt to save Spencer's life after Persephone had stabbed Spencer in the gut.

Karter pulled away from them. "What's going on?"

Andy's and Zoey's expressions fell.

"How could you?" Zoey asked Karter, her tone accusatory.

"How could I what?"

The white light faded, sucking the heat from Karter's body as it disappeared. He hugged his sides and shot them a glare, his teeth chattering. "What's going on?"

The cavern shook. The ground beneath Karter's feet split in two and opened into a black abyss. He scrambled to the side, tried to fly into the air, but it seemed as though he'd been stripped of his powers. He couldn't escape.

He fell into the abyss.

As the darkness swallowed him whole, he screamed. All around him, the familiar voice of a woman, the familiar voice of Asteria, the Titan goddess who'd told him Spencer needed his help in Hades, said, "You must be strong. Your destined greatness awaits."

Karter gasped, his eyes fluttering open.

There was thick forest overhead, the sun rising slowly. The smell of pine filled his nostrils, and sticky sweat soaked his skin. His head pounded, his throat parched, his stomach churning. The knife wounds on his side and thigh throbbed with hot pain.

He went to stretch, to climb to his feet and find some water, but thick rope bound his body tight. He cursed under his breath, remembering that Violet, Layla, and Xander had captured him for the crime of helping Andy and Zoey steal the Helm of Darkness and were taking him back to Olympus, where he'd face the punishment for his unforgivable sins.

He tried to move again, tried to conjure his inherited child-of-Zeus strength and break apart the rope, but a burning sensation shot through his chest. He cried out. His wounds were weakening him. How long would it take for them to kill him?

A low chuckle sounded beside him, and he jerked his head toward it, catching a glimpse of slick black hair and a crooked smile.

"Xander," Karter said, his voice hoarse.

The Son of Hermes kneeled beside Karter. "Good morning, traitor."

"Where are we?"

"Just a week or so away from Olympus. Don't worry, you'll see your father soon enough"—Xander sneered, then kicked Karter hard in the gut—"and finally get what you deserve. May I say, I cannot wait to watch?"

Karter caught his breath and prepared to snap back, but before he could say a word, the searing pain ripped through him again. *I'm dead*, he thought. *Whether I make it home or escape them, this is it for me.*

Violet, Daughter of Aphrodite, and Layla, Daughter of Ares, stepped into sight. Violet fluffed her blonde hair, batting her eyelashes. "Now, now, Xander," she said. "We still don't know what it is Zeus wants to do with poor, ugly Karter. No need to fill his head with horrors that will make him want to escape us."

Xander stood. "Zeus executed Syrena just for *trying* to bring the prophecy to fruition. Karter helped the mortals from the Before Time navigate the Underworld, steal the Helm of Darkness, and put Hades and Persephone in Tartarus. Don't think for a second Zeus would hesitate to kill even his own son for betraying the gods."

Violet placed a slender hand on her hip. "You're not wrong." She leaned over Karter, her opalescent eyes flashing. Karter avoided her gaze. If one stared too long into Violet's eyes, and they didn't have strong feelings for anyone else, they'd fall madly in love with her, which was the last thing he needed to happen right now. "However, Zeus has let him live this long, and it takes a special kind of power to do everything he's done. Perhaps the gods have something interesting planned."

Karter groaned. What was Violet thinking? Xander was right; Zeus wouldn't hesitate to kill Karter after everything he'd done.

The demigod trio gathered their things and threw Karter onto the back of a pegasus, then mounted their own and flew in the direction of Olympus.

* ～ * ～ * ～

When Andy opened his eyes, the first thing he saw was Diana kneeling over him as though she'd just finished healing his injuries. However, she didn't look near as sharp as usual; she looked fuzzy, like a low-quality photo. He reached up to his face and found his glasses were gone.

"Don't worry," Diana said. "Here you go." She pulled them out from behind herself and handed them to Andy.

He took them and shoved them back on, several scratches and a crack riddling them now. It didn't matter, though, because he was lucky they hadn't yet been lost. He had no idea how they'd survived the group's adventures thus far. "Thanks."

He held his hands up, flexing them and wiggling his fingers. They no longer stung, nor were they sore, and although the last thing he remembered was drowning while also being attacked by a lake monster, he was perfectly dry. What had happened? How much time had passed? And where were they?

He sat up and took in his surroundings. He was inside a two-story cabin he thought looked like the kind of place a fairy would make its home. Vines and orange lilies poked out and wrapped around the logs making up the walls and ceiling, sunlight pouring through the cabin's multiple windows. Instead of wood, tile, or carpet, the floor consisted of lush grass that tickled his skin, and the furniture looked to be made of oversized speckled mushrooms.

On either side of him, Kali and Darko sat. Luna stood next to Darko, her wing and legs looking good as new. Kali grinned. "Good morning."

Andy jumped to his feet. They were missing an important member of their group. "Where's Zoey? Is she okay?"

Someone tapped his shoulder, and he swung around to find Zoey. She looked beautiful as ever despite all she'd endured, her eyes bright. "I'm fine, but thanks for the concern."

"What's going on?" Andy asked. "We were trying to save Luna, and then . . ." Before he could finish his sentence, he caught sight of three girls standing behind Zoey. They were all short, about the height of Diana, and had to be around Andy's age. They wore flowing forest-green dresses. Wildflowers adorned their necks, wrists, and ankles.

The girl in the middle smiled and bowed. Her hair, long and auburn, hung in a braid over her shoulder. The soft curves of her body were pronounced, her cheeks plump. "Hello, Andy, one of the Chosen Two of the Prophecy," she said, her voice sweeter than vanilla ice-cream with chocolate syrup drizzled on top. "My name is Eugenia, and I am head of the Dryads in this division of the forest."

Andy raised an eyebrow. "Dryads? What's going on?"

The second girl hopped forward. Her skin and coiled locks were both deep shades of brown, and she wore a smile so cheerful it reminded Andy of daisies blooming on a spring day. "Dryads are nymphs of the trees and forests," she chirped. "My name's Harmony, by the way. It's *so* nice to meet you."

"Nymphs?" Andy said. "Those are kind of like gods, right?"

The third girl nodded, brushing back the wispy pieces of black hair that framed her sharp, pale face. "We are divine spirits who care for the plants and animals of our domain," she said. "I am Narcissa. Pleased to make your acquaintance."

"I mean, don't get me wrong, it's nice to meet you guys," Andy began. "But if you're like gods, why haven't you killed us already? You mentioned the prophecy, so you know who we are. And what we're planning to do, I'm assuming. So what in the hell is going on? Why haven't you killed us or something?"

Eugenia clicked her tongue. "How wonderful it is that our Chosen Two are both so clever. Both so full of questions. Allow us to explain ourselves, and surely that will clear the air."

The Dryads walked past the group toward the door on the other side of the cabin. "Please, follow us," Narcissa said, then opened the door. The Dryads stepped outside.

Andy shot the rest of the group a quizzical look, but they only shrugged in response. Luna sighed, blowing puffs of air out her nostrils. "We're as much in the dark as you are," Diana said. "They didn't want to say exactly what was going on until everyone woke up and was fully healed. They only told me they had 'pure intentions' and that we 'would be smart to trust them.'"

"Oh, and that they rounded up Ajax and Aladdin for us," Darko added.

Andy shrugged. "All right, sounds legit."

The group followed the Dryads out the door onto the cabin's deck, and when Andy stepped outside, his jaw dropped.

The cabin was one of many—Andy guessed there were at least thirty—clustered in the forest. Bushes and gardens full of flowers, fruits, and vegetables consumed the space between the homes. Unlike Deltama Village, this place had no gates or walls to protect it, and Andy guessed that because the inhabitants were Dryads and probably had special abilities like the gods, they didn't need protection from monsters; or maybe they had cast some sort of cloaking spell to keep themselves hidden.

Dozens more young girls dressed almost identically to Eugenia, Harmony, and Narcissa, whom Andy assumed were also Dryads, began gathering toward the group. Some slipped out from behind trees, some pulled themselves out of large bushes, and some seemed to appear from thin air.

Ajax and Aladdin trotted out of the trees and past the Dryads, whinnying with glee as they made their way to Kali and Luna. Kali smiled and hugged their necks, and Luna nuzzled their noses.

"Soooo," Andy began, turning toward Eugenia, Harmony, and Narcissa. "How did you guys save us from the lake monster?"

Harmony giggled. "Oh, humans are silly. There are no lake monsters around here, and we didn't save you from drowning. That was the Naiads."

Andy raised his eyebrows. "Naiads?"

"That would be us," a girl from the crowd said. Andy glanced over to see several young women waving at him. Although the young women appeared to be the same age as the Dryads, that was where their similarities stopped. These girls looked as if they'd just stepped out of a swimming pool, water dripping off them and creating puddles at their feet. They wore dresses woven from seaweed, their skin tinged with iridescent blue-and-green hues.

"Naiads are freshwater nymphs," Harmony said. "The lake you jumped in is full of them."

"Yes," Eugenia said. "Last night, when I saw our forest was ablaze, I rushed to the lake and asked the Naiads to put it out as quickly as possible. They can direct water with their hands, you see—and they sprayed water over the fire to stop it from destroying any more of our forest than it already had. Once they had finished their task, they discovered the five of you struggling to save your pegasus. We'd all heard rumors of the Chosen Two of the Prophecy storming into the Underworld and stealing Hades's Helm of Darkness, and when the Naiads found the Helm in your pack, they knew who you were at once, and that the rumors were true. They carried you to the bank and made sure to direct the water out from your lungs, and after gathering her strength, the Daughter of Apollo healed your ailments.

A few hours later, your other two pegasi came back, and we told them we would keep them safe if they would allow it."

"Thank you for putting out the fire and for saving us," Zoey said, giving the Naiads a quick nod of gratitude. She turned back to Eugenia. "From everything you've told us, I'm assuming you aren't too fond of the gods?"

"None of the nymphs in this division of the forest agree with what the gods have done to humanity," Eugenia said. "Nor what they have done to anyone else, really. Many of the world's inhabitants suffer at their hands. In a small act to fight against them, we are part of an underground association where nymphs and *astynomia* unite for the greater good, founded by a Dryad who, long ago, lost the love of her life to the gods' cruelty: a satyr *astynomia*. We help members of the *astynomia* who crave freedom escape the cities and reach Alikan Village." She gestured at the cabins. "Hence the houses. The forest is our true home, as fresh water is home to the Naiads. But we constructed these houses for any satyrs passing through, so they may have a safe place to rest before continuing their journey."

At the mention of *astynomia* and Alikan Village, Andy's heart sank, and he glanced at Darko, who stared down at his hooves. The satyr sniffled and rubbed his eyes. "That's right," he said. "My brother and I— Well, a couple weeks after we escaped Hermes City to get to Alikan Village, we stayed in a place like this. And the association you're a part of—someone else you work with, I mean—told us about Alikan Village and helped us get out of the city. But you guys don't look familiar, so I don't think I've met any of you before."

Harmony flashed Darko a smile. "You've never passed through here. I know for a fact. I would've remembered a satyr as cute as you." Darko shot her a wide-eyed glance.

"You said you have a brother, but you are the only satyr here," Narcissa said. "Where is he?"

Darko nibbled on his thumbnail. "Um—well, Phoenix is dead."

Harmony put a hand on her heart. "I'm so sorry for your loss."

"It's—it's okay," Darko said. "Him and I—we'd nearly made it to Alikan Village, but Medusa turned him to stone. Andy and Zoey slayed her, and we had her head—but I—I lost it when we were fighting the Chimera. I'm pretty sure it got burned up in the fire."

"It most definitely did," Diana said, shaking her head. "And now *everything* will be harder. What with Zoey's hand, Spencer's death, the loss of my father's help . . ."

At the mentions of Spencer's passing and her hand, Zoey's face fell, while the more Diana listed the group's troubles, the more Darko looked as if he were going to be sick.

Andy shot Diana a quick glare, then rested a palm on Darko's shoulder. "Hey, it's okay. It was an accident." Darko continued chewing his nail, saying nothing and going back to staring at his hooves.

Diana cleared her throat. "Uh, anyway, I hate to bring

this up, but you mentioned Alikan Village, so I have to. In case you didn't know, Alikan Village is gone. Zeus sent some demigods—Violet, Layla, and Xander—to kill everyone there."

Eugenia creased her brow and clasped her hands, and the rest of the nymphs in the crowd hung their heads. "Yes. We are aware of Alikan Village's tragic annihilation, Daughter of Apollo. We helped many satyrs escape the cities and find their way there, and when we discovered what happened, we were both outraged and full of sorrow. Which is why, when the time comes for you to wage war on the gods, we'd like to pledge our loyalty to you—as members of your army."

"We believe in your cause," Narcissa added. "And we intend to help you defeat the gods in any way we can."

Andy whistled. "Damn, that's awesome. We'll definitely need the help, thanks."

"Yes, we will," Diana said. "Thank you."

"No, thank *you*," Eugenia replied, bowing. She clapped her hands twice, and in a flash of white light, a small drawstring sack made of green vines and grass appeared in her hands. "Please, use the contents of this bag to get ahold of us when you have decided you need our help. I'd recommend contacting us a few days in advance, depending on how far from here you are, though."

"What is it?" Zoey asked, taking the bag from her.

"An orange daylily," Narcissa answered. "The officially appointed plant of our division of the forest."

Harmony grinned. "It's also my favorite flower. Except this one's a lot sturdier than the rest."

"How do we use a flower to get ahold of you?" Andy asked.

"Why, it's not just any flower, Chosen One," Eugenia said. "It's one of our messenger flowers. To reach us, burn it and ask the flames to allow you to speak with the ones who gave it to you. Now, I believe it's time for you to be on your way."

Diana mounted Aladdin, Kali Luna. "You're right," Diana said. "The world isn't going to save itself. Let's go."

"I'm not sure how we can ever repay you," Zoey said, following suit of Diana.

"Give everyone back their free will, and that will be enough," Eugenia said.

Darko climbed onto Ajax's back, and Harmony gave him a quick glance. "We'll see you again. Soon, I hope."

"Yeah, sure," the satyr squeaked, then swallowed hard. Andy stifled a chuckle. He knew all too well how hard it was to talk to a pretty girl; he'd had his fair share of awkward moments with Zoey, and he was sure there'd be more to come considering he still didn't know if she reciprocated how he felt about her.

The group waved goodbye to the nymphs. The nymphs waved back, and the group took to the sky.

They flew northeast for most of the day, and a few hours before the sun began to set, Diana directed them to land in the shelter of the forest.

"All right, guys, we need to talk," Diana said seriously as they climbed off the pegasi.

"Why?" Andy asked. "What's wrong?"

Diana crossed her arms. "Our circumstances have changed. Things are more dire than ever before, for a couple of reasons." Her gaze darted between Zoey and Darko.

"What do you mean by that, Princess?" Kali asked, hands on her hips. "I thought things were looking pretty good for us since we talked to the Fates."

"First of all," Diana began, "we're down a ton of magical resources. My father is Zeus's captive and is going to be put in Tartarus, and Spencer is . . ." She paused, her expression falling. "Well, you know. He's gone—alongside Syrena. Second off, we lost Medusa's head. Because of that, we're going to have to fight every monster we come across rather than just turning them to stone. And third, Zoey's hand got chopped off in Hades. I think that point is self-explanatory."

At Diana's words, Darko seemed to shrink in on himself with shame, while Zoey did so with sadness, and Andy balled his fists. "Is all this stuff such a big deal that we need to bring it up like this?" he said. "I mean, I'm really sorry about Apollo. I think we're all sorry about him. I know it's been hard for you that Syrena is dead, and it's hard for all of us to accept that Spencer is gone." A lump formed in his throat as he spoke Spencer's name. He gulped it down. "But—well, I think Zoey and Darko already feel bad enough about their stuff already. Can't we just drop it?"

Diana sighed. "Look, I'm not trying to make anyone feel bad. I'm not mad about Zoey's hand or the head. I'm just trying to emphasize the fact that things are going to be more difficult than before. We need to be aware of that, and we need to at the very least double the amount of time we're training every day, starting today, so we're prepared for anything regardless of our drawbacks."

"Is that it?" Andy asked.

"Well, yeah," Diana said.

"And did you have to make such a big deal about it?"

Diana opened her mouth as if she was about to argue, and Kali stepped between them. "Okay, quit, you two," Kali said. "We get it. Andy doesn't want anyone to have hurt feelings, and Diana thinks we need to train longer so we don't, you know, die. Is this really cause for a fight, or are you both just being touchy?"

Andy and Diana shared a look. He didn't want to fight with her; he just didn't want Zoey and Darko to feel any worse than they already did. *Then again*, he thought, *she isn't wrong. Things are about to become way more difficult with everything we have up against us . . .* Maybe she was right to bring it up.

"I'm sorry," Andy finally said. "You're right, Diana. This stuff might be hard to talk about, but we need to. More than anything else, though, we need to keep training for what's to come."

"Then let's begin," Diana replied.

CHAPTER THREE

PROMETHEUS

Zoey cursed and threw down her spear.

While she was getting her butt kicked by Diana, each fight between them more pathetic than the last, Andy, Darko, and Kali seemed to be having a grand old time a hundred feet away, laughing and joking as they battled each other. Any moment those three went unsupervised during training, they acted as if this were a spitting contest rather than incredibly important time when the group was supposed to prepare to take on the gods.

Zoey didn't hate them for having fun. In fact, a part of her wished she could join in. But she felt as if she sucked at fighting now. Earlier that evening, Diana had even announced to the entire group how much of a liability Zoey was since she'd lost her hand and how they needed to train twice as long every night because of it.

Sure, Diana had attributed the longer training times to the fact that Darko lost Medusa's head and the group's other disadvantages as well. However, Zoey was pretty sure the demigod wouldn't be making such a big deal about these things if Zoey weren't so incapable of defending herself now, and Zoey hated it more than anything. Somehow, she had to get her fighting skills back to where they'd been before.

"What's wrong?" Diana asked.

"When is this gonna be easier?" Zoey asked. "It seems like I'm doing worse than before I had any training at all."

Diana brushed some dirt off her dress. "It's not going to get easier for a long time. You lost a whole body part. Now you have to relearn things."

"I feel like a little kid. I can hardly do anything. If a monster came after me and I was all by myself—"

"Quit being so hard on yourself," Diana interrupted. "Things will get better with practice, which is why we're doing more of it." The demigod glanced over at the rest of the group as they goofed off. Kali knocked Andy over with the handle of her spear, and he face-planted into the forest floor. He sat up, blades of grass plastered to his cheeks, and Darko and Kali laughed and high-fived.

"Speaking of practice," Diana continued. "I think we have time for some more sparring before dinner. Why don't I get Andy over here to fight with you and I'll take on Kali and Darko? Then at least we'll know they aren't getting distracted again. If I didn't know any better, I'd swear they weren't above the age of ten."

Zoey giggled. "You're sure they *aren't*?"

Diana gave Zoey a mischievous smile and ran toward

Andy, Darko, and Kali, chucking two spheres of light at them. At the sight of the attacks hurtling toward them, Darko jumped to attention. He seized a couple of arrows from his quiver and loosed them one after the other at the spheres with incredible accuracy. As the projectiles whizzed through the spheres, their light dispersed into hundreds of golden sparks, then finally disappeared altogether.

"Holy gods of Olympus, Darko," Diana said, stopping in her tracks. "That was amazing. You're getting so much better!"

"Thanks," Darko replied as he gathered up his arrows. "I think watching you with your bow has helped me the most."

Diana stood up a little straighter at Darko's words. "Glad to hear it."

Kali poked the air in Diana's direction with the tip of her spear and grinned. "You're really choked up about this, aren't you, Princess?"

"As a matter of fact, I am," Diana said, then conjured another sphere of light, keeping her gaze on Kali's the whole time. "Andy, go spar with Zoey while I teach these guys a thing or two."

Andy scrambled out of the way as Diana began flinging attacks at Darko and Kali, then stood, wiped the grass off his face, and lowered his weapon.

"Get your spear ready," Zoey said, picking up her own as Andy walked to her side. "We're supposed to be sparring each other."

"I know," Andy replied. "But I was thinking, there's something I wanted to talk to you about."

"Okay, what's up?"

"I've been thinking that maybe from now on, whenever we're fighting a monster—or anything, really—you should wear the Helm."

"Okay. Why?"

"Well . . ." He scratched the back of his head. "Based on the stuff Diana brought up earlier, I think it would be safer for you if you stayed invisible to our opponents."

Zoey averted her gaze from his, her heart sinking. "I don't want to always have to rely on the Helm, though. Like, what if something happens, and I can't get to it? I need to be able to defend myself if things go wrong."

"I know," Andy said, stepping forward and resting a hand on her shoulder. "But I really think you should for now. At least until you get used to fighting with one hand."

Zoey laughed coldly and pulled away from him. "Look, I guess if it makes you feel better, I can use the Helm most of the time, okay? But I'm not going to improve any if we just keep standing around and talking about how much I suck instead of actually fighting, so could you please get your spear ready and fight me?"

"All right," Andy said with a sigh. He raised his weapon and they began to spar. Tears battled to spring from Zoey's eyes the entire time, but she held them back with all her might.

Later that night, when the sun had finally set, Diana

caught several rabbits and made a fire. The rest of the group set up camp. When it came time to prepare their meal, just as Diana was about to cook the meat over the flames, Kali made her way to Diana's side.

"Hey, mind if I take a crack at that?" Kali asked.

Diana raised a brow. "Take a crack at what?"

"Cooking the rabbit."

"What's wrong with the way I cook it?"

"Well . . ." Kali shared a knowing look with Zoey, who stood on the other side of the fire beside Andy and Darko, both of whom were chopping roots while the pegasi grazed nearby. "Nothing, really. I just thought it might be fun to try."

"Making dinner for everyone is a huge responsibility," Diana replied, shish-kebabbing the rabbits with a couple of sharp sticks. The rest of the group stifled laughter. "What's so funny?" Diana asked. "I'm being serious."

Kali took the sticks from Diana and began turning them over the flames. "I'll be honest with you, Princess. You burn the meat every time. Now, that's not necessarily a bad thing, but people like a little variety in their meals, and I think all of us are, quite frankly, sick of the taste of charred rabbit flesh. So, I'm taking the 'huge responsibility' of making dinner tonight. Because, well, I have skills."

"*You* have skills?" Diana said.

"In cooking, yes. Why do you think the feast in my village was so delicious? The folks of Deltama Village know how to eat."

Diana snorted and smiled mischievously. "I just hope you're a better cook than you are a fighter. Otherwise, we're all doomed."

Kali chuckled and shook her head, turning the rabbits. "I'm no 'Diana, Daughter of Apollo' when it comes to battle, but I've been known to hold my own, at least in comparison to everyone else in my village."

"Ha-ha," Diana said, her tone laced with sarcasm. "Sure."

When the meal was prepared and Zoey took a bite of what Kali had made the group, she quickly realized Kali wasn't kidding about possessing great cooking skills. The meat was tender, moist, and flavorful. How Kali pulled it off, Zoey wasn't sure, but she didn't really care. She hadn't eaten something this tasty since the feast in Deltama Village.

"Oh my God," Andy said as he chewed. "This is amazing."

Kali winked. "Learned everything I know from my beautiful mother, thank you."

Zoey swallowed her bite. "Where was your mother when we were in the village, anyway? We met Chief Agni, but—"

"She's dead," Kali said. "My mother is dead." Everyone went quiet, and Zoey immediately felt guilty for asking. She knew how hard it was to lose a parent.

Finally, Andy spoke. "I'm really sorry to hear that. How did she pass, if you don't mind me asking?"

"She got sick," Kali replied.

"What was she sick with?" Andy asked. "Do you know?"

Kali sighed. "We'll never know for sure. It came on so fast. It took her even faster, and none of our healers could decipher what it was. When Mother was alive and well, she ruled Deltama Village with more grace and beauty than any other chief's wife has—at least, that's what everyone tells me. And then, out of nowhere, she started to get dizzy all the time. She couldn't even walk in a straight line. She'd get headaches so painful she'd cry out in the night, and she'd even shake uncontrollably sometimes. That went on for a few weeks until she died. I was nine years old."

Andy set his food aside, scooted toward Kali, and rested a hand on her back. "I'm sorry for your loss. There aren't words that can make it better. I know from personal experience. But I'm still sorry. It sounds like she might have had a brain tumor of some sort."

"A brain tumor?" Kali said.

He nodded. "Yeah. It's a growth in your head that isn't supposed to be there. Back in the Before Time, my dad had a brain tumor, and it had cancer."

"Cancer?"

"Cancer is a type of sickness. A really, really bad sickness. Before my dad went to the hospital, the same things that happened to your mother happened to him: headaches, dizziness, seizures. He even threw up sometimes. The doctors and nurses were able to keep him alive for a while, but the cancer wouldn't go away. In fact, it kept reappearing in other places in his body, even after his treatments. I was twelve when he died."

"I'm also sorry for your loss," Kali said, her voice quivering.

Andy patted her back, then pulled away. "It's okay."

"Kali," Darko piped up. "Since you're Chief Agni's daughter, are you next in line to run Deltama Village? Or do you have a sibling who's going to do that?"

"The other children my parents conceived died during birth, so I'm the chief's only living child. I'm next in line to lead."

Zoey furrowed her brow. "Wait, next in line? Is that why Chief Agni didn't want you to come with us?"

"Yes. He believed the village needed me there."

"Why did you run away, then?" Darko asked.

Kali's gaze hardened. "Because if the Greek gods aren't defeated, my village will live in fear forever. Even if the monster attacks are few and far between, they still happen, and when they do, we all lose people we love. If the gods' tyranny isn't stopped, the people I care about will never really be free. By coming with you, I'm doing them a greater service than any other chief has."

"When this is all over, you're going back to Deltama Village, aren't you?" Zoey asked. At this question, Diana leaned forward as if she was listening intently.

"I have to. I'm the chief's only child," Kali replied. "My father will be furious with me, I'm sure, but if I'm alive and able to go home, the gods will have already been defeated, my village free. I'll marry a man Father picks for me—since I'll need to produce an heir—and when Father dies, I'll be made Chief Kali of Deltama Village."

Zoey's jaw dropped at the prospect of Kali being married to someone she wouldn't choose. How backward! Zoey could believe it, though—after all, when the world ended and fell under the gods' rule, it made sense that there would be some social regression. However, Kali had never said anything about an arranged marriage. In fact, she hadn't said much at all about her life in the village. She'd only spoken of plans to fight the gods, trying in every way she could to help the group on their mission and, of course, had teased Diana every chance she got.

At the thought of Diana, Zoey shot the demigod a glance. The Daughter of Apollo looked disconnected from the conversation now, staring into the crackling flames of the campfire.

"We'd better hurry up eating so we can get some rest," Diana said. "We've got a long way to travel before we reach Prometheus, and plenty more sparring to do."

They said nothing, finishing their dinner quickly. Within the next hour Diana and Darko paired up to watch for monsters, as it was their turn, and the rest of the group slept.

For the next several days, the group traveled toward Prometheus, training every night for several hours before dinner. Zoey took turns fighting with everyone. Diana continually insisted that Zoey was improving, even just a little—but Zoey wasn't so sure.

On the afternoon of the group's fourth day flying, dozens of levitating rocks in various shapes and sizes began to pop up throughout the sky. Diana yelled over the wind, "We've almost reached Prometheus."

Zoey peered into the distance, and as the group descended from the fluffy clouds, she spotted him.

He stood on a floating boulder, his ankles shackled with iron chains bolted into the rock. His wrists were bound with similar chains on a separate, smaller rock hovering above his head, and tons of other rocks and boulders levitated around him, as though he were imprisoned in the center of an asteroid belt. A jagged canyon resided hundreds of feet below, surrounded by mountains and forest.

As the group flew closer, weaving between boulders, Zoey could see Prometheus was a behemoth of a man. His bulging muscles were draped in grimy, blood-covered white robes that, although filthy, still accentuated his dark-olive skin, his black hair falling in shiny curls over his shoulders.

The group reached the edge of the boulder where he stood trapped. It wasn't big enough for all of them to land, so instead they circled it on their pegasi.

Prometheus looked to them, his face wrinkled as if he was in pain. "Who are you people?" His voice was deep and gruff. "What are you doing here?"

"I am Diana, Daughter of Apollo," Diana said. "And these are my companions. We're on a mission that will determine the fate of the world, and we need your help."

He chuckled. "What makes you think *I* could help you? Can't you tell I'm a little tied up right now?"

"The Fates themselves told us you could."

"And what makes you think I would?"

Zoey peered over Diana's shoulder at the Titan. "Prometheus, sir," she began. "From what I've heard about you, it sounds like you care a lot about humanity. You made people, and you stole fire from the gods for them. If you help us now, we could save humanity from the gods. We could give them back free will. In doing so, we could restore the world to what it once was." She eyed the chains binding him. "And you could be free."

Prometheus looked to Zoey. "Who are you?"

"My name is Zoey, and I come from the Before Time. Andy and I"—she gestured at Andy—"are the Chosen Two of the Prophecy." Prometheus stared at them blankly, and for a few moments no one said anything, waiting for him to respond. Wind whipped Zoey's curls backward.

Finally, Prometheus threw his head back and belted out a laugh so loud it echoed over the canyon. "You say you're the—HAHAHAHA—Chosen Two of the—HAHAHA—*Prophecy*?"

Andy rolled his eyes. "Well, yeah?"

"Oh my—HAHAHAHAHAHA!" Prometheus's face turned redder than a cherry. "You kids honestly believe in all that? You think you can change the world? That you can take on the gods? Look, the gods might be morons, I'll admit that much, but I'll tell you what they're not: weak and mortal, which both of you are. I can smell it from here. There's no way in Tartarus you'd last a second against them. They'd just blast you off Olympus, let you fall to your death, and call it a century."

"You're wrong," Zoey snapped. "We defeated Hades and Persephone in the Underworld and stole the Helm of Darkness. If we can steal Poseidon's Trident and Zeus's Master Lightning Bolt, we can—"

"Whoa, whoa, whoa," Prometheus said. "Let me stop you right there. Do you really expect me to believe *you* defeated Hades, King of the Underworld? Seriously? Do I look like an idiot to you?" He paused and glanced at the manacles binding his hands. "Actually, don't answer that question."

Kali reached into the sack tied around Luna and pulled the Helm of Darkness out. She held it high for Prometheus to see. "I guess you can choose not to believe them, but here's the evidence. How else do you think they got the Helm, other than defeating Hades?"

"Either it was pure luck—which I'm guessing is going to run out soon—or they didn't steal it on their own. Probably the latter." He looked to Zoey. "Who helped you?"

Kali put the Helm back in the bag, and Zoey cleared her throat. "Well, technically Persephone beheaded Hades right before we were about to fight him, but she turned on us and sicked the Furies on us, and then we had to follow her all the way to the edge of—"

"Just as I thought," Prometheus interrupted. "You couldn't have stolen it yourselves, and that's why you're here now. You think you're big and bad for taking on Persephone . . . HA! Let me tell you, no matter how powerful she seemed, she's nothing compared to the Olympians. Especially Zeus.

"You're just a couple of mortals. Not that mortals can't be amazing in their own right—I mean, I *made* the first few of 'em, of course they're amazing—but up against the gods . . . I'm sorry. I'm sure you have good intentions. But I won't help you. I can't."

Zoey creased her brow. "We're not just any mortals, though. The Fates themselves told us we're special before we even went on our first quest. And even if we don't know what they mean by that yet, they said we'll figure it out in time. I'm sure you're right about Persephone not being as big a threat as Zeus and the Olympians, but the Fates' input has to mean something to you, right? I mean, they're ancient and all-knowing."

Prometheus sighed. "Tell you what. You think you're so special, go ahead and prove it. Break these chains and get me outta here. If you can pull that off, I might *think* about helping you."

The group exchanged nervous glances, and Zoey squeezed Diana. "Do you think we could break the chains?"

"I don't know," Diana replied. "It was only possible for Heracles and Prometheus when they combined their power. Which is crazy, because Prometheus is a Titan god, and

Heracles, as a demigod child-of-Zeus, had super-strength. Unless . . ." Diana directed Aladdin toward Prometheus, then stepped off the pegasus and onto the boulder Prometheus stood on. In one hand, she conjured a blazing sphere, and with the other, she snatched an arrow from her quiver.

"What're you doing?" Andy asked.

"I'm going to try and break these," Diana said, kneeling next to the shackle around one of Prometheus's ankles. "Just give me a minute."

Prometheus laughed. "I know what you're thinking, and it's not gonna work."

Diana pressed the sphere of light against the shackle. "I have to try." She allowed the sphere to sit against the shackle for quite some time, until finally she raised the arrow above her head and slammed the head into the metal. The arrowhead shattered, not even making a dent in the metal.

"Gods dammit," Diana said, hurling the broken arrow off the boulder, then climbed back onto Aladdin.

"What'd I tell you?" Prometheus said. "Regular heat, regular *weapons*—those things don't do anything to chains forged by Hephaestus himself. Don't you think it's all been tried before?"

"What can we do, then?" Zoey asked.

Before Diana could answer, a bird's screech sounded above their heads, and the group directed the pegasi to turn toward the sound.

"It's the Caucasian Eagle!" Diana shouted. And it was

an eagle all right—if eagles were the size of helicopters. Its snow-white feathers shimmered, its eyes the color of blood.

"And the beastie returns, ready to eat my liver," Prometheus said. "Guess you can't bust me outta here if he's alive, so you better kill him first. If I'm being honest, though, I don't think you're gonna last five minutes, so it was nice knowing you. But thanks for providing me with some entertainment."

The Caucasian Eagle squawked, diving for the group.

CHAPTER FOUR

STATUE

As the eagle advanced for them, zigzagging through rocks, their pegasi whinnied and scattered. Zoey clung to Diana, her stomach clenching.

Darko readied his bow and arrows while Diana conjured a sphere of light. Kali took two spears out of the bag Luna carried. "Heads up," she said, tossing one to Andy.

He caught it and nodded. "Thanks."

Zoey wrapped her handless arm around Diana, trying not to slip backward while she grabbed her dagger with the other, but Diana looked back at Zoey and shook her head. "Just sit this one out."

"I can't just do nothing while you guys fight this thing," Zoey said.

The eagle threw his head back, screaming again, then spun through the air and veered toward the group. Diana chucked her sphere of light at him. They collided, and the eagle went somersaulting backward. "You need to do as I say," Diana said. "I'd rather you do nothing and stay safe than try to help and fall to your death."

As the eagle gathered his composure from Diana's attack, Darko sent an arrow at the monster. The projectile pierced the eagle in the stomach, and he screeched in contempt. He shot Darko a glare and flew toward Andy and the satyr. Darko nocked another arrow while Andy directed Ajax straight toward the eagle.

Andy readied his spear as he and the eagle came head-to-head, but before he could stab the eagle, the monster shot upward, seizing the spear with his beak. He flew high above them and clamped the weapon in his beak, snapping the spear in half.

"Shit," Andy said. Darko shot his arrow for the monster, but it just barely grazed the feathers of one of his wings.

Behind them, Prometheus laughed. "Oh gods, this is fun. Looks like the beastie wants to play with his food before eating it."

Kali directed Luna toward the eagle. The eagle screeched and flew toward the pair. Kali raised her spear above her head and let out a fierce battle cry, then hurled the weapon at the eagle. The monster swerved to the side, then continued flying toward Kali and Luna.

Kali made Luna dart beneath the eagle. He squawked, flipping around to come after them. Luna whinnied and darted out of his way. Diana threw a sphere of light at the monster, while Darko sent another arrow at him. He dodged their attacks with ease; it was as if the monster was anticipating their every move now.

Zoey gritted her teeth. "Guys, I'm not sure the usual monster-slaying methods will work on this guy."

"Well, do *you* have any bright ideas?" Diana asked, flinging another miniature sun at the eagle. He dipped out of the way of the attack and turned toward Zoey and Diana.

Zoey recalled how easily the eagle snapped Andy's spear with his beak, then how Diana had said it would be difficult to free Prometheus from the manacles. "I think I do, actually."

"Care to share?"

The eagle flapped toward them, and Zoey swung her legs onto one side of Aladdin. She planted her feet on the edge of his stomach.

Diana conjured another sphere of light. "What do you think you're doing?"

"I have an idea, okay?" Her heart skipped. "Well, sort of."

As the monster reached them, Aladdin veered to the right, toward Prometheus and his boulder. Zoey held her breath and focused. This was it.

As the pegasus's body jerked to the side to go the other way, Zoey used her legs to fling herself off his back. Time seemed to slow as she flew toward Prometheus. The rest of the group shouted her name.

She slammed chest-first into the edge of the boulder, her head ricocheting off it. Stars blinded her, the wind knocked from her lungs. She dug her nails into the rock to keep herself from plummeting into the canyon, her legs dangling over the edge.

"Well, that was valiant," Prometheus said. "And also very stupid."

Zoey pulled herself up and clambered to Prometheus's side, then crouched directly in front of one of his giant chained ankles, faced the eagle, and waved her hand in the air. "Oh, Mister Caucasian Eagle," she sang. The monster looked to her. "Don't you think I look scrumptious? You should fly over here and eat me instead of those guys."

Diana directed Aladdin toward Prometheus's boulder. "Zoey, stop!"

The eagle let out a vicious scream. He flapped his wings, making gusts of wind so strong Diana and Aladdin were pushed backward through the air. They crashed into a cluster of floating rocks, Diana clinging to Aladdin's mane. The eagle flapped toward Zoey.

"What exactly are you trying to accomplish?" Prometheus asked.

"We're about to find out," Zoey said, eyeing the clusters of floating rocks dozens of feet beneath Prometheus's boulder.

The eagle clacked its beak and dove for Zoey. She leapt off the boulder's side toward the rocks below.

A shrill *clang* pierced the air, reverberating across the canyon, and Zoey crashed into one of the boulders. Upon impact it teetered dangerously. She yelped, grasping its ridges, pain racking her knees and shins.

Above, the eagle let out a furious screech, and Zoey glanced to where she'd been crouched before, satisfaction rushing through her. The eagle's beak had rammed into the chains binding Prometheus's ankle to the rock, the metal fractured like a broken eggshell.

Prometheus laughed and shook his foot. "Hey, that was halfway clever."

The Caucasian Eagle glared down at Zoey, swaying side to side like a drunk in the street. He made a gurgling sound, then squawked, slowly flapping his wings to fly toward her. She reached for her dagger. *Left hand this time*, she thought, her pulse racing. *Hopefully he hit his head hard enough that I can take him now.*

"Hey, you ugly oversized dove," said the familiar voice of a boy above her.

She looked up to find Andy standing on another boulder which hovered above Prometheus's head. He swayed almost as badly as the Caucasian Eagle, the rock barely big enough to hold both his feet.

The eagle narrowed his eyes in Andy's direction. "That's right. I'm talking to you," Andy said. "Don't pay her any attention. I'm a far tastier snack." As if in agreement, the eagle shrieked and flew drunkenly toward Andy, but just before the monster reached him, he leapt off the boulder.

The eagle slammed beak-first into the rock. It shattered into pebbles, and Andy crash-landed onto a rock close to Zoey.

"Andy!" Zoey cried as the rock teetered, her friend slipping over the edge.

Andy grasped the boulder's ridges and pulled himself up, then chuckled nervously. "I'm okay, I think."

Above, the eagle screeched and began haphazardly spiraling toward the canyon below. As he passed Zoey and Andy, his wings collided with the rocks holding them and pitched them through the air. They screamed, limbs flailing as they plunged downward.

Within moments someone seized Zoey's forearm and she came to a halt midair, her shoulder feeling as if it were splitting in two. She cried out, then looked up to find it was Diana who'd grabbed her. Diana clenched her jaw and, with a massive tug, pulled Zoey onto Aladdin's back.

Zoey trembled and clung to Diana. "Andy—did someone catch him?"

"Yes," Diana said, and pointed to the left. Sure enough, Andy held tight to Kali on the back of Luna, while Darko and Ajax flew beside them. Zoey sighed in relief. *Everyone's safe.*

Far beneath them, the Caucasian Eagle let out a final weak cry, then plummeted so far into the canyon he disappeared.

Andy grinned and pumped a fist in the air. "Whoohoo! We did it!"

"Yes, we did," Diana said. "But in the process, you two almost got yourselves killed."

Zoey tensed. "Hey, at least my idea worked."

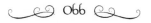

Diana looked over her shoulder and offered Zoey a mischievous grin. "Just try not to scare me so much next time, okay?"

Zoey relaxed. "I'll do my best."

Diana directed Aladdin toward Prometheus. The Titan's arms were free, although shackles still hung on his wrists like they did his ankles. His muscles bulged as he tugged on the chain around his remaining bound leg. Finally, he snapped the chain hooked to his ankle out of the rock, although the shackle remained.

"The Caucasian Eagle is gone, and you're set free," Diana said. "Now will you please help us into Poseidon's palace?"

Prometheus wiggled his hands and feet as if trying to shake the chains away. "Now, now, hold your pegasi. I said I'd help you if you freed me from these chains. Do I look freed of them to you?"

Zoey's stomach dropped. "But we *did* free you. You're not chained to those rocks anymore. You can go wherever you want now."

"Yeah," Andy added. "We did all we could. The least you could do is hold up your end of the deal."

"Did I ask for your help?" Prometheus replied. "Maybe I liked being trapped here, getting my liver eaten by the beastie every day. All I said was if you proved yourselves worthy of my help—by getting me out of these chains—I'd assist you. But as far as I'm concerned, you haven't done so."

"Well, I think Zoey and Andy proved themselves more

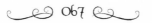

than worthy of your help," Kali said. "You're not being fair."

"Nothing in life is fair," Prometheus retorted. "That's just how it is."

"I don't understand," Darko said, shaking his head. "In the old days you did everything you could to help people, even if it meant being punished. And now it's like you're doing everything you can to avoid being a hero."

Prometheus sneered. "I've been chained up as punishment twice already. Tartarus is bound to be my next stop, and I'd prefer not to be thrown in there for the rest of eternity. If I thought you kids were worthy of my help—if I thought you had a chance of winning this war—I'd take that chance, but unfortunately you aren't worthy and you have no chance. So, sorry. It's time I save my own skin for once."

"What now, then?" Zoey said. "Are you gonna tell the gods what we're doing, where we are? Get us captured and wash everything we've worked for down the drain?"

The Titan chuckled. "Calm down, kid. I won't do that. If I turned you in to Zeus, he'd most likely assume I *was* working with you and put me in Tartarus anyway."

"Okay," Andy cut in. "You won't help us because we couldn't break you out of the shackles today. But what if we found something else, or someone else, to break them tomorrow? Or even in the next week, the next month? What if it was done later and on our behalf? Would you help us then?"

Prometheus scratched his chin as if in thought. Zoey held her breath.

"Tell you what," the Titan began. "If you bust me outta these chains within the next three days, I'll help you into ol' Poseidon's palace. But first I need to go to Aphrodite City, and I want you to escort me there on your pegasi. I would transport there, but my godly powers have been weakened because of these." He wiggled the chains. "There's some sorta enchantment on them, I think. Until I can get them off, I won't be at my most powerful."

Andy nodded. "That's fine. We can take you to Aphrodite City, and then once you finish up whatever you need to do there, we can start our three-day journey in finding a way to break your chains."

"No. The detour to Aphrodite City counts toward your three days."

Diana rubbed her temples. "You've got to be kidding me. It'll take us a whole day to reach that place, then we'll have to spend however long you want to be there, and then that will leave us with hardly any time left to find a way to break you loose."

"That's the deal I'm offering you," Prometheus said. "Take it, or you can find your own way into the palace."

"We'll do it," Zoey said. "If those are your conditions, we accept."

* ~ * ~ * ~

Karter had lost track of the days.

He did nothing but slip in and out of a restless, infection-and-nausea-induced unconscious state while the demigod trio carted him to Olympus. Over and over in his "sleep" the same nightmare plagued him . . .

Karter fell through the black abyss. If it were any other black abyss he would have been scared, and he would have screamed, but he didn't need to; there was no end in sight. The abyss went on forever. He could live like that, forever falling. But then his father materialized, green lightning bolt in hand, and suddenly he wasn't falling anymore. He stood in the Olympian throne room on New Mount Olympus.

He knew what was coming. He fell to his knees, begging for mercy. But his father didn't listen. Rather, he said, "The time has come."

Then he launched the bolt straight for Karter's face.

Each time Karter woke from the nightmare, his scar seared with familiar pain.

One night, as he slipped into unconsciousness again, he thought for sure he'd have the nightmare. After all, he'd had it dozens of times.

The dream played out the same as always, until— *Suddenly Asteria, with her burgundy hair and silver eyes, materialized.*

Karter furrowed his brow and reached for her. "Asteria? After I left Hades, I called to you, but you never came. What's—"

Before he could finish his question, the Titan goddess

disintegrated into thousands of miniature stars. They floated toward him, and once they reached him, they grabbed onto his robes like a glittering phantom and flew up, up, up.

"What's going on?" Karter asked.

"I could not come to you before," Asteria said, her voice echoing all around him. *"Zeus discovered Apollo helping Diana, and he suspected another deity had a hand in your choice to aid the Chosen Two of the Prophecy. He did not think you would have decided to on your own. I would have been caught if I came to you then, and if that were to happen, I would not have been able to help you any longer. But I have gathered my strength and bided enough time. Wake up, Karter. Wake up."*

With great effort, Karter opened his eyes, the edges of the lids crusted over with gunk. He lay on the forest floor. Pine trees loomed over him, stars twinkling in the night sky. Rope was still bound tight around his clammy, feverish body.

He glanced around. Violet and Layla slept on either side of a dying campfire, while Xander patrolled the surrounding area, their three pegasi tied to a tree.

Asteria popped her head into Karter's line of sight. "Do not be alarmed," she whispered. His stomach bubbled with nausea, his heart racing, his throat so parched he wasn't sure he could speak. Even if he *had* been alarmed at her arrival, he didn't think he was strong enough to react.

There were some snipping sounds, and the ropes loosened around Karter's body, then came undone completely and fell apart at his sides. Asteria wrapped him in her arms, her skin cool against his.

Karter closed his eyes for a moment, focusing on not retching all over Asteria, and the next time he opened them thousands of miniature stars carried him high above the forest. The demigod trio was out of sight. They traveled fast as light, but to Karter it felt as if they hadn't moved an inch from where they'd been before.

"Do not fall asleep until I say so," Asteria said, and Karter realized she'd taken the form of stars to carry him. "If you fall asleep, you may not wake this time. Your condition is graver than those three could have ever known or cared."

Where Asteria planned to take Karter, he had no idea, but until she said he could close his eyes, he'd use the last of his strength to keep them open.

* ~ * ~ * ~

Andy couldn't believe what he was seeing.

It had taken the group a whopping twenty-four hours, but the afternoon sun sat high in the sky, its golden rays shining on Aphrodite City far below them in the distance. Beyond the hills surrounding the location, acres of farmland and hundreds of thousands of stone-and-wood houses sat; they were spread for as far as he could see and appeared to make up the city's outer rim. Beyond them, in the center of the city, glistening gold-and-ivory statues and buildings held up by pillars were erected atop a mountain-like structure that stood taller than the trees.

Andy squinted. Massive hordes of people bustled about the city, and from up here, they looked like ants scurrying along sidewalks.

Ahead, Diana gestured for the group to land in the forest and directed Aladdin to descend into the trees. Everyone else followed suit.

Once they'd landed, Diana began relaying information. "All right, I know we're crunched for time, but no one can fly our pegasi or take any obvious weapons into the city. If the citizens or *astynomia* see anyone with pegasi or weapons, they're arrested on the spot." She glanced at the shackles still bound around Prometheus's hands and ankles, then looked him up and down, as if examining his giant size. Andy couldn't blame her; the Titan had to be over eight feet tall. "You're going to look really suspicious, too. Why is it that you needed to come here again? Are you sure a couple of us can't go in for you?"

"There's someone I have to see," Prometheus said. "That I have to speak with."

"Can one of us go in for you and bring out whoever you need to talk to?" Andy asked, but Diana was already shaking her head.

"No," Diana said. "Citizens can't leave the city. If they're caught, they'll be executed on the spot. Unless the citizens have permission from the gods to leave, they can't. It'll be much easier to sneak in and out rather than sneak in, sneak someone else out, then sneak back in, and so on. Prometheus will just need to disguise himself and the chains. If he doesn't, the citizens will be suspicious of him right away."

"All right," Prometheus said. "I should have enough power left in me to make a disguise at least." He clenched his fists and flexed his muscles. Veins popped up in his arms and legs, beads of sweat rolling down his forehead. Soon he began to shrink—first down to seven feet, then to six—and the shackles and chains melted and morphed until they were no more than cuff-like bracelets circling his wrists and ankles.

Once Prometheus finished disguising himself, he was still super buff, but now he could pass as a regular person and didn't look as if he'd just escaped prison or something.

Andy shot the Titan a glare. "If you could change the chains into those by yourself, why didn't you just do that in the first place?"

"They're not really changed," Prometheus replied. "They just appear to be. Titans and gods can alter their appearance and the appearances of others easily—Zeus and Poseidon were especially famous for disguising themselves in the old days to lure in unsuspecting women. Besides, I still can't get them off." The Titan pulled on the bracelets, but they didn't budge. "Anyway, the chains have drained most of my power, so this disguise is going to be difficult to maintain for long periods of time. You still have to find a way to free me of them, or you can kiss my help goodbye."

Diana crossed her arms and turned to the rest of the

group. "Whoever else goes into the city with him is going to have to steal some clothes for themselves. Especially Zoey, Andy, and Kali. You three will stick out even more than Prometheus would have without the disguise."

"Are not all of us going in?" Darko asked, biting a fingernail.

"I'm a fugitive," Diana replied, shaking her head. "By now everyone in the cities knows who I am and that the gods want me captured, so at the very least I have to stay hidden out here. The pegasi can't go in either, and I'd like one person to stay with me to help defend them in case any monsters show up while the rest of you are in the city."

"Why don't all of us wait out here while Prometheus goes in?" Andy asked. "Wouldn't that be safer?"

Diana smacked Andy's arm. "Are you stupid? Some of us have to go with Prometheus and make sure he doesn't try to escape before he helps us get into Poseidon's palace."

"Hey, I wouldn't do that," Prometheus said, then scratched his chin. "Well, actually, maybe I would."

Kali raised a hand. "I'll do the honors of staying in the forest with you, Princess."

Diana blushed, wrinkling her nose. "The *honors* of staying with *me*?"

"Oh, I must have said that wrong," Kali said, smiling. "What I meant to say is it's always an honor spending time with my pegasi—protecting them from monsters and such. You didn't think I'd trust you to watch them by yourself, did you?"

Diana crossed her arms and shook her head, chuckling slightly.

"Well, sounds like it's settled then," Prometheus said. "Diana and Kali can stay out here with the pegasi while the rest of us go in and take care of business."

Darko creased his brow. "Should we grab some weapons, too? You know, since the Caucasian Eagle kind of destroyed some of what we had?"

"Didn't Diana say it was illegal for anyone in the cities to have weapons?" Andy added. "How would we get any?"

"The *astynomia* always have weapons," Darko said. "I could sneak into one of their quarters and take some. They probably wouldn't ask any questions since I'm a satyr."

"Good thinking," Zoey replied, and the rest of the group nodded.

Prometheus started toward the city. "Well, I think we've covered everything. Let's go."

Andy and Zoey shared another look, and with that, the group followed Prometheus.

For a long time, they passed through forest. Once they'd arrived at the outer rim of Aphrodite City, acres of wheat farmland awaited them, people in loose brown clothes harvesting under the sun. The group crept along the field, careful to hide behind the tall grass and out of the people's vision, and soon they reached a neighborhood of wood-and-stone houses. Here, children and adults alike hung laundry out to dry, tended to household gardens, or gathered water from nearby wells with clay pots.

Andy, Zoey, and Prometheus scurried along the paths, careful not to draw attention to themselves and startle the citizens, while Darko clopped along.

"No one's seemed to notice us yet," Andy whispered.

Zoey nodded. "Yeah, but we still need to find some disguises."

Andy bit the tip of his thumb and eyed two nearby houses with ropes strung between them. Dozens of rust-colored cloaks, tunics, pants, and dresses were hung out to dry on the ropes. He didn't want to steal from these people, especially since he was supposed to be helping them by saving the world, but what other choice did they have?

He and Zoey looked around, making sure no one was looking. "Stay here and watch Prometheus for a few minutes while we get some new outfits," Zoey said to Darko, and the satyr nodded.

The two of them tiptoed toward the clothes. Andy grabbed a tunic, and Zoey grabbed a dress.

"No peeking," Zoey whispered, slinking behind a wall of clothes, and Andy nodded, his cheeks growing hot. He wouldn't do something like that; at least, not without Zoey telling him she wanted him to.

Andy concealed himself among the fabrics. After glancing around one last time to make sure no one could see, he tugged off his black T-shirt, tattered jeans, and filthy socks and sneakers, all of which he was sure smelled like a dumpster truck, although he'd grown accustomed to

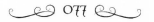

his own "natural" scent. He tossed his things into his bag and pulled the tunic over his head. To his surprise, it was comfortable: the texture that of lightweight cotton, the tip of its hem reaching his knees.

As he pressed his hands against the fabric, smoothing its wrinkles, Zoey stepped out from her fortress, her old clothes balled up in her hands. The new dress perfectly complemented Zoey's tan skin and curly brown hair, although it fell all the way to her ankles and hung straight off her body like a paper sack. Despite the way it fit, she was still gorgeous as far as Andy was concerned.

"Hey, that looks good on you," Zoey said, pointing at Andy's new getup. "Whatta ya think of mine?"

Andy smiled, careful to keep the nervousness out of his voice. "The dress is great."

Zoey stuffed her clothes into Andy's pack. "Thanks. It feels like it doesn't fit quite right, but we don't have time to play dress-up. We gotta hurry."

"Should we grab something for Diana and Kali? In case they'll need disguises later, too?" Zoey nodded and snatched another dress off the rope, then a long hooded cloak. She stuffed them into the bag as well, and the two scampered barefoot back to Darko and Prometheus.

"Do we look like proper members of Aphrodite City?" Andy asked.

"Yes, actually," Darko said, as though he was surprised.

Prometheus scratched his chin for a few moments, eyeing Zoey's attire. Finally, he snapped his fingers, and sparks crackled between them. In an instant, two shining golden ropes appeared in his hand, one noticeably longer than the other. He offered the ropes to Zoey.

"What are these for?" she asked, taking and examining them. "Won't this weaken you more? I thought your powers were limited."

Prometheus smirked. "It's a belt and a hair tie, and yes, I'm weaker than usual, but those shouldn't do me too much harm. Here, allow me." He snatched the gifts from her hands, then wrapped the longer one around her waist and double-knotted it, accentuating her prominent curves. "That'll spruce up your dress." He finished the ensemble by sweeping her hair into a low side ponytail which lay over her shoulder and stepped back to admire his work.

Zoey turned to Andy and Darko. "How does it look now?"

"Freaking beautiful," Andy blurted. Zoey blushed and looked away.

"Beautiful, but also similar to other women in the cities," Prometheus added. "No one will think she's out of place."

Zoey brushed Prometheus's gifts with her fingers. "Thank you."

For the next few hours, the group continued heading into the city. They eventually reached an even busier area that reminded Andy of the malls he'd visited in highly populated places from the Before Time, roars of chatter ringing in his ears.

Out of nowhere, a strange buzzing sensation filled Andy's chest like a swarm of flies beating against his ribs. He sucked in a sharp breath and closed his eyes. The image of a pillared white temple atop a hill flashed through his mind.

"This is the *Agora*," Darko said, and Andy snapped open his eyes, the buzzing fading away. "Every city has at least one. It's where the citizens go to buy things and socialize."

Rows of pillared shops lined the *Agora* for miles. Hundreds—no, thousands—of citizens clothed in dresses and tunics like Andy's and Zoey's, their arms and handbaskets filled with food, bustled in and out of the stores and along the cobblestone paths. Dirt roads wound every which way, leading farther into the city toward more neighborhoods and the shimmering white buildings erected high above all others. On the streets, men directed curtained, horse-drawn carts full of what Andy assumed were trading goods.

In the center of the commotion here, a golden fountain resided. Inside the structure, a sculpture of an inhumanly beautiful woman stood thirty feet high atop a large clamshell, her hair falling in waves all the way to her feet. Water cascaded from the mouths of several cherub statues—all of which stood around the woman's shell—and into the fountain. Pearls, jewels, and coins shimmered against its metallic floor, and as some citizens passed, they tossed more riches into the liquid, making it splash and ripple.

Zoey gazed at the *Agora* with wide eyes and pointed at

the statue of the woman inside the fountain. "That's Aphrodite, isn't it? The patron goddess of this city?"

Prometheus paused and nodded. "Goddess of Love and Beauty. Born from sea-foam when the Titan Kronos killed his father, Uranus, and threw the guy's, uh, genitals into the sea."

Andy shook his head. "Greek gods are so weird."

"What's weird to you might be completely normal for someone else," Prometheus replied, and Andy shrugged.

"Why are they throwing coins and stuff into the fountain?" Zoey asked. "Are they making sacrifices to Aphrodite or something?"

"Clever girl," Prometheus said. "Sacrifices for the goddess so she'll bless them and bring them prosperity."

"She looks nice," Andy said.

Prometheus snorted. "If by 'nice' you mean vain and conniving, you'd be right."

"Hey," Darko started, putting a finger to his mouth as though to shush the Titan. "We shouldn't be talking that way about a god or goddess in their own patron city, whether it's true or not. If any *astynomia* heard us, we'd be arrested."

"You're right," Prometheus said with a sigh. "Anyway, we're getting close. The bakery is only a few minutes away from here."

Andy snorted, wondering who in the world Prometheus needed to talk to there. "Let me guess, we came all this way to ask the baker for their famous cupcake recipe?"

Prometheus chuckled, walking along one of the larger paths into the *Agora*. "Nice try, but no."

Andy opened his mouth to speak again, but Zoey elbowed him in the side and gave him a look that said, *Shut up and be patient!*

Before they could follow Prometheus, Darko tapped Andy's shoulder. "Hey, it'll look strange to people if they see a satyr *astynomia* just hanging out with a couple of citizens. I'm gonna head toward one of the *astynomia* quarters and see if I can find some weapons we can steal."

Andy's pulse quickened. "Wait, you're gonna go all alone? Are you sure you'll be okay?"

"Well, yeah. You guys can't go with me to the quarters. Citizens aren't allowed there. But don't worry. I grew up in Hermes City. Even though every city is different, this is still sort of familiar territory. Just take care of whatever it is Prometheus needs to do and meet me at the fountain with the statue of Aphrodite by sundown. But no later, because that's curfew."

"Curfew?"

"Yeah, curfew. If the *astynomia* see you on the streets after the sun sets, they'll arrest you."

"Oh, lovely," Zoey said. "Okay. We'll see you here, at the very latest, by sundown."

Darko nodded and clopped away, and Andy watched, his stomach twisting in knots. He didn't like leaving Diana and Kali behind, and he definitely didn't like splitting up with Darko in the city.

Zoey tapped Andy on the shoulder, and he snapped out of his trance. "Prometheus is way ahead of us," she said, and the two of them hurried to catch up to the Titan, weaving through several citizens in the process.

Once they'd reached Prometheus's side, they slowed their pace, but the buzzing feeling snuck back into Andy's chest. He held his breath and willed it to go away, and soon it faded again.

Within less than five minutes of walking through the *Agora*, they reached a building that looked similar to the other shops but was certainly not like the rest. The unmistakable scent of fresh, savory bread mixed with sugary treats permeated the area surrounding the store, wafting into Andy's nose and making his mouth water. Prometheus paused in front of the bakery and clasped his hands, his expression almost fearful as he looked upon it.

Andy's stomach growled. "Is this the place you wanted to visit?"

"Yes," Prometheus said, then took a deep breath and marched toward the entrance. Andy and Zoey shared a look and followed the Titan.

As they stepped inside the bakery, the smells grew even stronger, the interior stuffy and warm. No customers perused the place, which surprised Andy, because it had the most delicious-looking food he'd seen since the world had ended, and possibly even since *before* the world had ended. Tables stacked with bundles of every kind of baked item Andy could imagine—bread loaves, biscuits, doughnuts, pretzels, muffins, bagels, and cookies—lined the shop from side to side. At the back of the store a young woman worked away, pulling trays of more goodies out of fiery clay ovens. She wore a tattered terracotta-colored tunic, her frizzy black hair pulled into a bun atop her head.

When Prometheus laid his eyes on the working girl, he halted and stared as though in a trance. She turned around and set a tray of steaming biscuits atop an empty spot at the nearest table, giving the group a dazzling smile when she saw them.

Andy blinked a few times, a little surprised at how attractive the girl was. She couldn't have been older than him and stood around his height, with a slim build, brown skin, and big dark eyes like circular pools of sweet Co-ca-Cola. Her ears stuck out more than the average person's, but coupled with the delicate lines of her face, it was cute.

"Good afternoon," she greeted them, her voice soft as a lullaby. She took off her oven mittens and set them aside. "Thank you so much for stopping in. What can I help you with today? Were you looking for anything in particular?"

For a few minutes, Prometheus said nothing, only staring wide-eyed at the girl. Andy would have said something, but he had no idea what. He didn't know why they were there; he just needed to fulfill Prometheus's requests.

Finally, Prometheus spoke up, clenching his hands at his sides. "Young lady, are you related to Nylah? The woman who owned this shop seventy-five years ago?"

The girl took a step back. "Well, yes. My family has

owned this bakery for over a hundred years. Nylah was my great-great-grandmother. But who—who are you? And why do you care?"

"My dear . . . if Nylah was your great-great-grandmother, then unless she had another child later in life, that would make me your great-great-grandfather."

Andy's jaw dropped, and he shared a look of shock with Zoey. Prometheus wanting to come to Aphrodite City finally made sense. This was where he'd met the woman he'd had a child with—the woman he'd been re-imprisoned for.

The working girl in the bakery ran to the entrance of the shop, slammed the doors shut, locked them, then swung around to face Prometheus with a frantic look in her eyes. "You're really him? The Titan? Prometheus? My great-great-grandfather?" She didn't take a breath between questions. Andy's head spun, and he wasn't even the one asking them.

Prometheus scratched his chin. "Well, did Nylah have any other children besides Mozes?"

"No. And Mozes went to live on New Mount Olympus and trained there and became a Warrior of the Gods and had an affair with a regular mortal named Jin who got pregnant and Mozes couldn't help her with the baby because of the gods so Nylah took care of them and—"

"Whoa, whoa, whoa," Prometheus interrupted. "Slow down, young lady. I hardly understood a word you just said. Did you say Mozes became a Warrior of the Gods? And had an affair with a regular mortal?" The girl nodded.

"What else do you know about my son's life?"

The girl sighed. "He died a long time ago—in battle. I wish I could tell you more about him, but that's all I know. My parents could have, but they're gone now . . . I'm so sorry."

Prometheus hung his head. "There's no need to apologize. It's been a long time." His voice cracked as he said it. He wiped his eyes and looked up. "What's your name?"

"My name?" She gave him a puzzled expression, as if she hadn't expected him to ask. "Why, it's Jasmine."

That's pretty, Andy thought, and Prometheus smiled. "Jasmine is the perfect name for such a lovely girl. You look . . . you look so much like her. Like Nylah. Beautiful, just beautiful."

Jasmine put her hand to her heart. "Thank you. I must say, I'm both surprised and happy you're here. I've been without family for so long now. I've been alone . . ." Her eyes grew sad, but she forced a smile and brushed a few disheveled curls that had fallen out of her bun behind her ears. "I have much to ask you. How did you escape the Caucasian Eagle, the gods?"

Prometheus drew closer to Jasmine, explaining to her how he'd been freed by Andy, Zoey, and the rest of the group—thankfully leaving out the part about how the group was trying to lead a war on the gods, and how if they took Prometheus to Aphrodite City and broke his chains, he'd help them into Poseidon's palace.

The strange buzzing sensation in Andy's chest started

up again, but this time it spread through his body, drowning out everything else. He closed his eyes, rubbing his temples, the same image from before—the one of the pillared white temple—flashing through his mind.

The temple is here in the city, he thought, although he had no idea how he knew. *It's here. I gotta find it.*

"What's wrong?" Zoey whispered, resting a hand on his shoulder. "Are you okay?" He gritted his teeth, the image of the building growing crisper in his mind. Somehow, he knew it held answers he needed to uncover.

Andy opened his eyes and looked to Zoey. "I gotta go."

"What the hell do you mean? We have to stay with Prometheus to make sure he doesn't try to run off."

Andy headed toward the bakery's entrance and shoved the bar locking the door out of place. The door *creak*ed open. "You're gonna have to stay with him. I'll explain later when I see you at the fountain with Darko."

"Andy!" Zoey cried, but he was already out the door and stumbling into a crowd.

Andy shoved past people along the paths, the buzzing reverberating through his body stronger as the seconds passed, his vision going blurry. He had no idea where he was, nor how to reach the temple from here. But at the same time, he did.

After a while of walking through the city, unsure of his purpose but knowing he must fulfill whatever it was, Andy paused. His vision cleared, and the buzzing subsided. He groaned, then rubbed his eyes and looked up.

Before him beckoned the temple in his mind, located in a more remote area of the city. Hardly any shops sat around it. It looked just as it did in his vision and stood atop a small hill, white and pillared and about the size of a narrow house.

Andy's breath caught in his throat, his pulse quickening. He'd never seen this place. He hadn't even known it existed before today. But now he felt as though he might explode if he didn't go inside.

He raced up the steps and barreled through the temple's entrance, then halted as he looked upon its interior. Metallic torches lined the walls. He could imagine them blazing with orange fire, but on this evening they hosted no flames.

Although the inside of the temple was dark, the sunlight pouring in from outside illuminated the walls, floor, and ceiling, which looked as though they were made of gold with swirls carved throughout. No one else was here, but at the back, hoisted on a golden stand, a tall statue of a young man with feathered, butterfly-shaped wings and a bow and arrow ready in hand gazed down at him.

Andy walked tentatively toward the statue. He wanted to get a better look at it; he wanted to figure out who it depicted. Something about it—he didn't know what—made him want to know more.

As he grew closer to the statue, the torches began to light with crackling flames, one by one, revealing thick dust which coated everything here. Chills rushed through him. What could be causing this? He glanced around. The temple was empty.

He took a deep breath. *Just focus on the statue. Who is it? Why did it call me here?*

How did I know it's even what called me here?

When he reached the statue, he looked around for something that would indicate who it was but could find nothing except a square plate bolted to the stand with something—he guessed a name or title—carved into it, indistinguishable because of the dust caking everything. *If I just wipe the gunk off . . .*

He went to brush the muck away with his hand, but as he touched the plate, an electric shock jolted through his body. The hairs on his arms and legs stood up straight, goose bumps rising all over his skin. But before he could pull away, before he could fall back, his body went still.

He felt as if he were petrified. He tried to call out, tried to scream, but he couldn't even part his lips. The only sound that came was a muffled grunt.

Dark clouds of smoke crept into the corners of his vision and swallowed him whole.

CHAPTER FIVE

PAST

Before Karter knew it, Asteria had laid him down on a stiff bed inside what she said was a healing shrine. She hadn't told him which one, and it could have been one of many, since every city had one—all of which were dedicated to a demigod child-of-Apollo from the old days, Asclepius— and Karter's vision was so blurred he couldn't determine which city he was in by building structure and décor alone.

Asteria whispered in Karter's ear, "Close your eyes now. You are safe. You will live." And he did as she said, almost instantly falling into a dreamless slumber.

When he woke again, the sun shone through the single window of the room he lay in. Asteria was nowhere to be seen, but a quick look at the room told him where he was: Hephaestus City.

The walls, ceiling, and door were crafted from a hodge-podge of metals. On one side of Karter's bed there was an iron toilet; on the other a steaming stove, its gears and cogs working away to keep the room at a comfortable temperature. On the other end of the room stood a stool and a grandfather clock. The clock was the biggest indicator Karter was in Hephaestus City, as Hephaestus was the only Olympian who allowed the people of his city to tell time with some of the same methods people from the Before Time used. It was quite odd in his opinion. However, as far as Karter knew, allowing this hadn't done Hephaestus any harm; Hephaestus's people seemed to love him for the most part.

Karter groaned, rubbing his eyes. Why had Asteria brought him to Hephaestus City? Had she struck a deal with the Blacksmith of the Gods himself to keep Karter concealed from Zeus? No, that couldn't be—Hephaestus may have been abused by the gods in the past, but surely he was no traitor. He had no reason to be. After all, this entire city was named for the god, with over one hundred thousand followers living here.

Karter's head throbbed with pain, his throat parched. Regardless of his discomfort, he had a feeling the people of the healing shrine had already done some work on him. The knife wounds he'd acquired didn't sting and were bandaged, his skin no longer clammy and feverish. *At least I'm not on the brink of death now*, he thought.

A light knock sounded from the door, and it opened. A young girl stepped inside, a bucket in one hand. She was probably ten years younger than Karter and a foot shorter. She wore purple robes, her sweet face chubby, her skin a light brown. Her dark coils of hair bounced with each step she took.

She made her way to his bedside and set down the bucket, some water sloshing out of it and onto the floor. "Hello, sir," she said in a straightforward, confident tone he hadn't expected from such a small girl. "My name is Ivy, and I'll be your primary caretaker for the duration of your time spent in the Hephaestus City Healing Shrine."

"Hello, Ivy. I'm . . ." He paused for a moment. He couldn't reveal his identity. These people would surely turn him in to Zeus the moment they discovered it.

"Erick," Ivy finished for him. "When your employer dropped you off, she told us all about you." Karter nodded slowly. Asteria must have pretended to be his employer and then created a fake identity for him. Was that all she'd done to disguise who he was, or had she altered his looks as well?

He reached up to the right side of his face, and his fingers brushed smooth flesh. *It can't be*, Karter thought. *My scar can't be gone. That's impossible.*

"Don't worry, Erick," Ivy continued. "We'll have you feeling better in no time."

* ~ * ~ * ~

When the smoke cleared, Andy found himself no longer in the strange, empty temple with the winged statue of a man.

He stood in a garden, one grander than he'd ever seen before. Cypress trees grew hundreds of feet tall here,

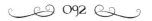

bushes with colorful flowers at every corner, their potent scents filling his nose. There were marble fountains with water flowing into ponds, and shining paths that looked as though they were made of gold. A vast black galaxy full of colorful planets and glittering stars looked down upon the garden. They seemed to hover so close Andy felt as though he could reach up and pluck them from the sky.

Somehow, this place felt familiar, although Andy knew he'd never been here before.

Up ahead a woman giggled. Who was there?

Andy walked along a path toward the laughter. Within moments, he reached a marble gazebo hidden behind bushes and trees. Under the gazebo a man and woman stood together, holding hands and swaying back and forth as though dancing to a tune only they could hear.

As Andy stepped closer, he recognized the man: he looked just like the statue in the temple, feathered butterfly-shaped wings and all. The man's dark hair was cut short, his features youthful. He wore white robes which reached his knees.

The woman appeared to be about the winged man's age, maybe a little older—but if so, not by much. Her flowing turquoise dress reached the ground, her brown hair falling in curls all the way down her back.

Andy slipped behind a rosebush. He didn't think these people would hurt him, but he felt as if he'd intruded on an intimate moment between them. The man stopped dancing and pulled the woman close, bringing his lips to

hers in a tender kiss.

The man pulled away, though still embracing the woman. "I love you, Calliope."

Andy's cheeks grew hot and he glanced away, for a moment reminded of his feelings for Zoey. He still hadn't told her how he felt, and he didn't know how to. After all, he'd never been in love before. How was he supposed to know if that's really what it was?

When he looked back at the man and woman, they were gone, the gazebo empty. The garden and everything in it began to disintegrate, breaking into tiny particles of matter, then coming together to form clouds of black smoke. The smoke engulfed Andy much like before, and he was transported to a new scene.

Andy stood in a dining hall now, one longer than a football field and taller than a four-story house. Candles and torches lined columns supporting the room's ceiling, where carvings depicting what seemed to be the Greek gods and goddesses were featured.

Hundreds of people stood in the chamber—all tall, gorgeous, and decked out in silk robes and fine jewelry— their attention focused on one hugely muscular, bearded man who floated high above them, his white robes curling around him as though blowing in a breeze that wasn't there.

Andy remembered the bearded man from the first vision Spencer had ever given Andy and Zoey. It was Zeus, King of the Gods.

"Fellow gods and goddesses," Zeus boomed, and Andy

realized, breath caught in his throat, that he must be seeing a vision of New Mount Olympus. "Today I gather you here to propose what is to be done about our—*problems* with humanity." The deities exploded into fits of nervous whispers.

"Now, now," Zeus continued. "I know it seems hopeless, my dear subjects. It seems as if humanity has forgotten us forever. It seems as if they will never again pray to us or give us beautiful sacrifices. I know many of you are frightened you will be the next god to fade away, never to be seen or heard from again, as am I. But I believe I have found a way to remedy this issue."

A goddess near the front of the dining hall scoffed. "Oh, really? And what might that be?"

Zeus gave them a sinister smile. "We will show humanity our power and make them bow down once again. To remind them of who once ruled the world, we must destroy the one they have created. In the process, many will die, but they will know of our greatness again." The crowd let out a collective gasp, and then everyone went silent.

Andy furrowed his brow, the realization hitting him. This must be a vision of the past, a vision of when the gods decided to destroy the modern world. But why was he seeing it now? He already knew what had happened. Diana and Spencer had explained it to him and Zoey.

"What will the other pantheons say? The Norse, the Egyptians, and the rest—will they not stop us?" a god in the crowd asked.

Zeus shook his head. "They will know nothing of it. I have seen many visions, a few of which revealed to me what we must do to rid ourselves of all other gods in order to execute this plan properly."

A goddess near Andy marched through the crowd toward the front, and immediately Andy recognized her as the woman in the garden—Calliope. *She must be a goddess*, Andy thought. The winged man stood behind her, only a few feet away from Andy, a look of concern etched on his youthful features. *And he must be a god. Just like I thought.*

"All of you, listen to me," Calliope shouted. "Destroying the world humanity has created will do nothing but anger them. They will not see us as great gods deserving of worship. They will see us as monsters, as demons. They will hate us, and it will only further lead us down a path of destruction."

Zeus narrowed his eyes at her. "Insolent fool. You are not King of the Gods, are you? You do not see visions of the future, nor do you know what is best for this pantheon. How dare you speak out with such foolishness."

Calliope balled her fists. "No, I am not King of the Gods. Nor do I see visions of the future. But I know humanity, and they do not need us anymore. As sad as that fact is, it is no reason to hurt them. It is the natural progression of the universe. Destroying what they have created, getting rid of the other pantheons—I cannot foresee these actions causing anything but total chaos and misery."

The crowd broke out into hushed conversation.

"Zeus has clearly lost his mind—"

"I cannot see this working out in our favor—"

"Calliope is right, you know—"

"The other pantheons would surely overcome us if we tried such a thing—"

Zeus snarled and balled his fists, sparks of electricity crackling in his hands and snaking up his arms. "Silence!"

The dining hall went quiet, and then it began to disintegrate, much like the garden had before. Soon all the gods disappeared, transforming into black smoke and consuming Andy again. Once it cleared, a new scene unfolded before him.

The winged god from both of Andy's visions wept at the foot of a marble statue inside a dark and empty temple, its cold air seeping into Andy's skin. The statue stood tall and beautiful, and Andy immediately recognized it as the goddess Calliope.

The winged god climbed to his feet, his body trembling. He brushed one of the statue's cheeks with the back of his hand. "My love, there must be a way to see you again. Even though you have faded away . . ."

Sobs escaped the god's throat, and Andy's eyes grew warm and watery. He almost let a tear or two slip himself. He knew how hard it was to lose a loved one. He'd lost his parents, his sister, his best friend Mark, and Spencer. If it weren't for the people he had now—Kali, Diana, Darko, and Zoey—he wasn't sure how he could go on, even if he didn't know them as well as he had his loved ones from the Before Time. Yes, saving the world was his job, but he knew he couldn't do it alone. No one could.

Andy waited for a long while as the god wept. Finally, the god wiped his eyes and took a deep breath, then looked to the statue of Calliope. "If there is a way to see you again, I will search the stars for it. Even if it takes a millennium . . . I will find it. I will see you again, my love. I promise." Just as the god finished his pledge, the vision disintegrated, and again black smoke overcame Andy.

He expected the smoke to clear, to transport him into another vision. But instead, the smoke grew darker. Sharp pain unlike anything he'd experienced before electrocuted his shoulder blades. It felt as if blasts of ice and fire battled beneath his flesh. His head spun. He cried out, falling to his knees and slamming his eyes shut.

For what seemed like forever, the pain seared Andy's back. He gritted his teeth; he pulled his hair. He writhed and screamed on the ground until finally the sensation faded.

He opened his eyes to find himself lying on the floor in the temple in Aphrodite City, his vision blurred as if he'd lost his glasses. Had they fallen off while he was out, or had someone come in and taken them?

He shot up, grimacing at the aches in his back. It was stiff and felt as if he'd worked his muscles until they'd torn open. But why were they sore? They had no reason to be, right? He shook his head. The pain didn't matter right now. He needed to find his glasses, and fast.

He climbed to his feet and looked around, raising his

brow as he noticed the frames in his peripheral vision. He threw his hands to his face, finding his glasses secure on his head.

Confused, he took them off, then glanced around the temple and gasped, unable to believe his eyes. His surroundings were perfectly crisp and clear: the temple's golden interior, the blazing torches, the statue of the winged man staring down at him, bow and arrow in hand.

Andy dropped his glasses. They clattered against the floor. For as long as he could remember, his sight had been terrible. How could he suddenly have great vision? Even when Diana had healed him, she'd never been so powerful she'd fixed his eyes. What the hell was going on?

Andy's gaze traveled from the face of the statue down to the plaque bolted to its stand. Dust still covered the writing; he hadn't been able to wipe it away before being swept into those crazy visions. Now that he'd been released from them, could he clean it up?

Andy reached out with a shaking hand, afraid of what might happen if he touched the plaque again. *I just need to find out who the statue depicts . . .*

He wiped the muck away, the plaque's metal smooth against his fingertips, and to his relief nothing happened.

Anteros
Son of Aphrodite and Ares
God of Requited Love
Avenger of the Unrequited

Andy shivered. *Anteros.* Why did that name sound familiar? What myth had he heard about this god from?

No, wait. Why was he suddenly so focused on stuff that didn't matter in the grand scheme of things? Who cared about this temple? Who cared about the statue, or who it was supposed to be?

What mattered was getting Prometheus out of Aphrodite City and freeing the Titan of his chains. What mattered was reaching Poseidon's palace and stealing the Trident, all the while keeping the Helm safe. Coming here had wasted precious time and effort. Why had he been so compelled to do it? Why had his body practically forced him to?

He put his head in his hands. What he really needed to do was find Zoey, Prometheus, and Darko, and get back to Diana and Kali. What he needed to do was continue his quest to save humanity from the gods.

Andy stumbled toward the entrance of the temple, grimacing at the pain in his back. When he got outside, he looked to the sky, his stomach clenching.

The sun had almost set.

* ~ * ~ * ~

Zoey's heart hammered in her chest as she stood in the bakery with Prometheus and Jasmine. She'd wanted to chase after Andy when he'd left. She was worried about him and wanted an explanation, but she couldn't leave

Prometheus for fear she'd lose him in the city.

What's going on with Andy? Where did he go? Is he okay?

Since he'd left, Prometheus and Jasmine had resumed their conversation. They'd discussed how after Prometheus had been re-imprisoned by the gods, Nylah, Jasmine's great-great-grandmother, had been left to raise their son, Mozes, by herself. When the boy had turned ten years old, the gods had brought him to New Mount Olympus, leaving Nylah all alone in the bakery.

"My parents told me Mozes ended up having a fling with a girl named Jin here in Aphrodite City," Jasmine said. "It was during one of his missions, but he had to end things because he could never marry her."

Prometheus glanced at Zoey. "The gods discourage relationships between demigods and regular mortals. They're scared of being betrayed, but they also know from personal experience how hard it is to control, uh, primal urges." Zoey bit her lip, nodding. None of this surprised her, since it seemed most of the gods she'd heard about had at least one demigod child. She guessed there were dozens of demigods on New Mount Olympus, too.

"Right," Jasmine continued. "But Jin had still become pregnant with Mozes's child, and later gave birth to Grandpa Qasim. Jin ended up living with Nylah in the bakery, as Nylah was thrilled to have a grandson. Grandpa Qasim grew up in the bakery and went on to marry Grandma Esi, and they had two children, Aunt Amari and my mother, Sadarah. Mother said Amari died when she was sixteen, but Mother grew up and married my father, Zaheer. I'm their only child.

"But, you see, Father was put to death about a year ago." Jasmine's eyes filled with tears. "The aristocracy of Aphrodite City had raised the taxes to an even more ridiculous amount than before, which they'd done eight other times since I'd been born. What's worse is they never even put the taxes toward the city. They just spend it on useless items for themselves. And, well, Father had had enough. He joined a protest group of other men and women like himself: hard-working business owners who were struggling to keep their homes afloat because of what the government kept doing to them.

"Our patron goddess, Aphrodite, didn't seem to care about what was happening to all of us, and she allowed the aristocracy to put the protesters to death. Shortly after the . . ." She choked on a sob, and Prometheus rested a hand on her shoulder. "S-sorry. Shortly after the e-execution, Mother died. The caretakers in our healing shrine said the only explanation was death of a broken heart. She'd simply lost her will to live. Since then, I've been all alone, caring for the bakery and doing the best I can to survive despite the fact the aristocracy has raised the taxes yet again.

"It's getting to the point where I can hardly keep the business running." She sighed. "I can't even afford to hire any help. I've had to let go of every employee that worked here before, and now I do all the work on my own. My life has become nothing but this place and awful memories.

Thankfully I still have loyal customers, so I don't have to worry about that."

Prometheus balled his fists. "Unbelievable. The gods can't expect worship if they allow their officials to continue mistreating their citizens."

"We hardly matter to our own patron goddess, let alone the whole pantheon itself," Jasmine replied. "The sacrifices we're required to make every month to Aphrodite and the rest of the gods don't hold a candle to the ones our aristocracy makes daily for them. I mean, sure, if we disobey the gods it's a huge deal, but other than that, they don't seem to care much about us."

Zoey thought for a moment, then joined in on their conversation. "Isn't Aphrodite the goddess of love? I mean, if you ask me, it doesn't sound very 'loving' that she just lets her government take advantage of the people in her city like that. I know you said she's vain and conniving, but allowing her own citizens to be executed for a protest just sounds plain cruel."

Prometheus sneered. "That awful Harpy embodies all of those things. Vain, conniving, *and* cruel."

"Forget I said anything," Jasmine said hurriedly, shaking her head. "Before Aphrodite—or someone else—hears us talking about this. Please. I don't want to get in trouble. I don't want to share the same fate as my parents." Prometheus clamped his mouth shut, lowering his gaze.

Zoey glanced out one of the bakery's windows, panic flooding through her as she realized the sun had already begun to set. She rushed to the Titan's side and grabbed his arm. "We have to go meet Andy and Darko. It's almost curfew."

"You can stay with me tonight," Jasmine said. "I mean, I don't know how long it will be before the gods discover Prometheus has come here, but it means everything to me that you helped bring him here and that I got to meet him. You're welcome in my home."

Zoey's chest tightened with guilt. After all, this poor girl had been alone for a whole year now, working herself to death and not gaining anything for it. She finally had a piece of her family back, but Zoey and Andy were taking him away. *It'll be for her own good*, Zoey thought. *Once the gods are defeated, she'll be free.*

"No, thank you," Zoey replied. "I'm sorry, but we have to go. It's important." Jasmine's expression fell.

Prometheus pulled away from Zoey's grasp. "Important to who? It's not to me."

Zoey's jaw dropped. "You can't be serious right now. We had a deal."

"That may be so," Prometheus replied. "But I can't go through with it. My family—or what's left of it—needs me."

"The entire world needs you," Zoey cried. "If you helped us save it, you'd be doing your family the greatest favor you ever could. Far greater than staying here with your great-great-granddaughter."

Jasmine glanced back and forth at Zoey and Prometheus, brow furrowed. "What are you talking about?" She locked eyes with Zoey. "What do you mean when you say the entire world needs him?"

Zoey sighed. "It's better for your safety if you don't know the details."

Jasmine opened her mouth to reply, but Prometheus stepped between them, narrowing his eyes at Zoey. "Which is why you won't be telling her a single thing. Now leave, before the sun sets and you and your friends get arrested."

"As if you care," Zoey spat.

What was the group supposed to do now? The Fates had given them one way to get into Poseidon's palace, and that was to ask Prometheus for his help. They'd freed him as best they could, taken him where he'd asked to go, and even agreed to break his chains before their three days with him were up—but he'd still backed out on the deal.

Zoey's fingers twitched with the urge to grab Prometheus by his hair and yell at him until he agreed to aid them, but she knew doing so wouldn't help and would only waste more time they didn't have. *No matter what I say, this guy's not going to help us*, she thought. With that realization, she held her chin high and swung around, then stomped out of the bakery.

When she reached the paths outside, she hurried through the *Agora* back to the fountain with the statue of Aphrodite. Very few people were out and about now, and most seemed to be wrapping up their business and heading into various surrounding neighborhoods. Satyrs that looked much older than Darko, with muscles like a bodybuilder's and horns nearly a foot high, crept along every corner of the marketplace, eyes on the citizens and weapons in hand.

It didn't take long for Zoey to reach the fountain, and when she did she saw Darko, a couple of big bags slung over his back. The satyr's worried gaze traveled up and down the streets. Andy was nowhere to be seen.

"Darko," Zoey called, racing to his side.

The satyr met her eyes, relief washing over his face. "Phew. You made it. I got some more weapons and some thread for the—" The relief faded, replaced with concern. "Wait, where's Andy?"

"He ran off. He said he had to go somewhere, but that he'd meet us here."

"And Prometheus?"

"He decided he's not helping us now. He has family here and wants to stay."

The color drained from Darko's face. "What're we gonna do?"

"I have no idea. Start over, I guess?"

Farther ahead, a satyr barked orders at a citizen. Darko eyed the scene, then grabbed Zoey's arm. "C'mon. The closer it gets to curfew, the more suspicious we'll look. We need to hide." The pair scurried between two buildings next to the fountain, now hidden from sight unless someone stepped straight in front of them.

"I'll watch for Andy," Darko said. "But we need to stay

quiet." Zoey nodded, and they waited together in silence.

As the sun fell farther in the sky, Zoey's heart raced. Where was Andy? What if he'd stumbled upon something he wasn't supposed to? What if he'd been discovered as one of the mortals from the Before Time? What if he'd been arrested, and she and Darko had to go break him out of whatever kind of jail they had here? If that happened, the gods would surely sniff out their trail.

Today couldn't get any worse, Zoey thought, and with that, a blanket of night fell over Aphrodite City. She and Darko exchanged nervous glances but remained where they were, the surrounding area so quiet Zoey could hear the blood pounding in her ears.

For a few minutes they remained like that, until the sound of hooves clopping and the familiar cries of a young man pierced the air. Darko squinted, peering into the dark marketplace. "A centaur *astynomia* got Andy," he whispered, his voice panicked.

Zoey pushed past Darko and looked into the *Agora*. Beside the fountain, Andy struggled against a shirtless man who, from the waist down, possessed the body of a black stallion. *A centaur*, she thought. *That's what Darko called him.*

The centaur stood nearly as tall as Prometheus when the Titan was in his true form. His cheekbones and jawline were as sharp as the daggers hanging from a belt around his waist, dark hair falling in braids down his back. He wrapped his beefy hands around Andy's throat and lifted the boy off the ground. Andy choked as if he couldn't breathe, struggling against the centaur's grasp. "What were ya doin' out past curfew, *peasant scum?*" the centaur asked, his voice gravelly and vicious.

Zoey's nostrils flared. She swung around and threw open the bag on Darko's back to find several weapons. She rummaged through the bag, then pulled out an axe that was almost identical to the one she'd been using before it had been sucked into Tartarus along with her severed hand. "Okay," she started, facing Darko. "We're gonna fight this guy, save Andy, then get outta here as fast as we can."

The satyr set his jaw, dropped the extra bags slung over his shoulder, and readied his bow and an arrow. "You got it."

Zoey and Darko bolted into the marketplace, side by side and weapons ready. "Hey," Zoey called to the centaur, brandishing her new axe. "Leave him alone!"

The centaur turned to her and Darko. "Another one? Hey, satyr! What're ya waitin' for? Get the girl." Darko shook his head. To Zoey's surprise, the centaur's eyes lit with excitement rather than darkening in anger, as she'd imagined they would when he witnessed a fellow *astynomia* breaking the rules. "So, we're dealin' with two peasants out past curfew—one of who thinks she's real tough since she stole one of our axes—*and* with an insubordinate little satyr? Me'n the boys are gonna have fun t'night."

Zoey gripped the axe's handle tight. She'd fought monsters and survived a battle against a goddess at the edge of Tartarus. Sure, she'd lost her hand and with it a good chunk of her fighting abilities, but she wasn't alone. Darko was with her; what did she have to be scared of? Together, they'd take this centaur down no problem.

Her resolve quickly faded as two more centaurs and four satyrs crept out from the shadows surrounding her and Darko, all of them nearly as huge as the one holding Andy captive. They smiled in malice, the blades of their weapons glinting in the moonlight.

Before Zoey could make another move, the centaur holding Andy flung the boy to the side. Andy crashed headfirst into the street, and the seven *astynomia* galloped toward Zoey and Darko.

CHAPTER SIX

DISGUISE

One of the centaurs charged straight for Zoey, sword ready. Zoey mustered her strength and slashed deep into his side. He cried out and fell back, blood spraying from his wound.

Beside Zoey, Darko sent arrows flying. They *whoosh*ed past her head. Within moments, two satyrs who'd been galloping toward them lay motionless on the ground, arrows sticking out from their chests.

A particularly large satyr—whose human torso and goat legs were so meaty he looked as if he could have been a sumo wrestler, the horns curling from his skull so massive they made him a foot taller than he really was—clopped toward Zoey, his body jiggling with every step. Dozens of small blades hung from his belt, even more held between his fingers.

Zoey readied her axe, preparing to attack again. The colossal creature brought his hands back, then launched the blades between his fingers forward. Four of the weapons shot through the air toward Zoey. She yelped, ducking and throwing her arms up to protect her head, but it wasn't enough to completely save her from the attack.

Three of the blades pierced her: one in each of her forearms and one in her thigh. Sharp pain seared from the wounds and she shrieked, dropping her axe and stumbling backward. She toppled into a cobblestone path, her eyes watering. Warm, sticky blood gushed from her injuries and seeped into her dress. A metallic odor filled her nostrils.

Darko launched an arrow. It sailed for Zoey's attacker, but the creature dodged the projectile with a speed Zoey could hardly believe. As the assailant regained his footing, he thrust his hands in Darko's direction. More blades went flying. Darko lunged to the side. However, he wasn't fast enough. Two of the weapons sank into his shoulder. He yelped, dropping his bow.

"Darko!" Zoey cried.

The centaur who'd originally held Andy captive clopped toward Zoey. When he reached her, he seized her by the throat and yanked her off the path. He brought her face so close to his she could smell wine on his breath.

The centaur's lips curled into a sinister smile. "Thought you'd get away with murderin' a couple'a hard-workin' *astynomia*, huh? Thought you'd get away with stealin' one of our own, gettin' him to betray us? How'd that work out for ya, little girl? Ya woulda just spent a month or two in jail and had to pay some hefty fines if you'd've cooperated in the first place, but now . . . oh, little girl, yer in a heapin' amount'a trouble. In fact"—the centaur gave Zoey's throat a hard squeeze, her vision going starry—"yer in so much trouble, the both a ya, I think it'd be best to kill ya now. That'll be more merciful than what the aristocracy will wanna do with ya, and it'll be more fun for *me*."

The centaur flung Zoey to the ground, and the three remaining *astynomia* dragged Darko to her side and kicked him down. All four of the *astynomia* gathered around Zoey and Darko, and the centaur raised his sword above his head, ready to strike.

Zoey closed her eyes. *I guess this is the end*, she thought. *I'm sorry, Diana. I'm sorry, Andy.* A tear trickled down her cheek, the handsome face of Spencer, Son of Hades, flashing across her mind. *I'm sorry, Spencer. I'm sorry you died for nothing.*

The sound of a blade slicing through guts filled the air. The centaur gasped.

Zoey's eyes shot open and she glanced up at the creature. A sword had been thrust through the centaur's chest, and Zoey guessed the weapon belonged to one of the other creatures she and Darko had knocked down earlier. The centaur's dark eyes grew wide, blood trickling from his wound and the corners of his mouth.

The weapon was twisted, then pulled from his body. He went stiff and fell onto his back. Andy stood before them, battered and bruised with a bump the size of a golf ball on his head, bloody sword in hand.

Relief flooded Zoey. Andy was up and fighting; they still had a chance to escape this.

Dread replaced relief as the two remaining satyrs—the huge one with dozens of knives on his belt, and a smaller one with a curved dagger in hand—knocked the sword from Andy's grasp. It clattered into the street. Andy groaned and swayed to the side, as if he was dizzy.

The smaller satyr brandished his knife in Andy's face. "Just for that, you'll be the first to die. Have fun in the Fields of Punishment, you filthy peasant sc—"

As if it had appeared from thin air, a long bulky chain swooped in from the left and wrapped itself around the smaller satyr's neck before the satyr could finish his sentence. Like a python snaring its prey, the chain tightened its hold. The satyr dropped his dagger and clawed at the iron links, but they only seemed to grow tighter. His eyes bulged. He choked for breath.

The last remaining centaur ran to the aid of the choking satyr and tried to pry the chain off his companion, while the larger satyr with the throwing knives turned to the left and glared into the darkness, where the rest of the chain remained suspended in the air. "Who goes there? Who else *dares* attack the *astynomia* of Aphrodite City?"

The chain rattled, and Zoey smiled as the familiar behemoth of a man stepped into view.

Prometheus.

The Titan's disguise had melted away to reveal his true form. He dragged the rest of his chains behind him.

The Titan narrowed his eyes at the *astynomia* and pulled so hard on the links wrapped around the smaller satyr's throat that the creature's skin turned blue. The satyr choked for a few moments, then went limp. Prometheus allowed the chain to loosen, and the *astynomia* fell to the ground.

The satyr with the knives snarled, thrusting several of his blades in Prometheus's direction. However, even as they pierced the Titan's chest, he barely flinched. Prometheus swung the chains attached to his wrists into the air toward the last two *astynomia*.

The links snaked themselves around the necks of the creatures, and Prometheus yanked his arms backward, securing the hold of his chains with titanic strength. The *astynomia* tried to cry out, but all they could muster were garbled sounds of panic.

For a few moments the *astynomia* remained that way, choking and clawing at their necks, until finally their skin turned a similar blue as their companion's, and they went still. Prometheus loosened the grip of his chains, and the satyr and centaur fell to the ground. The Titan pulled the links back to his side.

"You came back for us," Zoey said, her jaw clenched while she tried to ignore her wounds as they screamed in agony.

Prometheus chuckled, plucking the knives from his chest and tossing them into the street. "Way to state the obvious."

"What made you change your mind?"

"My great-great-granddaughter . . . the last piece of

Nylah I have left. All you need to know is if my chains aren't gone in the next two days, no one gets my help into Poseidon's palace."

Andy stumbled to Zoey's side, crinkling his nose at the dead bodies scattered around the *Agora*. "In other news, the people of Aphrodite City have a big mess to clean up in the morning."

"No," Darko replied, his voice strained with pain. "Wait. Watch them." Zoey raised an eyebrow at the satyr but did as he said, watching the bodies of the dead *astynomia*.

Within seconds, something incredibly strange happened. The blood splattered in the street—the blood of the satyr and centaur *aystynomia*—evaporated. Their torsos trembled and shrank, their limbs twisting and lengthening. Their skin shifted from various shades of brown into rich forest greens, and then sprouted a variety of flowers, thorns, and leaves. They shook for a while, then went still.

"What the hell was that?" Andy asked.

"It's what happens to all satyrs and centaurs when we die," Darko replied. "We weren't always *astynomia* in the cities, doing the gods' dirty work. In fact, we're more like the nymphs: nature spirits, but in physical form. When we die, our souls return to nature—as a bush, a tree, a flower, or whatever else the universe decides for us."

Andy knit his brow. "What about your brother? What about Phoenix? He was turned to stone. Will he ever return to nature?"

"I'm not sure," Darko said, his expression falling at the mention of his lost brother. "I don't know if Medusa trapped her victims or just killed them. I know his body won't change now, but I hope his spirit was able to escape at least."

"I'm sure it did," Zoey said. "There's no doubt about it."

Prometheus turned toward Zoey and Darko. "Get up. We need to leave."

Darko climbed to his hooves wearily, clutching his injuries, while Zoey placed her hand on the ground for support and tried to push herself up to stand. She cried out, sharp pain shooting through her arm and leg. Blood trickled freely from her wounds, making her head spin.

"That satyr really messed you up," Andy said. "Let me help you." He kneeled next to Zoey, then gently placed his hands on either side of her waist, and to Zoey's surprise, a sensation unlike anything she'd ever experienced whizzed from his fingertips throughout her entire body.

The feeling hurt but wasn't unbearable. It started where Andy touched her, then rushed through her body like dozens of tiny lightning bolts electrocuting her insides.

Zoey jumped, but within half a second of the sensation beginning, it ended.

"Whoa, you okay?" Andy asked.

Zoey raised an eyebrow and looked to him. "Did you not feel that?"

"Feel what?"

"The shock."

"The shock?"

"Oh my— Yes, the shock! I don't know how you *didn't* feel that."

Prometheus cleared his throat. "C'mon, you two. We don't have all night." He glanced at the buildings around them. "In fact, I'm not sure if we even have five minutes. More *astynomia* could show up at any time, and I'm not in the mood to kill anyone else tonight. At least, not right here and now. As we get closer to the edge of the city, I might change my mind . . ." He paused for a moment, scratching his chin. "Ahem. Well. As I was saying. We need to hurry. Get your stuff so we can skedaddle."

Andy tightened his grip on Zoey's waist and hoisted her to her feet. "You gonna be okay to walk?"

A wave of dizziness crashed through her. "You know, I'm not sure."

"We need to get to Diana, and fast," Darko said. He'd retrieved his pack and the bags from the alleyway, but he grimaced as he leaned down to grab the group's weapons. "I'm not feeling so good either."

"Do you want me to help you walk?" Andy asked Zoey, and she nodded. He kept one arm wrapped around her. "We need to hurry. You and Darko are seriously hurt, and like Prometheus said—we don't have all night." He looked to Darko. "Let me help you with our stuff."

"No, I can do this," Darko said, although the look on his face said otherwise. There were only a few items left to retrieve, but the satyr's arms trembled as if they'd been thrust into a snowstorm.

Prometheus stepped forward and grabbed the group's things off the ground. He snatched the bags from Darko's back, stuffed the items inside, and slung it all over his shoulder. "I've got it. Just take it easy, kid." The Titan took Darko's hand, as if to help the satyr walk. "Let's go."

Prometheus began leading the group out of Aphrodite City, toward Diana and Kali, his chains dragging behind him along the way.

$$* \sim * \sim * \sim$$

Since Ivy had left Karter alone earlier that evening—after cleaning and disinfecting his wounds, rebandaging them, and bringing him dinner—he'd finally been able to examine his reflection through the glass of the grandfather clock in his room in the Hephaestus City Healing Shrine.

The scar which usually twisted up the right side of his face like the branches of a brittle tree had been smoothed out, his once gaunt, pale, and almost-gray face now pink and plump like it had been when he was younger. His shaggy black hair had turned yellow and was cropped short, his golden irises a pale blue, just as his mother's were when she was still alive.

Now he lay awake, staring at the room's metallic ceiling, a sliver of moonlight peeking through his window. He wondered how long Asteria's disguise for him would last.

Would he be "Erick" for the rest of his life, or would this new identity fade away in time? A part of him prayed it wouldn't. Maybe then he could properly grieve for the loss of his two best friends; maybe then he could start his life over and have peace.

"Hello, Karter," said the familiar voice of Asteria. He looked over, and there she was, standing in his room with her burgundy hair and silver eyes, twinkling constellations dotting her midnight-black dress from top to bottom.

Karter shot up, his injuries groaning in protest at the quick movement. "Asteria—my face—"

"My powers are not limitless, and thus the disguise is only temporary," Asteria answered, as though reading his mind, and he dropped his head. "You must allow yourself to heal as much as possible before it fades away," she continued. "You must prepare yourself to fight and run. Once your true looks are restored, the people here will know who you are, and they will turn you in to Violet, Layla, and Xander."

"Those three are hunting me down, aren't they?"

"They are trying to, yes. You know as well as I their glory depends on bringing you to Zeus."

"If the disguise doesn't last forever, then what am I supposed to do when it wears off? What other choice do I have, other than to face my punishment? I can't fight and run forever. My father will catch me eventually."

Asteria took Karter's hands. "Oh, no, my dear. Your destined greatness awaits you now, in the next part of your journey. You must keep going."

Karter yanked himself away from the Titan goddess. "What's the point of greatness if everyone I love is gone? What's the point of greatness if I've betrayed my father, if I've betrayed the gods?" He put his face in his hands, trying to hide the hot tears filling his eyes. "Spencer and Syrena are dead. My mother has been dead for years. All of them are gone because of *me*, and my father is going to kill me for what I've done, or maybe something worse. I've spoiled my greatness. I've spoiled my destiny. I've ruined everything. If I had just reached Spencer sooner, if I had just protected Syrena . . ." He gulped down a cry. "If I had just never been born."

"It pains me to hear you speak this way," Asteria said, and Karter looked up at her. The goddess brushed a finger against his cheek, wiping away a few of his tears. "Even though there are many possible outcomes to everyone's destiny, the universe sometimes allows certain things to happen in order for others to take place. And, although I saw many different outcomes to Spencer's fate, the universe chose the scenario in which he was killed to unfold. But just because fate did not favor you that time, it does not mean hope is lost."

Karter's lip quivered. "What do you want to achieve by telling me that? It doesn't change anything."

"Your destined greatness awaits, Karter," Asteria said. "Whether you seize it or not, whether you fall into despair or rise above your sadness— Well, the universe has given you a choice. I suggest you pick wisely."

She kissed his cheek, then disintegrated into thousands of stars, leaving him alone with his thoughts.

CHAPTER SEVEN

DECEIT

For the whole trip out of Aphrodite City and back to Diana and Kali, Andy's head throbbed. However, it was nothing compared to the pain that still plagued his back muscles since he'd finished seeing those strange visions in the temple with the statue of Anteros.

A pitch-black sky loomed over them, their only guiding light that of the moon and stars, but thankfully the walk didn't take near as long as the one earlier that day had. The group only encountered a couple of *astynomia* along the way, whom Prometheus swiftly strangled with his chains before they could even try to arrest anyone. After death, they transformed into various plants, much like the others had earlier.

When the group finally reached the spot in the forest where Diana, Kali, and the pegasi awaited them, Diana immediately began tending to Zoey's injuries, as she said they were more severe than Andy's and Darko's.

While Diana healed Zoey's wounds, Andy, Zoey, and

Darko took turns telling Diana and Kali what had transpired in the city. Darko started by explaining how he'd gone off by himself and snuck into one of the *astynomia* quarters in order to steal the group more weapons.

The satyr pulled out a ball of brown thread from one of the bags. "After I snuck out of the quarters, I stumbled across a weaver's shop and was able to take this while the owner wasn't looking, too."

"Darko, we shouldn't steal anything unless our survival depends on it," Andy said. "Why would we need a ball of thread?"

"Because we need to know where we've been as we're walking through the Labyrinth," Darko replied.

"That's right," Diana said. "In the old days, Theseus used a ball of thread as a trail behind him so he could find his way to the center, then followed the thread back out to escape after he'd slain the Minotaur."

"Ohhhhhh," Andy replied. "I must've forgotten that detail, but it makes sense."

Once Darko finished his version of events, Andy and Zoey talked about going to the bakery with Prometheus and meeting Jasmine, then later encountering the *astynomia*.

Zoey made no mention of Prometheus abandoning the group, as Andy had suspected the Titan had done since Zoey seemed shocked when the Titan rescued them earlier, and given the fact that the Titan hadn't been with Zoey and Darko when Andy found them. Andy didn't mention to Diana and Kali how he'd run off on Zoey to go to the temple, either.

Once Diana finished with Zoey, she gestured for Andy to come next, but before she started healing him, she pointed to his face. "Whoa, where'd your glasses go?"

He sighed, shooting Zoey a dispirited glance when he caught her raising her eyebrows expectantly at him, arms crossed. "I'll explain later, maybe after we're all feeling better," he said. "It's a really, really weird story."

This answer seemed to be enough for Diana, as she began healing him. He hoped that after she did so the pains in his back would go away, but to his dismay, they remained. He didn't want to say anything just yet, though—Darko was in a lot of pain. Andy wanted Diana to heal the satyr before Andy addressed the pain in his back to her. Plus, he still had to explain to Zoey why he'd run off.

While Diana healed Darko, and Kali asked Prometheus more about Jasmine, Andy took a seat next to Zoey on a fallen log a ways from everyone else. "So, about earlier . . ." he began.

"Uh, yeah, care to explain why you left me alone with Prometheus in the bakery?" Zoey interrupted. "You scared the crap out of me, just so you know."

Andy nibbled on his thumbnail, guilt creeping through him. "This weird feeling just came over me, okay? There was this buzzing in my chest, and later the feeling spread all through my body. I kept getting visions of a temple, and like, it was so weird—I knew the temple was in Aphrodite

City, and I knew I needed to go to it. I didn't know why. But then I went there, and the buzzing feeling stopped. And there was this statue, and I touched it, and I got these visions of some of the gods . . ." He paused, hardly believing what came out of his mouth, although he knew it to be true. "I know it sounds crazy. But I swear, all of it happened."

"I believe you. Go on."

"Well, after the visions ended, I wasn't brought back to the temple. It was like I was trapped inside of clouds. And then the worst pain I've ever felt started up in my back. It seemed to last forever, and when it finally stopped, I was back in the temple. I looked outside. The sun was setting, and I knew I needed to get back to you and Darko fast. But the pain in my back never went away. It's still here, even after Diana healed me."

"We'll have to ask Diana what all of that could mean. Maybe there's a reason you had the visions. Maybe someone was trying to give you an important message or something like that. Is that when you lost your glasses, too?"

Andy put his head in his hands. "Oh my God, that's the craziest part about all this. When the visions were over, my eyesight was super blurry, and I thought my glasses fell off. But then I realized they were *on my face*. I took them off, and I could see everything perfect. I've *never* had perfect eyesight. I've always needed glasses."

Zoey went quiet for a few moments, a puzzled expression on her face. "This is weird. I'm not sure what to think."

"Maybe I was bitten by a radioactive spider?"

Zoey snorted. "Maybe. Anyway, when Diana is finished healing Darko, we need to bring what happened up to her. She usually has the all answers about this kind of stuff."

The sound of crunching grass and pine needles approached the pair, and Andy looked over. It was Diana. She walked toward Andy and Zoey, and once she grew close to them, she stopped and put her hands on her hips. It looked as though she'd finished healing Darko, who'd joined in with Kali and Prometheus's conversation.

Diana's breaths were labored, sweat seeping from her pores, surely from all the healing she'd just done. "Did I hear you say that I have all the answers?" The demigod winked despite her condition, then took a seat on Andy's other side. "Because if you did, you'd be correct. What can I help you with, O Chosen Two of the Dreaded Prophecy?"

Andy explained to Diana everything he'd just told Zoey, and Diana narrowed her eyes. "Hmm. Do you know who the statue was of? Did you get a chance to look, or did you just head out after you got the visions?"

"Oh, I looked. There was a plaque that said the statue was of Anteros. It said he's the God of Love, I think."

Diana knit her brow. "Anteros isn't the God of Love. He's the God of Requited Love, so, like, he's the god of love being returned, if that makes sense. He's a Son of Aphrodite and Ares. Well, at least, he *was*—back in the day, before he faded into nothingness since no one worshipped or remembered him anymore. What did you see in the visions, exactly?"

Andy explained each vision in the best detail he could: first of Anteros and Calliope in the garden, then of Zeus telling the gods about his plan to destroy humanity, and finally of Anteros promising Calliope that he'd see her again, no matter what it took.

For a while Diana fiddled with a few strands of her yellow waves, her expression thoughtful, until finally she spoke. "When I still lived on Olympus, and me and the rest of the Warriors of the Gods were taught about history and all that, we learned a little bit about the gods who faded away years before the Storm. We were told that when Anteros disappeared, Aphrodite was pretty upset about it. I mean, she doesn't have much of a heart for a lot of people, but figuring out her *son* was gone forever really messed her up, I guess. It's possible that she constructed that temple in his honor, probably in an attempt to bring him back into existence through worship, but from everything I've learned about when gods die, that just isn't possible. But through the temple—through people remembering him—it might be possible that bits and pieces of who he was are trapped there now, almost like a ghost or spirit."

"That would explain the visions since all of them involved him," Andy said. "But that doesn't explain the buzzing feeling I had and why I felt like I needed to go to the temple."

"It also doesn't explain how you knew where the temple was, why your back hurts now, or why you don't need glasses anymore," Zoey added.

Diana brushed her hair behind her ears. Her expression was that of worry, but she forced a smile regardless. "You know what? Don't worry about it. I'll think on it, and I'm sure once I pick my brain a little, I'll be able to come up with something logical." She climbed to her feet, wiping the sweat from her forehead with the back of her hand. "Anyway, now that everyone's healed and I'm feeling a little stronger, we should get going. Since you guys killed so many *astynomia*, everyone in the city is going to be looking for the murderer, and one of the first places they'll look is in the forest surrounding the city."

"Where'll we go next?" Zoey asked. "We only have two days to get the chains off of Prometheus, or he's not helping us into the palace."

Diana smiled mischievously. "While you guys were gone, Kali and I had a lot of time to talk about that—"

"Did you, now?" Andy asked. "And how'd that go?"

He shared a knowing look with Zoey, and a smirk formed on her lips. "Did you guys bicker the entire time, or did you finally decide to get along?"

Diana rolled her eyes. "We're never going to get along, so don't get your hopes up."

"For sure," Andy replied, chuckling.

"As I was saying, before I was so rudely interrupted," the demigod continued. "While you guys were gone, Kali and I had a lot of time to talk about how to get Prometheus's chains off. And I think we came up with something." She paused as if for dramatic effect. "We need to go to Hephaestus City."

"Hephaestus City?" Zoey asked, eyebrow raised. "What's in Hephaestus City?"

"And why would we go into another city after we just had to straight up kill a bunch of *astynomia* in the last one?" Andy added.

"Hephaestus is the Blacksmith of the Gods and the God of Fire and Metalworking," Diana said. "There are forges in his city—forges he built, similar to the ones where Prometheus's chains were created—and if the chains were made in a place similar to the forges in his city, I'll bet they can be broken there. I can't soften them with my light, but maybe they can be softened enough to break in the fire of those forges. Plus, since Hephaestus and Aphrodite are married, their cities are super close to each other. It'll only take around half a day to get there from here, which in theory should leave enough time to accomplish our task."

"Okay, makes sense—but I have a question. Why would Hephaestus teach other blacksmiths his skills?" Zoey asked. "Wouldn't that put the gods at risk for the citizens to revolt? Wouldn't that give them the tools to make their own weapons and stuff?"

"Not exactly," Diana replied. "Weapons aren't all the blacksmiths there make, and any weapons that are made are shipped straight to New Mount Olympus or to the city's *astynomia*. Besides, even if the citizens attained weapons and found the will to fight, the gods would squash them, no problem. The only chance anyone has at defeating the gods once and for all is by stealing their three main objects of power, like what we're doing."

"Okay," Zoey started. "This could work."

"But what if it doesn't?" Andy asked.

"Honestly, it might not," Diana replied. "But I can't think of anything else. And if I can't think of anything else, I'm pretty sure you guys can't either. No offense."

Andy shrugged. "None taken."

"It's settled then," Diana said. "Let's go."

While Andy and Zoey packed the group's things and prepared to leave, Diana explained the plan she'd concocted with Kali to Darko and Prometheus. They agreed it was most likely their best bet at freeing the Titan from his chains, and with that, the group headed northeast toward Hephaestus City.

After a few hours passed, Diana instructed the group to land and make camp, reasoning that they'd traveled far enough from Aphrodite City so that no *astynomia* would be able to find them. Andy, sure he wouldn't be able to sleep anyway because of the pain in his back, offered to watch for monsters while everyone else rested.

Within half an hour, the group had made camp and was sound asleep. Andy stared into the black of night and gritted his teeth, willing the spasms of discomfort in his back to go away. Memories of the visions he'd seen in the temple flashed across his mind. He wondered why they'd come to him, and if they meant anything.

"Andy?" Darko said from behind him.

Andy turned around slowly, trying not to agitate his back but grimacing as more pain arced up it. "Hey, Darko. What's up? Are you having trouble sleeping?"

"Well, kinda. I just— I mean . . ." The satyr sighed, and Andy knit his brow. Was something wrong? Had something bad happened when they'd been separated, and Darko hadn't come out and told the group? "Yeah, I'm restless. Watching those *astynomia* die earlier, and talking about Phoenix and everything . . ."

Andy was suddenly reminded of a time before the world had ended. It had been a hot summer night, and his mother had just finished a long day working a ten-hour shift at her retail job and completing her college home-work. She'd fallen asleep in her room right after dinner, and neither Andy nor his little sister, Melissa, ever bothered their mother more than what was necessary when she'd had a day like that.

"Andy?" Melissa had whispered while she stood in his doorway a few hours after he'd tucked her in for bed. *"I can't sleep."*

At this, Andy had immediately logged out of his com-puter game with Mark, texted his friend that he'd be on later, and turned his attention toward his sister. *"Well, that's no good, Mel-Mel. You've gotta get your rest. Maybe there's a way we can tire you out. Should we try watching cartoons, reading a book, playing games, or all of the above?"*

Melissa had squealed in glee at his proposition. *"All of the above!"*

And with that, Andy remembered, they'd done those things together. They'd watched a couple of episodes of Melissa's favorite princess cartoon, they'd read several chapters of *The Tale of Despereaux* by Kate DiCamillo, and they'd played board games until Melissa grew tired and fell asleep in her brother's embrace.

A thought came to Andy's mind. He didn't have a TV to watch shows on, nor did he have any books or board games, but there were other ways he and Darko could entertain themselves. Long before Andy's dad had died, when Andy was just a little kid, the man had taught Andy some of the games he'd played when he was younger that didn't require many materials.

"You ever play tic-tac-toe? Or thumb war?" Andy asked, and Darko shook his head. "All right, get comfortable. You're about to learn." Darko took a seat next to Andy, and Andy drew a three-by-three grid for tic-tac-toe in the dirt and explained the rules.

Darko's eyes lit with excitement as Andy told him how to play. "Hey, it's just like the game Phoenix and I used to play when I was little! We'd use white cloth and some ink. The higher-ups always scolded us for it. Yeah, it was just like tic-tac-toe, except instead of X's and O's, we drew axes and arrows." The satyr laughed. "I don't remember what Phoenix called the game, but that's what *I* always called it. Axes and Arrows, I mean."

"Okay, so you've played tic-tac-toe then, basically," Andy said. "But what about thumb war?" Darko raised his eyebrows, and Andy chuckled. "I'll take that as a no."

Andy quickly explained the rules of thumb war, and again, Darko recognized the game. "We used to play that one too," the satyr said. "Usually before bed. Except we pretended our thumbs were swords, and we called it Sword Fight."

"Okay, we can either play Axes and Arrows first, or we can play Sword Fight first. It's up to you."

"Let's do Sword Fight, then Axes and Arrows."

Andy grinned. "You're on."

And so, until Darko grew tired enough to sleep, the two of them alternated between playing Sword Fight and Axes and Arrows, laughing and joking all the while.

* ~ * ~ * ~

Karter awoke to soft knocks on his door.

He sat up and Ivy stepped into the room, a bucket of water and a rag in hand. "Good morning, Erick. How are you feeling today?"

Karter yawned, rubbing his eyes. After Asteria had left him the night before, it had taken him hours to fall asleep. He stretched and, to his surprise, none of his injuries hurt as he did so. "Uh, I'm feeling great, honestly."

Ivy set the bucket next to the bed and wet the rag in it. "I'm pleased to hear our treatments are doing their job so well. We have to keep you healing, though, so it's time to clean up. Strip down."

The first time Ivy had said "strip down" to Karter, his cheeks had practically lit on fire, and he'd had to ask her what she'd meant by it exactly. To his relief, she'd only meant to strip down to his undergarments so she could clean and rebandage his wounds. Not that Karter had never been naked in front of a girl before; he'd taken off his clothes for Violet and a few other young women plenty of times in his life. The difference was that because Ivy was so young, the command had caught him off guard. However, Ivy had tended his wounds several times now. He knew the drill.

He pulled off his robes, leaving only his undergarments. Ivy unwrapped his bandages and began cleaning his injuries with the wet rag, humming a happy tune.

Karter cleared his throat. "So, uh, how long have you worked here? In this healing shrine?"

Ivy stopped humming. "Oh, well, let's see"—she pulled away from Karter and wrung out the wet rag over her bucket of water—"I suppose since the day I could walk. I can't remember a time I wasn't caring for patients here. And how long have you been a farmer?"

A farmer. That must be what Asteria told them I was. "Uh, the same time as you. Since I could walk, I think."

"Well, isn't that wonderful?" She wiped away the last of the dried blood caked around Karter's stitches, then dropped the rag into the bucket and stood. "I must say, you're one of my most pleasant patients, Erick. In fact, you've already healed so much and in such a short time that I'd say you might have a little divine blood in you!" She chuckled, and Karter laughed awkwardly. *If only you knew*, he thought. "Anyway, I'll have your breakfast ready in the next half hour. Since you're feeling so good, perhaps later I can take you on a tour of the healing shrine."

Karter halfway smiled. "Perhaps." He'd never been inside one of the healing shrines in any of the cities; all injuries he or the other demigods had ever suffered from were healed by Apollo, or if a demigod was too far from Olympus and the gods did not answer their prayers, they would have to work through it on their own, lest they'd die.

Ivy smiled sweetly and gathered the bucket. She slipped out of the room, leaving Karter there and closing the door behind her.

Karter yawned and rested his head against his pillow, pulling his blanket up to his chin. Until Ivy returned with breakfast, he would rest.

After a while of sleep, Karter awoke to banging on his door. "Yes?" he called. "Ivy, is that you?"

"It sounds like him," hissed the familiar voice of a young woman on the other side of the door, sending chills down Karter's spine. "Let us in there, you filthy peasant."

"I can assure you," a voice that could only be Ivy said, "the Son of Zeus isn't here. He isn't one of my patients."

"Then prove it and open the gods-damned door!"

Someone—Karter guessed Ivy—pushed open the

door, revealing three familiar figures standing with her in the entryway.

Karter froze. It was Violet, Layla, and Xander.

* ~ * ~ * ~

The group landed their pegasi outside of Hephaestus City and overlooked it while hidden in the trees atop a hill, the sun rising at a steady pace. Even from this distance, Zoey could tell it was one of the most fascinating places she'd ever traveled to.

The layout of the city was nearly identical to Aphrodite City's, with farmland, neighborhoods, marketplaces, and temples. However, it was clear Hephaestus City's constructions and inner workings were far different. Instead of glistening gold-and-white buildings, its buildings, although they had similar shapes and pillars as Aphrodite City's, appeared as though they were forged with bronze and smeared with black soot. Citizens walked on stone paths which lined the twisting streets, where old-fashioned-looking cars hobbled along, spurting what had to be some sort of gas from their backsides. However, most interesting of all was what had been constructed near the center of the city: a rectangular copper-colored building with nine cylindrical towers of varying heights, all reaching for the sky and filling it with clouds of thick smoke which hovered over the city like a blanket of smog.

Diana pointed in the direction of the smoking building. "The forges."

Andy traipsed next to Zoey and whistled. "Whoa." Zoey nodded slowly.

"So, who's going in this time?" Darko asked. "And who's staying with the pegasi?"

Diana turned to the satyr. "Maybe this time you and Andy could stay out with the pegasi."

Andy and Darko shared mischievous grins. "When they leave, I'm totally annihilating you in Sword Fight," Andy said. Darko raised an eyebrow as if he was skeptical of Andy's words.

Diana rolled her eyes at the boys and continued giving directions. "Anyway, I'll go into the city and use the cloak you guys stole yesterday to hide my face so no one recognizes me; otherwise, it might take whoever goes in forever to find the forges, and we don't have that kind of time. We need to leave the Helm out here, too, in case we have any sort of run-in with *astynomia* like last time. It's best we do everything we can to make sure they don't know who we are and that they don't get ahold of our stuff."

"You think it'll be okay leaving only two people out here with the pegasi *and* the Helm?" Kali asked, putting her hands on her hips as she faced Diana. "What if they cross paths with a monster and they aren't able to fight it off or something? Maybe if it was you and someone else it would be okay, since you're a demigod, but they don't have powers or anything like that."

"You're right," Diana said, then smirked. "Would you

be willing to do the honors of staying out here with Andy and Darko and assisting them in protecting the pegasi and Helm?"

Kali did a little curtsy. "Anything for you, Princess."

"Thank you," Diana said, winking. She turned to Zoey and Prometheus. "All right, you two, it's up to us. We need to get ready and go quickly. We don't have any time to waste."

Zoey, Diana, and Prometheus began sorting through their supplies, discussing what could be brought into the city and what couldn't. Diana decided they may be able to conceal a few daggers in her cloak, but other than that, she didn't think it would be smart to take in any weapons. *At least this way we have a little more protection than last time*, Zoey thought.

Someone tapped Zoey's shoulder. She swung around to find Andy there, nibbling on his thumbnail. "Zoey—before you guys go in there—could I talk to you? In private?"

Her stomach flipped. "Yeah. Sure."

Andy turned, putting his hands at his sides, and walked farther into the trees. She followed, her mind buzzing with questions. What did Andy want to talk to her about? Why did it have to be done in private?

She thought back to the time at Deltama Village when Diana had told her that Andy was "practically in love" with her. Was Diana right—*did* Andy have feelings for her? Was he about to tell her that? If he did, what was she supposed to say?

How about, "I don't think about you that way"? she thought. *At least, I don't think I do. Right?*

She shook her head. It had taken forever to get over what Jet did to her, and the first guy she'd been attracted to since Jet was Spencer, who had not only been totally in love with someone else, but had also just *died*. She wasn't ready to start liking someone else—especially not someone she loved deeply as a friend.

If Andy did in fact have romantic feelings for her, how badly would it hurt him if she told him she couldn't reciprocate those feelings?

Finally, when the two of them were out of earshot of the rest of the group, Andy took a seat on a fallen log and gestured at the spot next to him. She plopped down at his side, brushing tangled curls behind her ears.

Andy cleared his throat. "Zoey—there's something I— there's something I wanted to tell you."

"What is it?" she asked, trying to mask her nervousness.

"Back before we—I mean—before we were brought *here*, you didn't seem to know who I was when you stood up to Jet for me. You asked me for my name and all that. I pretended not to know who you were, but I did. I'd known your name for a long time. Ever since the first day I saw you . . . I guess you could say I always really admired you."

Zoey's heart raced. "Admired me? For what?"

"Well . . ." His cheeks turned pink. "You're—*beautiful*." Heat rushed into Zoey's face. She knew now her suspicions had to be correct, and she still had no idea what she'd say when Andy told her he liked her. "But I didn't just admire you because you're pretty. People always talked about you. They always said you did some messed-up stuff when you were younger, and it seemed like you didn't have a lot of friends because of it. But it also always seemed like you didn't let it bother you. It seemed like you always chose to rise above the gossip—above the lies people told about you. It took me a long time to learn how to do that, and I still couldn't ignore Jet when he insulted my mom. But the fact that you ignored the stuff people said about you was really admirable."

Suddenly the fact Andy might have romantic feelings for her didn't matter so much. Zoey looked down at her feet. *He thinks they were rumors.* She recalled the day she'd stood up to Jet for him, led him out to her truck, and given him a ride to his car. He'd said he didn't believe the "rumors" surrounding her then, too. Back in Deltama Village, she'd wondered whether or not if he knew the truth, he'd still want to be her friend—even if he knew why she did what she did—and now she wondered so again.

"What if they weren't rumors?" Zoey asked. "What if it was all true?"

"But it's not," Andy said. "You're not that kind of person. You're an amazing person. You're strong, and smart, and selfless, and . . ." They locked eyes. "After all that's happened, you mean so much to me. You're the last normal thing left in my life."

"Would you still feel that way if the rumors were true?"

"Are you saying they are?"

"Just answer the question."

Andy turned from her and furrowed his brow. "I guess I don't know. Those things just don't sound like you. You're not like *that*."

Zoey stood, balling her fist at her side. "Like *what*? A slut? Say what you want. I've heard it all." Tears burned her eyes, threatening to run down her cheeks at any moment. *Don't cry*, she thought. *No one deserves your tears. Their opinions don't matter. They don't matter.*

Andy stared at her with wide eyes, and she clenched her jaw, willing herself to shut him out. She'd done it before to people she'd loved, and she could do it again. Shutting people out was something she'd grown accustomed to before the end of the world.

Wait, no. She didn't want to shut Andy out. She wanted to be his friend. She wanted him to know the truth about her, understand why she'd done what she'd done, and not judge her for it.

However, from the look on his face now, that would probably never happen. Could she backpedal and repair the damage she'd surely just inflicted on their friendship?

"I would never call you something like that," Andy said. "I wouldn't call anyone that. But—what everyone said about you is true, isn't it? Why didn't you just come out and say so?"

Zoey bit her lip. She had to convince him it was all

gossip. Rumors. Lies. She had to make her past go away. She had to escape it, like she thought she had when the world had ended.

She closed her eyes and focused on what she could say to make Andy believe her. Her throat began to tingle, as if her vocal cords were gently vibrating, and the words spilled from her mouth without a second thought. "Andy, of course none of what they used to say is true. You don't really believe I'd ever do something like that, do you?"

Opening her eyes to look at him, she rested her hand on his shoulder, and a shock—like static electricity—passed through her hand and up her arm. She flinched, pulling back, but Andy only smiled as though nothing had happened. "You're right, Zoey. Sorry. That was crazy rude of me to say."

Zoey blinked a few times. *What the hell?*

She backed away from him, ready to head toward the rest of the group and travel into Hephaestus City. As she spoke her last words to Andy, her throat began tingling again. "Well, I better get going. We gotta get those chains off Prometheus."

"You do, but there was something I needed to tell y—"

"You can tell me later, Andy."

And with that, she hurried back to the group to start their next mission. Andy followed her, saying nothing, and before she knew it, she, Diana, and Prometheus were walking through the forest toward Hephaestus City.

CHAPTER EIGHT

FORGES

Smoke from the sky snaked into the streets and curled into Zoey's throat.

She broke into a fit of coughing for what seemed like the hundredth time and looked to Diana—who had disguised her appearance with the long cloak Zoey and Andy had stolen from Aphrodite City—as the three of them walked along winding paths toward the forges of Hephaestus City. "How much longer do you think it'll take to get there?" Zoey asked.

The group had already trekked through some farmland and several neighborhoods, and were now marching through the city's *Agora*, which seemed to go on forever.

Diana pulled the cloak tighter around herself. "It shouldn't be too much longer."

"I hope not," Zoey remarked. "I don't wanna be out past curfew after what happened last time."

Prometheus chuckled. The Titan had disguised himself again, much as he had before entering Aphrodite City. His chains were now bracelets, and he'd shrunk down considerably. "We have plenty of time until then. The sun hasn't even hit its highest point in the sky yet."

Zoey set her gaze ahead. Even if Prometheus said they had plenty of time, she felt as though time were wasting away. However, she couldn't let herself worry about it. She needed to stay positive. They'd reach the forges, break Prometheus's chains, and get out of here. Then the Titan would help them. That *had* to be the way the situation would work out. At this point, there were no other options.

The group continued to pass through the *Agora*. Bronze-colored cars that looked as though they'd been plucked from 1920 puttered down the streets, while hundreds of citizens bustled in and out of shops and along the soot-smeared paths. Hundreds more worked away: some swept the streets, some shined shoes, and some stood next to carts full of a variety of items, insisting to every person strolling by that they needed to "take a look."

Hours passed, and finally they reached the rectangular building near the center of the city: the one Diana had said the forges were located inside. The building looked as though it were carved from copper, with nine smoking, cylindrical towers stemming from it, most of them so tall they seemed to touch the clouds. The building possessed no windows, but the sounds of fires roaring, hammers slamming against metal, and voices booming could still be heard from outside of it.

"This is it," Diana said, pausing in front of the building.

Zoey crossed her arms. "How're we supposed to get in there without being caught and questioned by someone?"

"We'll just say we lost our jobs," Diana replied in a hushed voice. "We could pretend we want to apply for work here, at least until we can steal some uniforms or something. I know they wouldn't like us snooping through their stuff if we hadn't yet been hired, so I think disguising ourselves as employees—after we're already in, of course—is our best bet at finding what we need."

The group headed toward the building's front entrance, where a ten-foot-tall bronze door loomed over them. "Do we just walk in, or what?" Zoey asked.

Diana grabbed a door handle and pried the massive entryway open. "Yup. Go ahead." They stepped inside onto an iron platform, and Diana shut the entrance behind them. A rush of blistering heat slammed Zoey in the face and blew her hair backward, and after catching sight of what lay before them, she gasped.

The building seemed to go for miles belowground, all the way until it stopped at a pit at the very bottom, where several more forges resided. Working in the pit at these forges were mammoth-sized bald men clothed in rags. The men's leathery skin was drawn tight over their veins and muscles, and instead of two eyes, they had one giant eye in the center of their sweaty, wrinkled foreheads.

"Cyclopes," Diana said, pointing at the colossal one-eyed men. "The elder Cyclopes were the creatures who constructed the Helm of Darkness, Poseidon's Trident, and the Master Lightning Bolt for the gods as a gift when Zeus freed them from the Titans. Centuries later, their descendants were known to herd sheep and eat men passing through their domains. Now some torment people in the forests along with the other monsters, while some live here."

Above the group, hundreds of balcony-like structures were situated on all sides of the building's walls, each one complete with its own personal flaming forge—however, these ones had regular people working at them instead of Cyclopes. Three to four people worked at each balcony-forge, wearing coats, gloves, and masks with dark goggles attached. Smoke and steam rose from the forges into the cylindrical towers high above.

"How do the workers get to their stations?" Zoey asked, and Diana pointed to the side of the platform at four barred doors which led to small chambers in the wall. Zoey squinted, looking around at the rest of the walls. Upon closer inspection, she realized there were dozens more of the barred-door chambers moving up and down and side to side within the walls, carrying people to and from their work stations, gears and cogs spinning to keep the machinery suspended.

"They're elevators," Zoey said. "We had the same kind of contraptions in the Before Time. They were a little different, but same idea. How do the Cyclopes get to their station? The elevators don't look big enough for them."

"They never leave," Diana said. "They're slaves. They're given room and board here by Hephaestus, but he wants to keep them trapped their whole lives. That's why they're down in a pit."

One of the Cyclopes let out a long wail, shaking the building and making everyone jump. Once the creature quieted, Zoey put her hand to her heart. "That's so sad."

"Don't worry too much about it," Diana replied. "Cyclopes are like most of the other monsters we've faced. They'd eat you the first chance they got."

A tall man at the closest forge to the group paused his hammering and turned to them. He lifted his mask, then shouted over the commotion. "Hello, strangers, and welcome. How can I help you?"

Diana stepped forward and yelled back. "We're looking for work."

"Oh! Give me a minute, please." He scurried past the other workers at his forge and slammed his hand down on a large button in the wall. Within moments, an elevator made its way to his station and creaked open. He stepped inside, and in no time it transported him to the platform the group stood on. He made his way toward them.

He was young, probably in his mid to late twenties, with skin and eyes a deep shade of brown, his black hair falling in waves over his shoulders. He had a large, pointed nose stained with soot, equally big ears sticking out on either side of his slender head.

The man gave the group a smile, his teeth straight and white. His eyes crinkled kindly around the edges. "You say you're searching for work?"

"That's right," Diana said. "Could you take us to whoever is in charge here, so we can ask if there are any jobs available?"

"You're looking at one of 'em," the man said, and stuck out a gloved hand to Diana. She gingerly took it and gave it a shake. "The name's Troy, Master Blacksmith of the Hephaestus City Forges. The other one in charge would be my twin sister, Marina, who I believe is in the break room now on lunch. I do think we have a few openings available, but Marina would be the one to talk to about it, as she does all the hiring. Would you like to speak with her?"

"Yes, please."

Troy turned around and walked back into the elevator from which he'd come, gesturing for them to follow. "All right, c'mon then."

Zoey and Prometheus looked to Diana, who set her jaw. "When we get to the break room, we'll knock out anyone in there and steal their uniforms," she whispered. "Then hurry to one of the forges, soften Prometheus's chains, break them, and get out of here." Zoey and Prometheus nodded, and the group followed the Master Blacksmith into the elevator.

There were rows of numbered buttons on the elevator's left wall, and Troy punched several. The machine roared to life, then began traveling up, up, up. They passed dozens of forges where men and women alike worked on what looked like car and clock parts, weapons, and other various items. She gripped one of the door's bars tight, not daring to glance at the pit where the Cyclopes worked below.

"Has anyone ever fallen off their forge and down . . . there?" Zoey asked, cocking her head in the pit's direction.

"Only the stupid ones. The fall is big enough to kill them instantly, but they prove themselves useful still."

"How can they be useful if they're dead?" Zoey asked.

"Oh, they make good treats for the Cyclopes," Troy answered. "Those guys never do stop whining, so even though it's tragic when someone falls down there, at least the rest of us get a day or two of peace before they start it up again."

Zoey gulped as another Cyclops let out a long, solemn wail. "Good to know."

Finally, the elevator stopped at another platform. The door opened and they stepped out, another door waiting for them ten feet ahead. Troy swung the door open and held it for them. "C'mon then, head inside."

They did as he said, walking into the break room. This one was made of metal, too—lined with several long tables with meat, fruit, bread, and copper glasses scattered atop them. Six men and women sat together eating at one of the tables. They wore normal civilian clothes, their uniforms piled beside their feet.

A young woman with shoulder-length black hair turned around to face them, her brown skin smeared with soot. Her nose and ears were similar in size and shape to Troy's, her eyes the same dark color as his.

The woman smiled, which made her look even more like the Master Blacksmith. "Hey there, strangers."

"Marina, these fine folks here are searching for work," Troy said to the woman, shutting the break-room door behind him. "I thought we had some openings, but I wanted to talk to you first before making any promises."

Marina pursed her lips, eyeing each member of the group up and down. "We do have quite a few openings, yes, and these people look like they'll make great additions to the team. I'm sure we can find something easy to do for the cripple."

Zoey flinched at the word "cripple" but chose not to reply. *Just keep up the act, and soon we'll be out of here.*

"We'll go to my office and fill out the proper paperwork," Marina said as she stood and crossed her arms. "You'll all start your training tomorrow, so you can be working in the forges within the next few months."

With one hand, Diana kept the cloak pulled tight around her face. With the other, she conjured a sphere of blazing sunlight. "Sorry to disappoint you, but I'm afraid we're just stopping in for today."

Diana launched the attack for Marina, and to Zoey's surprise, Marina didn't try to dodge it. Instead, she threw up her hands. From her palms, streams of flames erupted. The flames collided with Diana's sphere of sunlight, and both disintegrated, the smell of smoke filling the air.

The rest of the men and women in the break room shot up and grabbed cutting-knives off the table. Behind the group, Troy blocked the door.

Marina chuckled. "For that little outburst, I'm going to need you folks to explain who you are and what exactly you're doing here, unless you'd like to be burned to crisps."

* ⁓ * ⁓ * ⁓

Karter paced his healing shrine room, panic brewing in his chest.

The demigod trio hadn't taken him away earlier that day when they'd burst into his refuge, as they hadn't been able to see through his "Erick" disguise, but none of them had been convinced the Son of Zeus wasn't in the city altogether.

Xander had laughed, almost maniacally. *"He's here, somewhere, and he's going to be sorry for running off on us when I get my hands on him next."*

"We'll stay in the city and watch for him," Violet had said, her opalescent eyes glittering with malice. *"He can't hide from us forever."* And with that, they'd left Karter alone again. Ivy had brought him breakfast, and he'd pretended as though nothing were bothering him even after he refused her tour of the healing shrine.

He ran shaking hands through his hair. How much longer would this disguise last? What if it wore off while he was still in the city, and the demigod trio caught him? *I'm dead anyway*, he thought. *Either way, Father will have me back eventually.* Tears filled his eyes, anguish clawing at his insides and threatening to pull him into its black abyss. He knew if he allowed it to this time, he'd never escape again.

"Your destined greatness awaits," Asteria had said. *"Whether you seize it or not, whether you fall into despair or rise above your sadness— Well, the universe has given you a choice. I suggest you pick wisely."*

Karter paused and tried to even his breathing. Perhaps Asteria was right: perhaps the universe had a greater plan for him than he'd expected. Although he blamed himself for the deaths of everyone he loved, although it felt as though he had no hope left for the future, maybe there was a reason he was still here after all this time.

A knock sounded at his door, and Ivy stepped inside. "Hello, Erick, I just wanted to check on y—" She stopped, her eyes going wide at the sight of him.

He turned to her. "What's wrong?"

"Your—your hair. But that means . . . the Daughter of Aphrodite . . ."

He lunged toward the grandfather clock and looked into the glass. The reflection staring back at him made his blood turn cold. His hair, once yellow and short because of Asteria's spell, had changed back to shaggy and black. *The rest of my disguise is going to fade away soon, too*, he thought.

He turned to Ivy. "I swear, this isn't what it looks like."

Ivy darted out of the room and down the hallway. "Guards! Guards, come quickly!"

Karter ran to the window, then balled a fist, conjured his inherited child-of-Zeus strength, and punched it. The glass shattered. He picked a few stray pieces from his stinging, bleeding knuckles, then jumped outside into the streets of Hephaestus City.

* ~ * ~ * ~

"I think it's my turn to teach you guys a game," Kali said, scribbling away the latest three-by-three board Andy had drawn in the dirt.

While Andy, Darko, and Kali guarded the Helm and pegasi in the forest, they'd decided to pass the time by playing Axes and Arrows and Sword Fight. Kali hadn't known how to play either, but the names had intrigued her, so Andy and Darko had explained the rules. At first, she'd lost every round, but once she'd gotten the hang of things, she'd beaten Andy and Darko at both games several times.

After the disaster Andy had created trying to express his feelings to Zoey, explaining the games to Kali and playing them with her and Darko had proved to be a good distraction to keep his mind off his embarrassment—and off the everlasting pain in his back.

Andy plucked up a pebble and flicked it into the air. "Okay, Kali, what's this game of yours called?"

"Five Stones," Kali said, climbing to her feet.

"And what do we need to play?" Andy asked.

Kali looked down at him and cocked her head.

"Five . . . stones?"

Darko burst out laughing. "I thought the name gave it away."

"Probably did," Andy said, smiling.

Kali gathered five rocks around the same size, took a seat in front of Andy and Darko, laid the stones before them, and explained the rules. There were eight steps, and Andy understood the first few—something about throwing one stone, at the same time picking another one up, then catching the one that was thrown, and every round the amount of stones that were picked up increased—but Kali talked so fast he hardly caught the minor details, not to mention how one went about winning the game.

"I used to play Five Stones with my mother," Kali said, once she'd finished explaining the rules. "Before, well, you know."

Andy opened his mouth to reply, but before he could say a word, the unfamiliar but seductive voice of a young woman said from behind them, "My, my, what an interesting scene I've stumbled upon here. What do you peasant scum think you're doing outside the city?"

Andy shot to his feet. Sharp pain arced down his back. It hadn't stopped hurting all day, but he couldn't let that hold him back. Ignoring the sensation, he unsheathed his sword and swung around to catch sight of a tall and unbelievably beautiful girl who had to be only a few years older than himself. Her wavy blonde hair hung all the way to her hips, her eyes glittering pink, green, and silver—as though her irises were made of opals.

"Who're you?" Andy asked.

The girl flipped her hair. "I am Violet, Daughter of Aphrodite, the Goddess of Love and Beauty."

Andy's nostrils flared. Hadn't Violet been one of the demigods who'd destroyed Alikan Village and slain everyone there? Was this demigod one of the monsters who took away Darko's last hope for a normal life?

The group's three pegasi, who'd been quietly grazing a ways away from the group, reared back and squealed as they spotted Violet stepping closer. With what seemed like minimal effort, Violet swiftly reached into her robes, pulled out three pink darts, and flung them one, two, three at the pegasi. The darts pierced the pegasi in the necks, sinking deep into their flesh.

"Ajax!" Kali cried. "Aladdin! Luna!" The winged horses calmed, dropping on all fours, then began to sway. Within moments, they toppled onto the forest floor.

Violet sneered and turned toward the group. "How curious that a satyr and two peasant scum would have pegasi in their dirty clutches. No matter, I suppose. I'll have them back on New Mount Olympus in no time."

Kali seized her spear and brandished it at Violet. "Over my dead body."

Violet narrowed her eyes. "Even with that pathetic excuse for a weapon, death can be easily arranged for you."

"Bull," Andy said. "There are three of us and one of you. We'll take you down easy."

"Think again," Violet said. "One of your friends has already fallen under my spell. Satyr, get ready to shoot them."

Andy's gut clenched. Beside him, Darko nocked an arrow. Andy looked over. Darko's irises were shifting between brown and shimmering opalescent—an opalescent much like Violet's eyes—until finally settling back to brown. His expression was blank, and he aimed his weapon straight for Andy.

"What the hell did you do to him?" Andy said.

Violet cackled. "The satyr looked into my eyes, as you all did, but because he is in love with no one, he has fallen deeply in love with me. So deeply, in fact, that he's now under my control."

CHAPTER NINE

CAPTURE

Andy swung his sword at Violet. "Let him go."

"I'd rather not," Violet said, twirling a blonde wave with her fingers. "Satyr, take your arrow and point the tip at your own throat. If either of your former companions try to hurt me, stop you, or run away, I want you to skewer yourself."

Darko raised the arrow to his neck. "Anything for you."

"No!" Andy cried. "Don't hurt him!"

Violet strode toward Andy. "My, my, this is a strange development: the pig-faced mortal boy seems to care for the incompetent satyr. Didn't you know the gods would have you both killed for less?"

"Please," Andy said. "Stop."

The demigod laughed. "If you don't want the satyr harmed, then I'd advise you to drop your weapons." Andy threw his sword to the ground, while Kali tossed her spear aside. "Oh, get rid of the dagger too."

Andy took the knife from his belt and pitched it into

the dirt. "Okay. We're unarmed. Now would you please let Darko go?"

"Tell me," Violet started, eyeing the group's supplies bags, "what do those packs carry?"

"Our stuff," Andy said.

"Empty them, or the satyr dies."

Kali put a hand on Andy's shoulder. "Andy, I'm not sure we should do as she says," she whispered. "The Helm."

"I know what you mean," he replied. "But we can't just let her kill Darko. Besides, even if we did fight, she might have more of those dart things, knock us out, and get someone else to take the Helm anyway. At least this way we can fight later."

After coming to the agreement that it was better to save Darko's life instead of overpowering the demigod, Andy and Kali did as Violet instructed: they opened the bags and dumped out the contents inside. Their things came tumbling to the forest floor, including the Helm of Darkness.

Violet burst into a fit of cackling. "Oh my gods, you're the two mortals from the Before Time, aren't you?"

"I'm not," Kali said.

"But he is, isn't he?" Violet continued, pointing at Andy. "Does this mean the Daughter of Apollo is in Hephaestus City? It must. Tell me, did you really think you'd be able to get away with such heinous crimes?"

"It's not like you can take the Helm from us, anyway," Andy blurted out, desperation flooding his senses. "And I'm sure you know that. Diana does, and Spencer did. You

amazon Gift Receipt

Send a Thank You Note

You can learn more about your gift or start a return here too.

Scan using the Amazon app or visit
https://a.co/i13fbaR

Poseidon's Trident

Order ID: 112-5485873-6302623   Ordered on December 14, 2020

can't touch it. It'll suck your life force away."

"I may not be able to," Violet replied, "but there are others who can. You, the girl, and the satyr." She pointed at Darko. "Satyr! Grab the Helm of Darkness, conceal it inside one of the bags, and carry it for me. As for the two of you," she continued, looking to Andy and Kali. "The Olympians will be pleased when I deliver you to them in chains."

* ~ * ~ * ~

"What should we do?" Zoey whispered to Diana and Prometheus, her heart racing, as Troy, Marina, and the rest of the workers in the break room of the Hephaestus City Forges cornered them. She'd brought her dagger into the city, sure, but was it smart for the group to battle these people?

Prometheus allowed his disguise to fade away. He grew taller and taller, his bracelets melting and morphing back into their true forms. "We should fight."

Marina wiggled her fingers, orange flames curling from them and into the air. "I wouldn't recommend it. You're outnumbered. Now, would you like to cooperate and tell me who you are and what you're doing here, or am I going to have to kill you?"

"We may be outnumbered," Diana said, "but that hasn't stopped us before." She ripped off her cloak, threw it aside, and conjured a blazing sphere of sunlight in each hand.

One of the workers pointed her cutting-knife at Diana. "It's the Daughter of Apollo!"

"Didn't she aid the Chosen Two of the Prophecy in defeating King Hades and Queen Persephone and stealing the Helm of Darkness?" a man asked.

Marina locked eyes with Troy, and they gave each other a nod. She allowed her flames to disintegrate, and they raised their hands as if in surrender. "Stand down," Troy said. "We can't defeat the Daughter of Apollo in a fight."

"What are you on about?" another man said. "She's a traitor, and so are these other two just for associating themselves with her. We can't let them get away. If we do, we'll be killed."

The man lunged for Diana, but before the demigod could attack him, Marina leapt into the air and kicked the man in the back of his head with such force he dropped face-first to the floor and fell unconscious. Zoey gasped. What was Marina doing? What in the hell was going on?

"Marina, what have you done?" a woman said, staring wide-eyed at the man on the floor. "You know the law. When the *astynomia* find out you defended the Daughter of Apollo, you'll be executed."

Troy stepped forward, cracking his knuckles. "Good thing none of them will be finding out what went on today then, right?"

The five remaining workers in the break room snarled. "Traitors," one said. They raised their cutting-knives and thrusted themselves toward Troy and Marina, but within moments the black-haired twins slapped the utensils from the workers' hands and knocked them unconscious.

The siblings dragged the workers, one by one, to a nearby closet and stuffed them inside. "We have to go," Marina said. "Quickly."

Diana held the spheres of light up as if to shield the group from the twins. "And why would we trust you?"

Troy grabbed a ring of keys from his robes and used one to lock the closet door. "Maybe because we just took out our own employees to protect you?"

"He has a point," Zoey said. "They must be on our side—well, at least somewhat."

"Just cover yourself, Daughter of Apollo," Marina said. "And follow us. We can explain later. But it's vital to your safety that we leave this area immediately."

Diana retrieved her cloak and pulled it back on, and the group followed Troy and Marina out of the break room, onto the platform outside, and into another elevator. Once everyone had gathered inside, Troy punched in a few numbers. The wall behind them *creeeaaaaak*ed as though another door was opening. When the sound ceased, the elevator shifted backward, farther inside the wall. Soon Zoey couldn't see any of the forges below, the inside of the elevator growing dim.

"Where are you taking us?" Diana asked.

"To our workshop," Troy replied. The elevator began traveling downward.

Marina turned to Diana, peering at the demigod

through dim light. "What are you really doing here?"

Diana grabbed the links of Prometheus's chains and held them out to Troy and Marina. "This is the Titan god Prometheus. We need to break his chains."

"Why?"

Prometheus chuckled. "Because they want help getting into Poseidon's palace, and I'm their only lead. But if I'm going to help them, I want something in return: to be completely free."

"You plan to steal the Trident next, don't you?" Marina asked. "Like how you stole the Helm?" Diana nodded.

Troy ran his fingers along the chains. "These were forged by our grandfather himself. I smell an enchantment on them, too."

"Wait," Zoey started. "Hephaestus is your grandfather?"

"Yes," Marina replied. "That's why Troy is such a talented blacksmith, and why I possess the gift of fire. We aren't demigods, so we aren't forced to live on New Mount Olympus, but some divine blood runs through our veins."

"Then why are you helping us?"

Bright light flooded the elevator; it came to a jarring halt, and Zoey had to catch herself on the bars as the stop hurled her forward. She gathered her footing, and the door creaked open. Troy and Marina made their way out of the elevator and gestured for everyone to follow. "Come on then," Troy said. "Don't be shy."

Zoey squinted into the place they'd come to, the light

practically blinding her after standing for a few minutes with barely any. Once her vision adjusted, she stared wide-eyed at what lay before them. It was the most fascinating location she'd seen so far today.

The room was huge, probably even bigger than the entire third floor of Zoey's high school from the Before Time, and smelled like a mechanic's garage. Dozens of lightbulbs hung from the ceiling. The walls were made of turning gears and cogs, steaming pipes, ancient weaponry, and various tools. Contraptions littered the floor—what looked like car and clock parts, wires, batteries, cell phones, laptops, and other bits of technology from the Before Time, and many other inventions that appeared way more high-tech than anything Zoey had ever seen, and that she couldn't identify. At the back of the room, a large hole in the wall looked as though it had been drilled, a forge constructed in the empty space.

Zoey, Diana, and Prometheus followed Troy and Marina into the workshop. "You never answered my question," Zoey said as she glanced around at the items on the floor. "If Hephaestus is your grandfather, if you're related to the gods, then why are you helping us?"

"The Daughter of Apollo is rumored to have led this whole expedition against the gods, alongside the late Daughter of Poseidon," Troy said, laughing. "Why can't we help out? We have our reasons."

Marina hurried toward the forge. She conjured flames in her hands, then launched them into the coals. "That's no kidding. Just because Hephaestus is our grandfather, and just because he is more merciful to his citizens than the other gods, doesn't mean we support him and the rest of our twisted immortal family."

Prometheus grimaced as if in wry amusement. "They've always caused more pain than joy, that's for sure."

"Our mother, Helen, was a Daughter of Hephaestus," Troy said, making his way to Marina's side. "She was incredibly useful to the gods, possessing both a talent in metalworking and the power of Hephaestus's fire. But she made a grave mistake. She got pregnant by a regular mortal man, and she tried to trick the gods about her twin babies so they could live with her on Mount Olympus."

"That was you guys, wasn't it?" Zoey said.

"Yes," Troy said with a sigh. "Our mother lied to Zeus. She said we were another demigod's children and that we had enough divine blood to not be thrown off Olympus after our birth. But once we were born, she couldn't lie anymore. Zeus knew right away we didn't have enough divine blood for our parents to both be demigods."

Marina stared hard at the flames in the forge. "Zeus executed her in front of hundreds, if not thousands. He would have killed us too, for her crimes I mean, even as infants, but Hephaestus pleaded with him to allow us to live. Not because he cared for us, I know, since we've only met him a handful of times, all incredibly impersonal. Not because he loved our mother, since he did nothing to stop her murder, even though she only lied because she knew we'd be taken from her if she didn't. He just wanted to see what we would be capable of with only a quarter of his divine blood. At least, that's what Father always said." She smiled sadly. "If we can break Prometheus's chains for you, Hephaestus may find out that begging to keep us around and charging us with running the forges of his city were some of his worst mistakes."

Troy grabbed a double-sided tool off the wall—one side was a hammer, the other a chisel—and gestured for Prometheus to come to the forge. "Let's begin. We'll do the hands first, then the feet. Now, just know this will be painful. Marina's fire is used to light the forges here; it's one of the closest things in temperature to Hephaestus's own flames, and she'll be shooting more at the chains while they're sitting in the coals. Not to mention when I bring the chisel down to break the metal, it'll probably cut you open. But if combining our powers like this can't break your chains, I don't know if anything will."

"Don't worry about hurting me," Prometheus said. "I had my liver ripped outta me by a beastie every day for centuries, then for another seventy-five years when I was imprisoned for the second time. Pain isn't a problem for me."

"Whatever you say, Titan. I'm just trying to prepare you," Troy said. He pointed at the coals. "Put 'er there."

Prometheus rested a hand in the fire so the chain around his wrist lay in the center of the burning coals. Marina conjured fire in her hands and blasted it at the metal, over and over. Less than a minute passed, and the metal began glowing red. Prometheus gritted his teeth, sweat seeping from his pores, the smell of burnt flesh filling the air.

Troy raised the chisel side of the tool above his head, then rammed it against the chain. Sparks whizzed into the air, but not even a dent was made in the metal. Troy raised the tool and brought it down again and again, but it was no use. The chain wouldn't budge.

Troy dropped the tool and wiped his brow, his breaths labored, and Marina allowed her fire to disintegrate. "I'm sorry to say, but I don't think anything will break these. Not unless Hephaestus himself does it." Zoey's heart sank. What else could they do?

Prometheus ripped his hand from the forge and clutched his arm, his skin blistered red and black with burns. "That can't be. In the old days, when Heracles and I combined our strength . . ."

"Your old chains must have been forged differently," Marina said, resting a hand on Prometheus's back. "They must not have been enchanted. But these ones are. And, although we're powerful, we can't break an enchantment cast by an Olympian. Maybe if it were cast by someone else, but . . . I'm sorry. We've done all we can."

Diana clasped her hands. "Prometheus, I know we were supposed to break your chains for you. I know that was the deal. But please, help us get into Poseidon's palace. If you don't, we'll never be able to defeat the gods . . ."

Prometheus said nothing to Diana; he only looked away.

Zoey bit her lip. What could she say to convince Prometheus to help them into Poseidon's palace, even though they couldn't break his chains in the time he'd given them?

She closed her eyes and thought of her conversation with Andy earlier that day. The way her throat had tingled, the way the right words to sway the conversation back in her favor had spilled from her mouth with no thought.

Finally, Prometheus spoke. "The deal was if you proved yourselves worthy of my help by breaking these chains, I would get you into Poseidon's palace. But you didn't."

Zoey's throat began tingling like earlier—again, as if her vocal cords were gently vibrating. She opened her eyes and looked up at the Titan. "What about Jasmine, Prometheus?" He hung his head. "I know we couldn't follow through with the deal, but does that mean you're just going to let your great-great-granddaughter suffer at the hands of the Aphrodite City aristocracy?"

"I could help her, assure her workload is lessened significantly," Prometheus said. "I could work for her for free for the rest of her days, then for her children and her children's children, until I'm discovered and re-imprisoned."

"But would that really help her in the end?" Zoey continued. The tingling in her throat began to subside, the tone in her voice now brewing with the same panic coursing through her. "Would she ever truly be free of the gods' tyranny? And—and what about Nylah? What would Nylah think if you turned your back on the world? What would she say to such a selfish decision? Wouldn't that make you just as self-serving as the rest of the gods? Wouldn't it make you no better than any of them?"

For a long time, no one said a word, the only sound that of Prometheus's charred flesh cracking as it healed itself.

Finally, Prometheus held his head up and looked to Zoey. "I'll help you into Poseidon's palace. Not for you or your cause or because I believe in you, but for my son. For Nylah, and for my great-great-granddaughter."

Diana let out a long sigh of relief. "Thank you so much. Even though we couldn't get the chains off now, maybe someday we can. Should we head toward the Labyrinth, then?" Prometheus nodded.

Troy and Marina stepped forward. "We're ecstatic you'll be able to enter Poseidon's palace, and we don't want to keep you here much longer," Troy started. "But there are a few things we wanted to give you before you go. You may or may not find them useful for your journey. I'm hoping you do."

"We'll take any and all help we can," Zoey said. "What is it?"

The siblings shared a glance and a nod, and Marina turned back to Zoey and Diana, her eyes lighting with excitement. "The first thing is something we've been working on for a long time." She scurried over to the workshop's nearest wall and plucked two small objects from it. They looked like shiny, copper-colored wallets.

"These are highly experimental," Marina said, walking back to the group and placing one in Diana's hand, then the other in Zoey's. Zoey rubbed her thumb over the contraption. It was made of cold, smooth metal. "In fact, we've never even been able to properly test them."

Diana held hers up to the light, squinting at it. "And what are they, exactly?"

"I like to call them 'Pocket-Sized Submarines,'" Troy said.

"Wait, what?" Zoey asked. "Did you say pocket-sized *submarine*?"

Troy chuckled. "That's right. They're built to be small enough for your robe pocket until you get them wet, in which case they unfold until they're a submarine big enough to hold around five people."

"Okay, a few questions," Diana said. "First, what in the world would ever possess you to build something like this? Second, how did you figure out how to build it? And third, how do you even know it works?"

"We're grandchildren-of-Hephaestus," Marina answered. "He creates, so building things is in our blood, but more than anything we like to be challenged by our projects. Troy read about submarines in an old book we found when we were kids, and when he told me about them, we became fascinated with the idea of using our powers to build several. However, we didn't have a good place to put them, so we decided we needed to make them small enough to fit in a robe pocket, and design them so they would only expand to full size when touched by liquid. We had to use a combination of enchantments we stole from others and our own powers to build them, and for the most part I think the endeavor was successful. We don't know for sure if they work—that's why I said they're experimental."

"Why haven't you been able to test them?" Zoey said.

"We can't leave Hephaestus City," Troy replied. "And there aren't exactly any large bodies of water around that we could try them out in, so we've just kept them down here."

"Thank you so much," Zoey said.

Prometheus smiled. "Once we go through the portal to the palace, there's no way to know if we'll be able to make it back through. These could come in handy if we can't."

"That's the goal," Marina said. "There was one more thing we wanted to give you, though, and that would be our allegiance to your cause. After hearing about how the Daughter of Apollo and the Chosen Two of the Prophecy defeated Hades and Persephone, stole the Helm of Darkness, and survived it all, we swore to each other if the chance arose, we would join the army waging war on Olympus."

"Not only did the gods murder our mother," Troy added, "but they also murdered our father, because they found out he told us the truth about our mother. When we were kids, we had no idea what the gods did to her. But when we turned twelve years old, Father told us. The first chance we got, we asked our grandfather why he let it happen. Father was executed within the next week."

Zoey swallowed hard. "Killed just for telling his children the truth."

"I think Hephaestus didn't want us to hate him for what happened," Marina said. "He saw our potential, and he wanted us to be his good little workers. But he was too foolish to see that by telling Zeus that Father gave us the truth about our mother—by being the reason our father is dead—he was only solidifying our hate for him."

"I'm sorry for your losses," Diana said. "And I thank you for all the help you've given us today, but the sun should be setting soon, and I think we've been away from our friends for too long. We need to get back to them so we can start the next part of our journey."

"Of course," Troy said. The twins walked past Zoey, Diana, and Prometheus and pressed the button to summon an elevator. Within minutes one showed up. They climbed inside, Troy punched in a code, and they began their ascent. While they traveled up, Prometheus morphed back into his disguise.

"What will you do about the employees in that closet?" Zoey asked.

Marina pursed her lips. "Don't you worry about us. We'll figure something out."

"They might make a good snack for the Cyclopes if they don't keep their mouths shut," Troy said, and Zoey stifled a laugh.

Soon they got so high in the elevator they could overlook the forges. Once it reached the building's entrance it stopped, and then its barred door creaked open.

Zoey clutched her Pocket-Sized Submarine. "Thank you again for all your help, and I hope this isn't goodbye forever. How will we find you later, when we need you?"

Marina winked at her. "We install tracking devices into all our inventions. When word reaches the city about how the Daughter of Apollo and the Chosen Two of the Prophecy stole Poseidon's Trident right from under the Sea God's nose, we'll track you using the submarines." Diana and Prometheus bowed to the siblings, and Zoey hugged each.

After finishing their farewells, Zoey, Diana, and Prometheus exited the elevator and walked across the platform. When they opened the entryway doors, stepped outside, and looked at the sky, Zoey sighed in relief. The sun was still high up.

"We have a while before sunset," Diana said, pulling the hood of her cloak tightly to cover her face. "If we hurry, we can get out of here before curfew."

The group hurried through the streets of the *Agora*, toward the edge of the city. No one recognized them; no one stopped them. In fact, hardly anyone spoke to them, except for a few merchants attempting to entice them with "deals they couldn't resist."

Soon they reached a more crowded area, where hundreds of people and satyr and centaur *astynomia* were gathered in the wide street and the sidewalks lining it. Cars were parked on either side of the mob or were making U-turns and hobbling back to where they'd come from—Zoey guessed the drivers couldn't get past the people.

"What's going on?" Zoey yelled to Diana and Prometheus, trying to be heard over the roar of the crowd.

"I don't know," Diana said, glancing around at the people and shops surrounding them. "Let's cut through the buildings and get to another street. They can't all be this busy." The demigod jogged toward a shop to their right, holding her hood in place all the while, and Zoey and Prometheus followed suit.

"Let it be known," a young woman cried from behind, her powerful voice commanding attention and projecting over everyone else's, "that on this day in history, Layla, Daughter of Ares, and Xander, Son of Hermes, captured the treacherous Son of Zeus in the streets of Hephaestus City. He will not escape us again. We will take him to New Mount Olympus, and he will finally answer to his father for his crimes against the gods."

The crowd cheered, but Zoey stopped dead and swung around. *Treacherous Son of Zeus?* Were they talking about Karter? The black-haired, golden-eyed demigod with the horrible scar on his face? The one who'd tried to get Spencer back on the gods' side, had tried to kidnap Zoey, and had struck Diana with lightning—but had ultimately helped Zoey and Andy steal the Helm of Darkness and put Persephone in Tartarus in order to save Spencer's life?

Zoey hadn't seen him since the group's trip to the Underworld, and she hadn't given him much thought other than hoping he'd be okay, but that didn't change the fact that without him, Zoey and Andy wouldn't have been able to steal the Helm of Darkness and could have even died that day in Hades, regardless of the motives behind the Son of Zeus's actions. If he was in trouble . . .

"Zoey," Diana hissed through clenched teeth, seizing Zoey's hand. "What are you doing? I know Layla. I was her friend and teammate. And I know Xander, too. If they see us, we're done for. We have to get out of here."

Zoey yanked her hand from Diana's grasp. "Didn't you hear her say they captured the Son of Zeus? Isn't that Karter, or are there other children-of-Zeus that just so happen to have betrayed the gods?"

Prometheus stomped toward them. "What do you care?"

"Karter helped us! Without him, we wouldn't have been able to steal the Helm, not to mention escape Hades alive."

"Please don't tell me you want to repay the favor," Diana said, her expression full of fear.

"We can't just leave him," Zoey said. "The gods will have him executed or worse for helping us. There's no doubt about it."

"And that's not our problem. He could have come with us. Don't forget I gave him that option. But he chose not to."

"Because he'd just watched his best friend die," Zoey

cried. "He didn't want to leave Spencer. And I understand that, because I didn't either, but you made me."

Diana let out a cold laugh. "You know who else was his best friend? Syrena. Did you know he had no problem letting the gods kill her? Did you know he held Spencer back from saving her? Spencer himself told me so. Karter was fine to capture me right after his father executed her. He was fine with bringing me to Zeus. To have me suffer the same fate Syrena did. Forgive me if I'd rather just leave him to the mercy of the gods."

"All that happened before he helped us," Zoey retorted. "And before he'd redeemed himself so much in Spencer's eyes that Spencer gave him the last golden apple from Eris and refused to take it back. Spencer was willing to *die* for him that day. We can't let them take him after what happened in Hades. We just can't." She paused, looking back at the crowd. "And I won't." She darted into the crowd.

"No!" Diana cried from behind. "Zoey, stop!" But Zoey didn't stop. She was already shoving through the horde.

She focused on what she could say to save Karter, focused on what to say to reach him, and her throat began tingling again. "Get out of my way!" she screamed over the yells. "Get out of my way and *let Karter go!*"

Within moments the people surrounding Zoey quieted and stepped aside, clearing a path for her to walk. She ran down the path toward the center of the crowd, the citizens and *astynomia* staring at her blankly. "Let Karter go," she said. "Let him go."

The laugh of a young man pierced the air ahead. It was cruel, almost taunting. "What do we have here?"

Zoey reached a small clearing in the street at the center of the crowd. Karter lay on the ground there—Zoey recognized him. He looked exactly as she remembered. He was battered and bruised, struggling to keep his eyes open, his breathing labored.

On either side of Karter stood who Zoey assumed were the demigods who'd overtaken him today. The girl—she must have been Layla, Daughter of Ares—was several inches taller than Zoey, a bush of tight burgundy coils piled atop her head, the sweat on her medium-brown skin glinting in the sunlight. Lean muscle showed on her arms and legs. The boy—he had to be Xander, Son of Hermes—was around Zoey's height. His frame was slender, his skin a dark-olive shade, his black hair slick and shiny, a crooked smirk plastered on his lips.

Layla brandished a sword in Zoey's direction. "What do you think you're doing, peasant girl?"

Zoey grabbed the dagger from her robes. "I'm saving Karter from you, that's what. Now let him go!"

Layla and Xander shared looks and glanced at Zoey in amusement, but soon Diana and Prometheus appeared on either side of Zoey, and the demigods' expressions shifted into that of confusion. A mixture of relief and determination flooded through Zoey at the sight of her companions.

Prometheus allowed his disguise to fade away, his manacles clanking as they reappeared. Diana stepped forward, still clutching the hood of her cloak so it wouldn't come loose. "Just let the Son of Zeus go," Diana said. "And no one will have to get hurt."

Layla squinted. "Diana?"

Diana cursed under her breath, then let the hood of her cloak fall. Layla's jaw dropped, and Xander burst into a fit of laughter. "Oh my gods," Xander said. "It seems like fate is leading us to all our enemies today." He looked to Zoey and Prometheus. "Is the pathetic little girl one of the Chosen Two from the Before? And you, with the chains— who are you? No matter, we'll get both of you. Zeus will be pleased with this turn of events."

"No," Diana said, conjuring two spheres of light. "He won't be pleased, because you're not catching any of us today."

Diana chucked the spheres at the demigods. One hit Layla square in the stomach, sending her flying backward, but Xander dodged the other with lightning speed, literally: as he ran, avoiding the attack, his body blurred he moved so fast. Within a quarter of a second, he was behind Zoey. He knocked the knife from her grasp and grabbed her arms with one hand. With the other, he held a dagger to her throat.

Prometheus turned to face Xander, swinging his chains. "You must be a very powerful demigod for Zeus to have sent you on such an important mission. Why would you waste your efforts on a fight against a regular mortal girl, when you could battle a Titan god?"

Xander pressed the cold metal of his knife against the upper corner of Zoey's mouth and sliced it, dragging the blade all the way across her cheek. "Destroying a Titan god does sound like fun, but I think the most fun would be in mutilating you both." Pain seared Zoey's skin, a few drops of warm blood trickling into her mouth. She spit it out, but a metallic taste lingered on her tongue. The demigod shoved Zoey into the street and kicked her hard in the back, knocking the wind out of her. She gasped for breath.

Prometheus hurled his chains at Xander, but Xander dodged the attack with what seemed to be super-speed. At the same time, the crowd broke from their trance—some began yelling while others watched as if in fear as the fight raged on.

Zoey looked over to find the Daughter of Ares charging toward Diana, sword ready. Just as Layla reached Diana, the Daughter of Apollo leapt into the air like a ballerina and pitched a sphere of light at the Daughter of Ares. Layla swerved out of the way. The attack rammed into the street.

"Why?" Layla cried. "Why are you doing this? Why have you turned away from the gods? It didn't have to be this way."

Diana's eyes blazed with fury. She conjured two more attacks. "How have you forgiven them so easily? They let Pearl die." She launched the spheres at Layla. The Daughter of Ares somersaulted to the side, and the light exploded in the street.

Karter stumbled to Zoey's side, his expression full of

confusion. "W-what's going on? What are you doing here? How did you find . . ." He looked around, his eyes going wide as if he'd finally realized what Zoey and her companions were trying to accomplish. He turned to Zoey, eyeing her cut, then offered his hand to help her up. "Are you okay?"

Zoey caught her breath and took his hand. He pulled her to her feet. She let go of him and retrieved her dagger. "I'm fine. Just help us defeat these guys so we can get outta here."

Karter nodded and conjured a golden bolt. He launched it at Xander, who swiftly dodged the attack as he grabbed the end links of Prometheus's chains. Prometheus wrenched his hands back as if trying to pull the chains out of Xander's grasp. Xander held tight with a smirk, allowing Prometheus to pull him closer. When they were only a few feet apart, Xander raced circles around Prometheus faster than ever, links still in hand. Within seconds, the Titan was tangled in his own chains. Prometheus fell to the ground, squirming. Xander plunged his blade into Prometheus's temple. The Titan went still.

"Prometheus!" Zoey cried.

Xander raised his eyebrows at Zoey and laughed. "Did you say *Prometheus*? Well, that would explain his size, and the chains. Don't you worry about him though, girl. Immortals always regenerate after they're killed. Save your concern for when Zeus finds out the traitor escaped his prison."

Zoey snarled and lunged for Xander, dagger ready. The demigod ripped his weapon from the Titan's head, jumped into the air, and kicked Zoey's wrist. Her knife went flying. Xander landed, then punched Zoey so hard in the gut sour vomit rose in her throat. He punched her again, chuckling as he did so, as if he enjoyed this.

Karter tackled Xander into the street. They struggled against each other, kicking and punching. Karter snarled at the demigod as they fought, but Xander kept up his laughing. Finally, Karter pinned Xander down, one hand wrapped around the Son of Hermes's throat.

Xander smiled. "What are you waiting for, coward? Snap my neck. You're strong enough." Karter's expression hardened. He tightened his grip on Xander. The demigod began making choking noises. He spat out globs of saliva although his lips were still pulled back in a sneer.

Layla appeared behind Karter—across the clearing, Diana lay unconscious in the street. Layla balled a fist and reared it back, then slammed it into the back of Karter's skull. Karter went limp and fell to the ground, his hand falling away from Xander's neck.

"Hear me, citizens of Hephaestus City," Layla shouted. "Today, Xander and I have not only captured Karter, Son of Zeus, but also Diana, Daughter of Apollo, the Titan god Prometheus, and one of the Chosen Two of the Dreaded Prophecy. We will need assistance to properly arrest these traitors." At this, several satyr and centaur *astynomia* shoved through the crowd to help Layla and Xander. One seized Zoey by her hair. "But once we can be sure they are secured, we will rejoin our companion, the Daughter of Aphrodite, and bring these prisoners to New Mount Olympus together."

Some of the people in the crowd clapped and cheered, while others slipped away in silence.

CHAPTER TEN

CELL

Karter's chest ached.

He sat in the corner of a cell in the Hephaestus City jail, his wrists and ankles chained to the floor. After he'd awoken from being knocked out, he'd found himself being dragged to the jail by the demigods and several *astynomia*. Soon they'd locked him up.

Through the dim light of a lantern hanging from the ceiling, he watched as the mortal girl, Zoey, sobbed next to the door, pounding her fist against it until her knuckles bled. The *astynomia* hadn't put her in chains, so she was able to move freely in the space given to them, which wasn't much—the cells could only hold up to two people, as they were about half the size of Karter's closet back home. The cells were made of solid iron, and Karter couldn't hear or see anything outside the cramped metal box. Somewhere else in this building, Diana and Prometheus were locked together in a separate cage.

Prometheus, Karter thought. *It's crazy to think Diana*

even got him in on her ridiculous scheme. How did she man-
age it? Think of it?

After a long while, Zoey seemed to give up on hitting the door. She let out a shaky breath and rested her
bloodstained cheek against a wall. "This is all my fault."
Karter looked up at her and cocked his head. "I . . . I'm the
one who wanted to save you from Layla and Xander," she
continued. "I was so stupid. I really thought we could just
march up and—"

"You wanted to save *me*?" Karter blurted. "I mean, I
knew it couldn't have been Diana. But still, why?"

Zoey kept her gaze down. "Spencer was my friend. And
I knew how much . . . how much he loved you, because of
some visions he gave Andy and me during our training.
Then because he tried to give you his golden apple, even
though giving it to you would mean he'd die in Hades . . ."
She gulped. "Not only that, but you helped us steal the
Helm. And, I mean, if it weren't for you, I'd be in Tartarus
right now. You grabbed me from Persephone when she was
dragging me in."

She glanced up, and they locked eyes. Hers were red
and puffy from crying, but the irises shone a brilliant blue
like a clear midday sky. For a few moments neither of them
said anything, only staring at each other.

"I guess what I mean is," she continued, breaking their
eye contact, "I couldn't let them take you after you helped
Andy and me like you did. After you helped Spencer."

"I wish I had done more for Spencer. More for Syrena. Maybe then they'd still be alive . . . Anyway, it was incredibly courageous of you to try and save me. I don't deserve it—but thank you."

"You're—you're welcome. I just wish it hadn't put me and my friends in jail cells."

Karter looked away. *She's going to die because of me.*

They fell into silence.

* ~ * ~ * ~

Andy didn't know where Violet was taking him, Kali, and Darko.

Sure, he knew they were in Hephaestus City, and he knew if he made one wrong move Darko would pierce his own neck with an arrow. But he didn't know where they were going, or why Violet was bringing them this way if she planned to cart them to Olympus. Then again, he also didn't know which direction Olympus was. Maybe this was a stop along the way?

As they passed through the city's *Agora*, people stared at Violet and whispered to each other, but Andy couldn't hear about what exactly, nor did he try to listen. Instead, he prayed Zoey and Diana would reach the group's pegasi and realize something bad had happened before the demigod could send someone to fetch them like she said she would. Or better yet, that Zoey and Diana would cross paths with Violet and end this madness since Andy and Kali couldn't.

Soon they reached a tall building surrounded by iron gates. Centaur and satyr *astynomia* stood guard at all corners. As Violet approached a barred door which must have been the entrance, the *astynomia* guarding it bowed to her.

"These were allies of the Daughter of Apollo," Violet said. "But now they are my prisoners. Would you be so kind as to escort them to their cells?"

"Of course," one satyr said. Within a minute the *astynomia* had Andy, Kali, and Darko handcuffed.

"Any news on the Son of Zeus?" Violet asked.

A centaur turned to her. "Your companions captured him earlier today. Along with the Daughter of Apollo, the Titan Prometheus, and one of the two mortals of the prophecy." At this news, Andy's stomach twisted in knots.

Violet's expression lit with surprise, then morphed into one of pure satisfaction. "Excellent."

* ‿ * ‿ * ‿

For what seemed like hours Zoey and Karter sat in absolute quiet. Zoey was fine with it, though. She didn't know Karter well enough to have a full-blown conversation with him, and it gave her plenty of time to think about how badly she'd screwed up today.

How could I have been so stupid? she thought, over and over. *How could I have thought for one second that I was unstoppable? That we could take on those demigods and rescue Karter?*

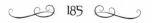

Okay, calm down. Think. How can I fix this? How can we escape?

As Zoey's mind reeled with ways she could remedy the situation and get herself and Diana back to Andy, Darko, and Kali, Karter suddenly spoke. "I'm sorry."

Zoey jerked her head to look at him. "What? Why?"

"We're going to die, and I'm sorry for that."

"We're not going to die. Not if we can get out of here."

Karter sighed. "No. Even if we get out of here, they know your face now, and I can't hide anymore. They'll hunt you down; they'll hunt me down. And when we get to Olympus, Zeus will kill me first. Then Diana. Then you, and he'll put the Titan back in his prison—or worse, in Tartarus. And I'm sorry for that."

"Try to think positively. Maybe we could get out of here and fight those guys off if we found my friends and worked together." She thought back to what she'd been hearing about all day: the gods' cruelty. How Zeus didn't allow demigods to keep their children on Olympus with them if they didn't have enough divine blood, and how he'd executed Troy and Marina's mother just for lying to him about their father's identity. How, when their father finally told them what really happened to their mother, Hephaestus informed Zeus and their father was executed.

Maybe Karter was right about what Zeus would do to him, but it wasn't productive for Karter to be thinking so negatively. "Besides, isn't Zeus your father?" she asked. "I can't imagine he'd wanna kill you first, or that he'd do it himself, no matter how much messed-up stuff he's done before."

"Oh, Zeus might be my father, but he'd kill me without hesitation after what I've done. He gave me this for much less." He gestured at the scar on his face as best as he could with his wrists in chains.

Zoey's breath caught in her throat. Zeus had given Karter that awful scar? "What did you do? What happened?"

Karter hung his head. "Several years ago, Spencer and Syrena tried to leave New Mount Olympus without permission. I told my father if he could just refrain from punishing them, I'd make sure it never happened again. He asked me then if I took responsibility for their crimes. I didn't want them to suffer, so I said yes. He said since I took responsibility for them, and because I disrespected his ruling, I would suffer their punishment, but that it would be increased tenfold. My punishment was a lightning bolt to the face. My eyes turned from brown to the color of the bolt he used, and I was left with this scar. After that, I was considered a disappointment to everyone on New Mount Olympus. I had to work for years to get my father's trust back. And now, because I tried to save Spencer in Hades, my father is going to kill me, and I'll be known forever as a disgrace."

Zoey studied Karter. She gazed at the lines of his face, of his scar, and at his odd golden irises that shone bright even in the dark. At one time she'd thought these things tarnished what could have been a handsome face, but now she wasn't so sure.

"I understand what it's like to be a 'disgrace,'" she said, reminded of the way her classmates used to treat her after Jet told everyone what she'd done to pay her apartment rent. "I was, too. Back in my own time. I also . . . I understand what it's like for a parent to hurt you. My mother—she used to hit me or yell at me almost every day, for who knows what reason. Maybe she thought I disrespected her, and maybe I did. Regardless, no kid should ever have to be scared of their parents."

"You know, I was never scared of my mother. She was wonderful—at least, in the time I was able to spend with her. I'm sorry yours hurt you."

"And I wasn't scared of my father. He was amazing, until I never saw him again. I'm sorry yours scarred you."

In that moment, Karter held an expression Zoey had never seen on him before. It was soft, tender.

Zoey cleared her throat. "So whaddya say? Do you wanna come up with a plan to escape this place together, get Diana and Prometheus, and join our group? Someone as powerful as you could be a huge help to us on our quest."

Before Karter could reply, the cell's iron door was pulled open. In the doorway stood Layla and Xander. Karter frowned at them. "Come to gloat?"

Xander shot Karter a glare, then stomped into the cell. "Oh no, something much less exciting. I've come to get the mortal while Layla has a word with you." Xander snatched

Zoey by the arm and yanked her to her feet. It hurt, but Zoey hardly noticed the pain—she was more concerned with what Xander had just said. What did Layla need to talk to Karter about?

"Why do you need to speak to me alone?" Karter asked. "Why are you afraid of her hearing what you have to say?"

Layla put her hands on her hips. "We're not at all. We're just following orders."

As Xander pulled Zoey into the hall, she glanced over her shoulder at Karter and, for a few moments, they locked eyes.

Layla closed the cell door.

CHAPTER ELEVEN

DECISION

"What do you want from me?" Karter asked Layla, glaring at her.

"I don't want anything from you," Layla replied, examining her nails. "Zeus wants me to tell you something."

"Which is?"

"After Xander and I captured you and your little friends, Xander requested to speak with Zeus." Karter nodded. Xander had two major powers as a Son of Hermes, Messenger of the Gods: the first being his exceptional speed, the second being his ability to contact the gods any time he wished, no matter where he was. He'd wave a hand and say the god or goddess's name, then he would appear before him or her, and they would appear in front of him, both far away from each other but solidified as if in the flesh. Hermes had the same power, except he could also physically transport himself to any of the gods as he wished.

"We told him everything," Layla said. "We were sure

he'd be furious that you'd run away from us, that you'd tried to escape your punishment again. But instead, he seemed happy. He said all was unfolding according to plan."

"According to plan?"

"Yes. He informed us he never really planned to execute you, at least not for this screwup. A few months ago, he had a vision of your future. He said the vision is your true destiny and that he would be an idiot to try and sway it."

"Wait, what? My destiny? What did he see, and why did he wait so long to tell me this?"

"He was waiting for the right time to tell you, and apparently this was it. As far as what he saw, he explained that first he witnessed Xander, Violet, and I capture you and the Daughter of Apollo. Then he saw you realize the mistakes you've made and swear your loyalty to the gods once again—he already knew you'd betray the gods in Hades before he sent you to capture Diana.

"Anyway, in the vision you brought Diana to Olympus—to her execution—but instead of Zeus killing her, as he did Syrena, you were the one to kill her. You made green lightning, something everyone knows you've never accomplished, and you struck the Daughter of Apollo with it. Without any hope of help left, without any direction, the mortals from the Before Time lost the war. Peace was brought to New Mount Olympus and the rest of the world. And last, because of your heroic deeds, Zeus saw you live forever, a god among the rest, seated on your own throne in the palace for eternity."

Karter's heart skipped. *Your destined greatness awaits*, Asteria had said. Was this what she meant? Was this the "greatness" he was bound to achieve? He'd kill Diana, which would inevitably end the upcoming war on the gods, and he'd become an immortal? Very few demigods had completed such incredible feats that Zeus rewarded them with their own godship, his brother Heracles being one of them. Yes, Karter was powerful, but it was hard to believe he'd be able to create and control green lightning and stand equal among the gods.

"Even if Diana dies, the war won't be over," Karter said. "Those mortals will never give up. They're strong and persistent, regardless of the fact they have no powers. They'll find a way to keep fighting. I witnessed it myself in Hades."

Layla laughed. "No matter what you believe, that's not what Zeus saw in his vision. Besides, we have them and the rest of their friends in custody. Violet caught the boy earlier, along with another girl and a satyr. How can they keep fighting if they and all their allies are executed alongside Diana?"

"Are you telling me I'm meant to kill the rest of them, too?" Karter asked, his stomach churning.

"No, Zeus wants them for himself. However, we do need your help to transport them to New Mount Olympus. Zeus has appointed a few of the Cyclopes from the Hephaestus City Forges to make us cages and carry them, but we'll still need you to help guard them as we travel. When we reach home, a public execution will be scheduled, you'll stand by your father's side and help him carry it out, and then you'll be made a god."

"How can I trust you're telling the truth?"

She bent down next to him, pulled a key from her robes, and unlocked each of his chains, one by one. "Why else would I let you go? You're meant to end the war. You're meant to bring peace to the world, and one day, you're meant to be made a god."

* ~ * ~ * ~

Andy wasn't sure how long he'd been chained up in the prison cell.

He'd been separated from Darko and Kali, as the cells were too small to hold all three of them. Violet had locked those two up somewhere else, then taken Andy away and done the same to him. Since then, he'd been able to do nothing but worry about what was going to happen to them next.

We're all captured, he thought. *And Darko is under that sick love spell. What are we going to do?*

As if in reply to his thoughts, the cell door opened, and a girl covered in bruises and cuts was thrown inside, blood smeared on her face like streaks of red paint.

"Zoey!" Andy cried. He went to reach for her, to throw his arms around her and bury his hands in her curls and never let her go, but his chains held him back. The door closed behind her, then locked.

Zoey climbed to her knees and looked to him with fear in her eyes. "Andy? W-what's happening? How'd you get in here?"

"A psycho Daughter of Aphrodite found us while we were waiting for you guys to come back. She put Darko under this crazy love spell and then used him to threaten us. We had to follow her back or else she was going to make Darko kill himself. How did you get here?"

"We'd just left the forges. Karter was—was in the city. I don't know how or why. But two demigods—Layla, a Daughter of Ares, and Xander, a Son of Hermes—were going to capture Karter and take him to Olympus. I knew that would mean certain death for him, and after what happened in Hades, I couldn't stand by and let that happen. We tried to save him, but we couldn't, and they captured us all."

Andy gulped. "What are we going to do?"

"I don't know," Zoey said, her voice cracking as if she was about to cry. "This is all my fault."

"No, it's not," Andy replied. "We can still figure this out. We just have to work together. That Daughter of Aphrodite said something about taking us to Olympus. If that's the case, they can't keep us in here for—"

Pain unlike anything he'd felt before interrupted all other thoughts, all other words, arcing up his back like lightning. He screamed, his throat ripping raw. His vision faded between red and black. What was happening to his body? Was he splitting in two?

A hand cupped his cheek, and Zoey begged him to tell her what was wrong, begged him to be okay. Her voice was barely audible over his shrieks, but as the pain consumed him, it became his only solace in an ocean of agony.

Finally, the electrifying sensations faded into a dull, throbbing ache. Andy's breaths were shallow. Sweat seeped from his pores.

Zoey sat just inches from him, cupping his cheek with her hand. "Andy, what's going on? What *was* that?"

"My—my back," he said between breaths. "It's . . ." He paused for a moment. A new feeling plagued him; what felt like warm, sticky liquid trickled down his spine. His pulse quickened. He couldn't be bleeding, could he?

"What's wrong?"

"I— I— Zoey, look down the back of my shirt."

"What? Why?"

"Please just do it. Something—something is wrong."

She pulled her hand away and stood, lifted the back of his shirt, then peeked down it and gasped.

"What is it?" Andy asked.

"It—it looks like you have wings. Small, bloody wings."

"What in the hell do you mean I have *wings*?"

Zoey kneeled in front of him, her blue eyes wide. "F-feathered wings. Like a bird's. Except yours are tiny in comparison to your body—like, they're maybe the length of a pencil, and they're covered in blood. Did they rip through the skin, or . . .?"

"You're not serious."

"I am. Andy, do you think—"

The cell door creaked open, and in the doorway stood Violet, a young woman with curly burgundy hair Andy assumed was Layla, and a young man with a crooked and sinister smile who must be Xander.

Violet strolled toward Zoey. The demigod's opalescent eyes flashed with malice, her hips swaying with every step. The demigod leaned down and grabbed Zoey's chin, then lifted her head so Zoey and Violet were at eye level.

Andy remembered the way Darko had fallen in love with Violet upon seeing her and was forced under the demigod's control; how, because he was in love with no one else, he'd fallen in love with Violet just by looking into her eyes.

Andy clenched his teeth. "Leave her alone."

Violet dug her nails into Zoey's face, drawing the girl closer and batting her eyelashes. Zoey stared fearfully at the demigod. "Is she the reason you didn't fall for me, little boy? Why you were able to evade my love spell?"

Andy opened and closed his mouth, refusing to answer the question.

Violet released Zoey and walked back to the other demigods. Zoey gave Andy a wide-eyed glance. "Oh, you're in luck. She must feel the same. Otherwise, she'd have fallen desperately for me and wouldn't have turned away like that. Unless . . ." She giggled. "Unless she cares for someone else. That's always awful. For the one whose feelings go unrequited, anyway. Luckily I've never had to experience heartbreak. I'm always the one breaking hearts."

The girl who must be Layla rolled her eyes. "Quit taunting them and talking about yourself. We have a job to do." She stomped into the cell and unlocked Andy's chains, only to bind his hands behind his back using her own. Her grip was like stone, and he wondered if one of her powers was super-strength. She pushed him out of the cell and into the hallway.

"I like it when you talk about yourself," the boy who had to be Xander said to Violet, smirking as he looked her up and down. Violet blew him a kiss, then cocked her head at Zoey. Xander sauntered into the cell, grabbed Zoey, and hoisted her to her feet.

The demigods shoved Andy and Zoey through a dimly lit metallic corridor lined with *astynomia* and the doors of other cells, until finally they reached the end of the hall, where the tallest door of all awaited them: the one through which they'd entered the jail or prison or whatever the hell the place was called earlier that day. Violet unlocked the door. She threw it open and allowed Layla and Xander to lead Andy and Zoey into the building's courtyard. Massive iron gates circled the enclosure, blocking it off from the rest of Hephaestus City and keeping its prisoners from escaping, the moon a sliver of silver in a star-dotted navy sky.

Several *booms* sounded from the left and shook the ground. Andy stumbled backward into Layla. His bleeding "wings" screamed in torment as they collided with the demigod. He cried out. Layla took hold of his shoulders and steadied him, his back throbbing with pain. Andy clenched his jaw, then looked over to find what was causing the booming and shaking, his breath catching at the sight.

Two pairs of men clothed in dirty rags and at least five times Andy's height approached them, along with two centaur *astynomia* who carried bags that Andy assumed held the group's things—including the Helm of Darkness. *Zeus will want that*, Andy thought.

Each pair of the gigantic men worked together to carry two large iron cages, their leathery skin drawn tight over bulging muscles. The tips of their ears were pointed like Diana's arrows, their noses wide and bulbous. Yellowed, fang-like teeth poked out of their mouths in the nastiest underbites Andy had ever seen, and instead of two eyes, they had one giant eye in the center of their foreheads.

"Uh—those are Cyclopses, aren't they?" Andy asked.

Violet laughed. "The correct word would be 'Cyclopes,' boy, and 'Cyclops' would be the singular term."

"Uh-huh," Andy replied. "I didn't need you to correct me, but thanks for wasting your breath."

Violet turned toward the Cyclopes and smiled. "Disgusting creatures, aren't they?"

As the Cyclopes grew closer, Andy realized the cages they held were not empty. In the first pair's cage, the group's three pegasi stood cramped against each other in their confinement, no longer unconscious but blinking drowsily, as if they'd just awoken from deep sleep. In the second pair's cage, Diana, Darko, Kali, and Prometheus sat together. However, their cage looked as if it had room left for more hostages.

"Lock the rest up," Violet said. "And we'll start for Olympus."

The pair of Cyclopes holding Diana, Darko, Kali, and Prometheus dropped the cage. Diana and Kali clasped hands, while Darko and Prometheus hung onto the enclosure's bars. The cage banged into the ground, making the earth tremble.

"Promise us first that if we do as you say, we'll truly earn our freedom," one of the Cyclopes said, his voice like boulders crashing down a mountain. "Promise us that Zeus will let us roam free in the forests—that he will let us feast on the flesh of any mortal outside the cities . . . We cannot go back into that pit."

Violet scrunched up her nose as if she'd smelled something foul. "I already promised you those things and more. Now, you can get these two in their cage, or you can kiss any chance at freedom you may have had goodbye, and I'll have some Cyclopes who are willing to follow my orders carry the traitors to Olympus. I think they'd love to frolic through the trees and cook people into stews just as much as you would."

The Cyclops said nothing to Violet. Instead, he plucked open the cage's door. The demigods shoved Andy and Zoey inside, and the Cyclops locked the door. Zoey threw her arms around Diana and Kali and the three girls embraced, but when Andy approached Darko, the satyr wouldn't even look at Andy. He only hung his head.

"After Violet let me go, Kali told me what happened," Darko said. "Why didn't you just fight her?"

"If we fought her, she would have killed you," Andy replied.

Darko shook his head. "That would have been better than all of us getting captured. I've ruined everything again."

Andy grabbed the satyr by the shoulder and pulled him into a hug. "Don't say that. None of this is your fault."

From outside the cage, Violet laughed. "As much as I love watching reunions this touching, it's time for us to leave."

"We can't go without Karter," Layla said. Andy noticed Zoey perk up a little at the mention of the Son of Zeus. "The vision included him. It was centered around him, really."

"I would never imagine leaving dear Karter behind," Violet said. "Where did he run off to, again?"

"I'm right here," Karter said from above. The scar-faced demigod descended from the night sky, free of chains and captors. *If the demigods were out to capture him before and he managed to escape, then why would he come back to them now?* Andy wondered.

Karter landed at Violet's side, and Zoey furrowed her brow. "But what— I don't— What's going on?"

"He's helping us take you to Olympus," Xander sneered. "Does that upset you?"

Diana bolted forward, conjuring a sphere of sunlight. She chucked the attack in Karter's direction. "*Bastard!*" He swerved out of the way. "We tried to rescue you from them, and this is how you repay us?"

"You didn't succeed in saving him, so he owes you nothing," Xander said. "Besides, even if you had, he'd still come back to our side. Destiny demands it."

"What the hell do you mean?" Zoey asked.

Violet twirled her golden waves with her fingers. "Zeus saw Karter's future. He is meant to publicly execute the Daughter of Apollo, which will end the war on the gods. As a reward, he'll become an immortal god."

Diana seized the bars of the cage. "That can't be true. Andy and Zoey are meant to lead the war. My father's prophecy says so."

"They already tried leading the war," Violet replied. "When they put Hades and Persephone in Tartarus and stole the Helm of Darkness. But now they're in our custody. They've failed."

"No!" Diana shouted, shaking herself against the bars. "My father's prophecy says, *When the sky is black and green, and the heavens cry, they will lead a war. A war on the gods.* Has the sky been black and green lately? When was the last time it rained on Olympus? My father told me years ago that he saw them himself, riding on the backs of pegasi to Olympus with an army behind them. He saw it!"

"I don't know when it rained on Olympus last, but I'm sure Zeus will welcome them into his arms with blasts of green lightning and a storm unlike any other the world has seen," Violet replied. "They will ride up to Olympus when we take them there, their 'army' being everyone who's present now. Honestly, Diana, it's not that hard to piece together. Give up already. It's over." Diana let go of the bars and collapsed on the cage's floor.

Violet, Karter, and the other demigods started for the gates, the two centaurs Andy assumed carried the group's things clopping close behind. The pair of Cyclopes who had dropped the cage with the group inside it earlier lifted it off the ground and followed the demigods' suit, shaking the ground with every step.

Andy looked over at Zoey to see her scowling in Karter's direction. "Why would you help people working for the gods if you feel even an ounce of guilt for Spencer's and Syrena's deaths?" she asked. "I can't imagine they'd be happy if they saw you now. I'd bet my life Spencer would regret giving you the golden apple."

Karter continued walking, casting Zoey a quick glance over his shoulder. Andy couldn't be sure, but he thought he saw a trace of guilt in the Son of Zeus's expression. "It doesn't matter what Spencer and Syrena would have wanted for me. I have no choice. This is my destiny."

"Everyone has a choice," Zoey said. "No one can make you do anything you don't want to do."

Before Karter could reply, Layla swung around to face Zoey, her eyes narrowed into tiny slits. "You don't know anything about destiny. You don't know anything about duty to the gods. How could you?" The demigod's skin shifted from brown to the same burgundy shade as her hair. "Keep your mouth shut, unless you want me to gag it."

They traveled out of the courtyard gates and into Hephaestus City, then toward the outskirts of the city and eventually into the surrounding forest. Zoey said nothing, and neither did anyone else.

CHAPTER TWELVE

FAREWELL

Long before dawn, the party reached a large circular clearing in the forest, where Violet decided they would rest until morning. Violet, Layla, the Cyclopes, and the *astynomia* slept around a campfire, while Karter and Xander patrolled the surrounding area. The Cyclopes' snores were so loud they reverberated through the air and shook the ground.

For the whole night, all Zoey had done was sit in this prison and glare at Karter, but he wouldn't even give her the satisfaction of hating him properly. He wouldn't meet her eyes.

How could he have chosen to help the people who had surely been plotting to kill him? How could he help cart Zoey and her friends to Olympus to die when he knew she'd risked everything to save him, and when he knew he would have been welcome to join their group?

What would Spencer have said had he been here?

Spencer probably wouldn't have said anything, she thought. *He would have just found a way to get rid of the asshole once and for all.*

If only.

Andy and Darko sat on either side of Zoey, while Diana, Kali, and Prometheus sat across from her. Wind whistled through the cage, chilling the air. Goose bumps prickled Zoey's bare arms.

Kali began shivering. Diana eyed Kali with concern, then pulled her cloak off over her head and offered it to Kali.

"Oh, I'm fine," Kali said. "I don't need anything."

"Yes, you do," Diana replied, then laid the cloak over Kali's shoulders like a blanket. "You're cold."

Kali pulled the garment tighter around herself. "Thank you." Despite their dire circumstances, Zoey smiled at Diana's gesture.

After a few minutes, Karter and Xander made another round across the campsite and disappeared into the trees— they were as far from earshot as they'd been all night—and Andy leaned toward Diana and whispered, "If we're going to try and escape, I think now would be the best time."

"If I thought there was a way out of this, I would have already told you about it," Diana replied. "But there isn't."

"We have to try," Andy said. "We can't give up now. After everything we did to get the Helm, after everything we've done to reach Poseidon's palace, we can't just let them win."

Diana sighed. "I'm afraid this is a battle we can't win, Andy." Her voice cracked as she spoke. "Even if we did manage to break out, we'd still be forced to fight four powerful demigods, four Cyclopes, and two centaurs—with no weapons. Trust me, I've given it plenty of thought."

Andy's face fell, while Zoey shared grim looks with Darko and Kali. *Diana is right*, Zoey thought. A lump formed in her throat and tears trickled down her cheeks, the realization hitting her fully. *There's no way out of this one.*

She thought of everyone who had placed their faith in the group to save the world—the citizens of Deltama Village, the nymphs who had saved the group from drowning, Jasmine, Troy, Marina, Syrena, Spencer . . .

How many countless others still hoped for a world where they would be free of the gods' tyranny? How many people would fall into despair when they discovered the Chosen Two of the Prophecy had been publicly executed on New Mount Olympus?

Not only that, but what would happen *after* death? Before the world had ended, Zoey had always considered herself an atheist. But now, after meeting gods and traveling into the Underworld itself, she knew she had a soul. Would she go to Hades when she died, or would she travel into some other unknown land of the dead? Would Spencer and Syrena be there? What about the people she'd known from the Before Time? What about her mother? Her father? As Zoey contemplated the possibilities, her insides twisted into knots.

"This is all my fault," Zoey said. "If I hadn't tried to

help Karter, we would never have been in this mess."

Diana shook her head. "No. Even if we hadn't helped Karter, Violet would've still found a way to take Andy and Darko and Kali. We would have had to go back to save them, and then we would have been captured."

"It's destiny, isn't it?" Kali asked. "Just like those demigods said. It's destiny that we failed today."

Prometheus scowled, lifting his manacles and turning toward the bars of their cage. "You know what? Screw destiny." He wrapped the links around most of the barrier on his side of the prison and pulled them back, his muscles bulging at the effort. "I have an idea. Back up, ladies."

"What are you doing?" Diana whispered, her tone laced with panic. She and Kali scrambled to the other side of the cage.

The bars began to bend with the chains as Prometheus tugged harder. "I'm breaking us out of here."

"It won't work," Diana replied. "These things were forged by the Cyclopes themselves specifically for the task of taking us to Olympus. Don't you see how thick the metal is?"

Prometheus grunted. "They may have been forged by the Cyclopes, but my chains were forged by Hephaestus himself and, as we've already discovered, can't be broken very easily."

"What do you expect us to do even if you break us out, then?" Diana asked. "The odds are most definitely not in our favor."

"You kids have fought countless monsters, and you survived a trip to the edge of Tartarus. You'll figure something out. And if you don't, at least you will have tried. Now get ready to fight these guys."

The bars snapped and caved in with loud *clang*s, and Prometheus scrambled out of the broken cage toward their pegasi's prison, manacles ready. From beside the campfire, Violet, Layla, and the centaurs woke from their slumbers and jumped to attention, their own pegasi neighing as if to alert them. The Cyclopes stopped snoring, blinking open their bloodshot eyes in confusion.

Diana looked to everyone in the group, nodding at them although her expression was fearful, as though to say, *Even if we can't win, we have to try.* And with that, the group shot to their feet and darted out of the cage together.

The centaurs drew their swords and charged for the group. Diana leapt ahead and conjured two blazing spheres of light, then chucked them at the centaurs. The attack hit both creatures in their stomachs. They flew backward and crashed into the trees.

Andy and Darko sprinted side by side toward the two bags holding the group's weapons. Violet grabbed darts out from her robes and held them between her fingers. With a flick of her wrist, she sent them soaring for Andy and Darko. The pair bolted in different directions, avoiding the darts by inches.

Violet readied more darts and flung them in Andy's direction, but Andy somersaulted out of the way and skidded next to the bags. He seized them and dumped their contents onto the ground—two bows and quivers of arrows, spears, daggers, a sword, an axe, and the Helm of Darkness. With an urgency Zoey had never seen in him before, Andy kicked the bows and arrows toward Darko and shoved a spear, an axe, and the Helm of Darkness back at Zoey and Kali, dodging Violet's darts all the while.

Layla bounded toward Andy, blade ready, her skin and eyes shifting into as deep a red as her coiled hair. Andy grabbed the sword and darted out of Layla's way just before she could reach him. Layla screamed in fury and pivoted toward him, ready to bring her weapon down, but before she could, Diana blasted her with a sphere of light and sent her flailing backward.

The Cyclopes fumbled to their feet, each of their booming movements sending shudders through the earth. Zoey pulled the Helm of Darkness over her head, vanishing, and seized her axe while Kali took the spear, two Cyclopes stepping toward them. The other Cyclopes walked toward Prometheus as he wrapped his chains around the bars of the pegasi's cage. Their steps shook the ground so much Zoey could hardly keep her balance.

"Foolish human girl," one Cyclops boomed, reaching in Zoey's general direction with a giant calloused hand. "There is no escaping your fate today. Perhaps Zeus will let me have you for a snack if I can catch you and retrieve Hades's Helm."

The Cyclops's hand hovered over Zoey and grabbed the

space around her. She darted to the left, then the right, avoiding the monster's grasp. He grabbed for her a third time. As his hand came down, she channeled her strength into her left arm and hand. Using all her might, she swung her axe at his thumb. The blade cut deep. Zoey wrenched the weapon from the Cyclops's flesh, blood squirting from the wound. The monster bellowed and pulled away.

Beside Zoey, as the other Cyclops tried to pick up Kali, the girl shoved her spear through his palm. His hand *crunch*ed from the attack. She ripped the weapon back out and the monster shrieked, falling back.

Across the camp, Prometheus cried out. Zoey looked over to see him on his hands and knees, the remaining Cyclopes standing over him. Karter circled the air above them, a golden lightning bolt in hand. The pegasi were still trapped in the cage; Prometheus had not yet broken the bars.

The Cyclops Zoey had injured stepped forward, shaking the forest floor and grabbing the air around her. Zoey charged on the monster and swung her axe at him. The blade cut into his wrist. He yelped, but before Zoey could wrench her weapon away, the monster flung his hand backward. The momentum flipped Zoey around and sent her toppling into the dirt, the Helm flying off her head and sliding away. The monster ripped her weapon from his wrist and flicked it across the clearing.

The Cyclops plucked Zoey off the ground and tightened his grip around her waist, then brought her to his nostrils and sniffed. "Mmmmmmmm. Perhaps instead of waiting for Zeus to give me permission to eat you, I'll just go ahead and do it."

A bright lightning bolt, one the color of rubies, flashed past Zoey's head and blasted the Cyclops in the cheek. The Cyclops whined like a child, and Zoey glanced over to see Karter, more red bolts arcing and hissing in his hands. "You won't do anything to her unless my father orders you to," Karter said. "This is your only warning."

The Cyclops's bottom lip quivered. "Yes, Son of Zeus."

Karter gave the Cyclops one last stern look, then swooped toward the brawl below. Kali must have come to Prometheus's aid, because the two of them zigzagged between the feet of the remaining Cyclopes. Kali stabbed them in the toes and ankles with her spear, while Prometheus used his chains to whip them in the legs. Both sent the monsters hopping and howling. Diana and Darko fought against Layla and Xander, arrows and blasts of light whizzing through the air. Andy battled Violet and the centaurs tirelessly.

Karter flew toward Violet, but before he could land next to her, he launched his ruby-red lightning bolts at Diana and Darko. The force sent them stumbling to the forest floor. Layla and Xander ran forward and secured Diana's and Darko's hands behind their backs.

"No," Zoey cried, squirming in the Cyclops's hand. "Diana! Darko!"

Karter conjured two more red bolts and turned toward

Kali and Prometheus.

"Kali, Prometheus, look out!" Zoey yelled, but they didn't seem to hear. Karter threw the attacks and knocked Kali and Prometheus to the ground. Before they could stand, two Cyclopes plucked them up as the one holding Zoey had.

Zoey looked to Violet and the centaur *astynomia*. The centaurs grabbed Andy by the shoulders—*No, not him!* Zoey thought—and Karter conjured a final red bolt and chucked it at the boy. The bolt blasted Andy's sword from his grasp, knocking it into the dirt, and the centaurs bound Andy's wrists behind his back.

Zoey slapped and kicked her captor as best as she could, but to no avail. *This can't be the end of it*, she thought. *Not when we were so close.*

A faint crackling sound tickled Zoey's ears, and her eyes fluttered open. Tiny balls of orange fire appeared in four corners of the clearing. Zoey furrowed her brow as the balls grew taller and wider and more rectangular, until they'd morphed into walls of flame standing as high as the trees, separated by twenty-foot gaps where no fire burned. For a moment the walls remained in their respective corners, not spreading into the forest or the clearing or growing any bigger. Everyone paused and stared at the walls in confusion. What was going on? Where could they be coming from?

Suddenly the fiery walls roared, curving inward, then raged into the clearing like waves crashing toward a beach.

The demigods and centaurs shrieked, releasing their prisoners and dashing for the closest gap between the fires. Everyone else followed suit, the ground tremoring from the Cyclopes' lumbering strides. Karter and the demigod trio's pegasi leapt into the sky.

The Cyclops holding Kali reached a gap first, but just as he was about to pass through it and into the trees, his head reared back so hard Zoey thought she heard his neck crack. He tumbled back-first toward the ground, Violet and Layla racing out of his way, then crushed a centaur under the weight of his massive body. For a moment his fingers went slack, and Kali rolled out of his hand and onto the ground.

The creature keeping Zoey captive jumped over his fallen companion, keeping her secure in his hand. Her stomach reeled. Midair, he rammed into an invisible barrier, then fell backward as well. Zoey screamed. It felt as though she were barreling down the tallest track of a roller coaster, her only seat belt the Cyclops's grimy fingers.

The monster landed with a loud *thud* on top of his companion. Upon impact, his grip on Zoey loosened a bit, and she scrambled from his grasp and tumbled to the forest floor.

"Where is that fire coming from?" Violet screeched, her beautiful face twisted with fury. "Who is doing this?"

As if in response to the Daughter of Aphrodite, the fiery walls charging the party stopped, then crept back toward where they'd come from and finally disappeared altogether, leaving the air hot, dry, and smoke-filled. Karter and the demigods' three pegasi descended into the clearing.

"I'm waiting," Violet said. "Stop your tricks and fight us face-to-face."

Like a spark leaping from a pile of ash, a familiar woman with shoulder-length black hair burst from the darkness before them, her palms blazing with orange flames. She ran to face the fallen, disoriented Cyclopes. They turned their heads toward her, blinking in disbelief as if the realization of who she was hit them.

Zoey gasped. "Marina?"

Marina brought her fiery hands behind her head and launched her attacks straight for the Cyclopes' eyes. The flames set their corneas ablaze. They writhed and screamed, clawing their faces, an acrid stench filling the air. After a few moments Marina waved her hands and the flames died. However, the damage was already done. The Cyclopes whimpered, tears streaming down their faces, the whites of their eyes now smoking and scarlet.

Marina crossed her arms. "If you interfere with the Daughter of Apollo and the Chosen Two of the Prophecy again, I'll ruin more than your sight."

The Cyclopes nodded hurriedly, and the Granddaughter of Hephaestus ran to Zoey's side, panting—probably from the effort she'd just exerted to help save the group. Zoey wasn't sure how quickly grandchildren of the gods drained their energy when using their powers, but she guessed it was probably quicker than for demigods considering they had far less divine blood running through their veins.

Troy appeared from the forest and hurried to them as well. A large hammer and a bundle of rope hung from his belt.

"But how— What's going on?" Zoey asked.

Troy grinned. "When Zeus recruited some of the Cyclopes in our forges to help take you guys to Olympus, we knew we had to help you escape, so we tracked the submarines. Did you like our trick with the fire and the ropes in the trees?" Zoey smiled and nodded.

The rest of the group—other than Prometheus, as one of the uninjured Cyclopes still had him in hand—rushed to Zoey's side. Kali clutched a spear and handed Zoey the Helm of Darkness; once she pulled it over her head, she drew her dagger. Andy had his sword in hand. Diana made spheres of light, and Darko nocked an arrow.

Karter conjured two golden lightning bolts while Layla, Xander, and the remaining centaur readied their weapons. The last two Cyclopes stood behind them like guards.

Violet put up her hands as though in surrender and walked forward. Her hips swayed with every step. "Why don't we take some time to talk about this instead of mindlessly killing each other?" she said, batting her lashes, her opalescent irises flashing even in the dark. "I for one would prefer not to die today."

Andy glared at Violet. "Don't look the Daughter of Aphrodite in the eyes. If you don't already have feelings for someone else, she'll make you fall in love with her and turn you against us." Troy and Marina turned their gazes away from Violet altogether.

The Daughter of Aphrodite scowled at Andy. "Fine, then. We'll fight." Violet backed away until she stood close to Karter. She caressed his shoulder—at this, Zoey inhaled sharply—and flashed him a flirtatious smile. He looked at the demigod, his eyes full of confusion.

"I don't like them one bit," Violet said. "I know we're supposed to keep them alive for the execution, but could you at least give them some bruises? Maybe a few black eyes? For me?"

Before Karter could reply, the Cyclops with his hands free took booming footsteps over the demigods toward the group, and the centaur clopped alongside him.

Marina rushed toward the Cyclops and centaur and began throwing balls of fire at the creatures. Troy ran past her, toward the demigods, and started clobbering Xander and Layla with his hammer, dodging Karter's lightning bolts and Violet's darts.

At the same time, Prometheus swung his chains at the face of the Cyclops holding him captive. The links slapped the Cyclops in his eye, and the monster bellowed so loudly the trees shook, dropping Prometheus and fumbling backward. The Titan rolled as he landed, then gained his footing and joined Troy and Marina in battle.

Andy brandished his sword as if ready to help as well, then cried out and fell back, dropping his blade and falling to his knees.

"Andy!" Darko cried. "What's wrong?"

"I'm—fine," Andy said, grunting. "Just—just get my sword." Darko nodded, snatching up the boy's blade, then sheathed it for him.

Zoey kneeled at Andy's side and rested her hand on his back, but recoiled quickly—warm, sticky blood had seeped through the fabric of the boy's clothes. His "wings" looked as if they'd grown several inches. They now poked out of his shirt.

"Andy . . . the wings," Zoey whispered. "They're bigger than before."

Diana stepped in front of Zoey and Andy, spheres of light ready in her hands. "I have to help Troy and Marina fight so Prometheus can break out the pegasi. The rest of you . . . start running. I'll send Prometheus after you."

Kali grabbed Diana's wrist. "I won't let you hold them off by yourself."

"I won't be by myself," Diana said. "I'll have Troy and Marina. Besides, Zoey and Andy will need Darko and you more than ever if I can't escape."

"Please," Kali replied, holding tight to Diana.

Diana looked over her shoulder and offered Kali a small smile. "I'll catch up with you when I'm done here, all right?"

Kali hesitated, staring hard at Diana. Finally, Kali took a deep breath, then leaned down, closed her eyes, and pressed her lips against Diana's. The demigod froze for a moment, her spheres of light disintegrating, but soon she softened her shoulders and closed her eyes as well, leaning into the kiss.

A short time passed, and Kali let go of Diana's wrist and pulled away. "Finish up with the monster-and-demi-god-slaying so we can do that again, okay, Princess?"

"O-okay," Diana stammered.

Zoey took off the Helm, handed it to Darko, and hurried forward to give Diana a quick hug. "Please be careful."

"Of course," Diana replied, then turned around and sprinted into the battle before them.

Kali rushed to Andy's other side and took his hand. "Are you okay? Do you need help walking?"

He shook his head. "I'm good. Maybe just to stand?" Kali pulled him to his feet. He stumbled forward, but she caught him before he could fall.

"Let me help," Zoey said. She wrapped her hand around Andy's waist and laid his arm over her shoulder. Kali did the same on his other side.

"Do you think Diana will be okay?" Darko asked.

Zoey swallowed hard and forced a smile. She wasn't sure what was going to happen now. "Of course. She'll be fine. You heard her yourself. She'll catch up with us later. Now c'mon, we need to get out of here."

"Lead the way, Darko," Kali said.

Darko clopped into the trees, the Helm and a bow in hand, a quiver with only a couple of arrows left in it slung over his back. Zoey, Andy, and Kali hobbled along as fast as they could. The conflict raged on behind them.

* ﹏ * ﹏ * ﹏

Karter jumped into the sky and flew over the battle, toward the trees he'd seen Zoey, Andy, the satyr, and the tall dark-haired girl escape into. Karter didn't know what they were planning, but while his companions overtook the rest of their enemies, he would stop them.

Once he spotted them below, limping through the forest, he swooped down.

Before Karter even landed, the satyr caught sight of him. The satyr aimed an arrow for Karter and loosed it, but Karter dodged the attack with ease. The satyr shot another arrow. Karter darted to the side. The arrow missed him by inches.

The satyr reached into his quiver to pull out another arrow, but none remained. Karter smirked and landed before them. He conjured a golden lightning bolt.

The tall dark-haired girl lunged for Karter, a dagger in hand. He leapt up and kicked her arm. The blade went flying, but she snatched his ankle and yanked him to the forest floor. He landed on his back with a hard *thud*, his bolt disintegrating, and suddenly the girl was straddling him, sending punch after punch to his jaw. Rage etched harsh lines into her face.

The punches caused hardly any pain—in fact, Karter would have bet it was hurting the girl far more than him—but he still wanted her off. He focused on conjuring his child-of-Zeus strength, then grabbed her wrists, stopping the blows. He released her and thrust his legs upward. The girl went flying. She landed back-first onto the forest floor several feet away.

Karter sprang to his feet to see Zoey as she slipped the Helm of Darkness over her head. She disappeared, but he concentrated on the ground, watching the grass and dirt shift under her weight as she charged at him. In seconds she was upon him. He snarled, grappling with her until he was able to pull the Helm of Darkness off her head.

The Helm's metal stung as though hundreds of needles were pricking his flesh, and as soon as he had the item out of Zoey's reach, he threw it aside—he couldn't risk the magical item sucking away his life force any more than it may have already in the short time he'd touched it. It clattered to the ground.

Zoey snarled and raised one of the satyr's loosed arrows above her head, but Karter knocked it aside easily. He grasped Zoey's shoulders and held her in place. She struggled against him, but she was no match for his child-of-Zeus strength.

Andy lay unconscious far ahead. What was wrong with the boy, Karter didn't know. Had he been wounded during the fight? *It doesn't matter*, Karter thought. *No need to worry for him.*

"Why are you doing this?" Zoey cried. "You could have helped us."

"I'll do as my father commands me," Karter said. "What destiny has planned for me."

"Why would you help a person who murdered millions of innocent people for power? Who killed one of your best friends right in front of you? Who mutilated your face?"

Karter paused, locking eyes with Zoey. Her gaze seemed to plead with him, as if begging him to do the right thing.

But what *was* the right thing to do, really? Sure, Karter's father and the rest of the gods murdered millions of people—but only because the gods had been fading away from lack of worship from those "innocent" mortals who, Karter could argue, were no more innocent than the gods themselves. Mortals lied, cheated, and murdered too.

The gods existed long before humans ever did, and they controlled everything: the lands, the skies, the seas. Why should the lives of mortals matter more than the lives of gods? Regular mortals and demigods alike were only specks of dust in the grand scheme of the universe, swept away in the blink of an eye. However, the gods, despite their character flaws, were divine beings able to grant and destroy life with a snap of their fingers. They would last longer than all the stars in the sky so long as they received worship.

Yes, sometimes the gods made questionable decisions. Sometimes they were petty and dishonest and cruel. Karter had been the victim of their abuse more than once. But who was Zoey to question their will? Who was he to do the same? They were not eternal, and neither of them were capable of understanding the universe in the same way the gods did. Besides, if Karter was to be *made* a god . . .

Well, why would he allow his frail human emotions to control him, when his destiny had always been to become so much more?

The neighs of pegasi sounded above them. Karter looked up. Prometheus, manacles and all, sat on the back of one of the three pegasi Karter and his companions had imprisoned, descending from the night sky toward them. The other two followed suit.

Karter's stomach fell. If Prometheus had been able to free those creatures and escape the other demigods, Diana wouldn't be far behind. Zeus had only mentioned seeing Karter executing Diana in his vision and was sure Diana's death would end this war before it ever truly began.

Karter couldn't go back to Olympus—he couldn't fulfill his destiny of becoming an immortal god—if Diana escaped.

Prometheus landed the pegasus and started for Karter. However, instead of fighting, Karter let go of Zoey and jumped into the sky, beginning the flight back to his companions. If he went back to them now and allowed Zoey and Andy to go free, but kept Diana in custody, everything would work out the way it was meant to.

At least, Karter hoped it would.

CHAPTER THIRTEEN

WINGS

Andy wasn't sure how he'd arrived in the garden.

He'd been following Darko through thick forest, the pain in his back so bad Zoey and Kali had to hold him up to walk. He'd closed his eyes for just a moment, the agony unbearable, and when he'd opened them again, his surroundings had completely changed. His pain faded.

The garden he was in now looked identical to the one from his visions in Aphrodite City, when he'd touched the statue of Anteros and saw Anteros and Calliope under a gazebo in a garden. There were cypress trees, bushes of flowers, marble fountains, golden paths. Planets and stars gazed down at him, lingering so closely he felt perhaps he could reach up and touch them.

From behind, a woman's voice said, "Greetings, Chosen One."

Andy swung around. A pretty woman who looked to be around thirty stood before him. She was pale, with curly red hair, her silver irises glittering. Twinkling stars dotted her black dress.

"Who are you, and how do you know who I am?" Andy asked. "What's going on? Where am I?"

"I thought you'd be taller, like him, but I suppose you have similar mannerisms," the woman said, almost absent-mindedly, then gestured at their surroundings. "Do you not remember this place? You have visited it before."

"I was thinking it looked like the one from a vision I've had."

"The garden you saw then is the one you stand in now."

Andy raised a brow. "You know about that? About what I saw?"

"Yes."

"Uhhhhhhh, I've never met you before. You wanna explain how you know about that vision?"

The woman curtsied. "Allow me to introduce myself. I am Asteria, Titan goddess of stars, prophetic dreams, and necromancy. I dreamt of you. Well, in a way I dreamt of you, I suppose. I saw the visions you were given in Aphrodite City, and I knew I needed to speak with you at my first opportunity."

"If you're a god, then how did you find me? The Fates' spell keeps Zoey and me hidden from the gods so that they can't reach us."

"I have kept a close eye on Karter, Son of Zeus. Through him, I found you. You are in a compromised state, and so it was easy to enter your mind. But do not fret. I mean you no harm."

"Wait. If you're a goddess of prophetic dreams, does that mean this is a dream?"

"Perhaps it is. Perhaps not."

"What the hell does that mean?" He rubbed his temples. "Lady, please, I've had a long couple'a weeks. I don't need vague riddles to ponder. Just be up front with me. What do you want?"

"I want to warn you and your friend of the coming adversary."

"Which friend? I have a couple."

"The girl. The one you love."

Zoey's face flashed across Andy's mind. He began backing away from the Titan goddess. "Okay, this is weird. I've never explicitly told *anyone* how I feel about Zoey. And you know what, I don't know if what I feel for her is actual love. I've never even kissed a girl, okay? So why the hell would you say I love her?"

"Because your affection for her has been fated for centuries. It is what brought you where you are now."

He shook his head. "No way. I'm here because I'm meant to fight the gods. I'm here because my life thread or whatever the Fates called it turned white and started to glow when I died, and they didn't let my soul pass on because they knew I had more to accomplish."

"Have you ever wondered why your thread did what it did when you died? Have you ever wondered why, out of all the mortals the universe could have picked for this task, it picked you?"

"Well . . ." He thought for a moment. Why had the universe picked him? He was scrawny and nerdy, and before the world had ended, he couldn't even properly defend himself against bullies. At least now he could fight monsters with the help of his friends.

When the group had visited the Fates the first time, hadn't Zoey asked them why Andy's and Zoey's threads were so special? *"We cannot say,"* they'd answered. *"In time, you will discover it for yourself."*

"I guess I haven't thought about it in a while," Andy said. "I kinda had a lot on my plate. It was hard enough wrapping my head around the fact that my best friend and family were dead, that the Greek gods are real, and that people are counting on me to save the world. Plus, the Fates told Zoey and me we'd find out more of the 'whys' eventually. I guess I forgot about it. Once we started fighting monsters and stuff, it just didn't cross my mind anymore."

"The truth is coming," Asteria said. "And it will be hard to accept. This is your and the girl's coming adversary. But you cannot fight the truth, Chosen One. You cannot question it. If you do, you will be at war with yourself—you will be at war with your friend—and neither of you will survive the coming battles."

"What truth? What are you talking about?"

"I wish I could say, but I can only warn you of the future, lest I sway your destiny. I can only advise you to accept the truth. When the time has arrived, you will know what I mean by all of this." The Titan goddess disintegrated into millions of shimmering stars and floated into the sky.

Once the last of Asteria had disappeared, the vegetation of the garden shifted from deep greens to pure black, the dark sky swallowing the planets and stars. Andy closed his eyes and then floated aimlessly through empty space like strips of seaweed in an ocean. Blissfully, with no care in the world, his mind finally at peace.

"Andy?" he heard Zoey call, somewhere far away. "Andy, it's time to wake up."

He opened his eyes.

He lay on his back in a cave, what felt like a mattress made of fluffy clouds beneath him. The rays of a sunset peeked through the jagged crevice of the cave's entrance. Zoey, Darko, Kali, and Prometheus hovered over him, and the group's three pegasi rested in the far corner.

Andy groaned. His back was sore, but the intense pains he'd experienced before had dissipated. "W-what happened? Where are we? Where's . . ." His stomach dropped. "Where's Diana?"

Zoey took Andy's hand. "We escaped Karter and the others last night. You've been passed out this whole time. We're a long way from Hephaestus City, and only a day away from Poseidon City, but Diana and the twins who helped us—Marina and Troy—didn't get away. Based off what those demigods said about Zeus's vision, Diana won't be executed until they reach New Mount Olympus, and Prometheus says they won't be able to get there for another five to six days since they're mostly traveling on foot. We think she's still alive."

"And the siblings?" Andy asked, remembering the flame-throwing woman and the hammer-wielding guy. He hadn't known who they were, but Zoey had seemed to, so he'd assumed she'd met them in Hephaestus City and, judging by their actions last night, it seemed as if they wanted to help fight the gods.

Zoey's eyes grew watery, her lip quivering. "I don't know about Marina and Troy. I don't know if they'll be kept alive that long. I hope so."

Andy sat up. "There's time left to save them—all of them. We have to start for New Mount Olympus or try and intercept the demigods."

"No," Prometheus said. "We have to go to Poseidon's palace."

"We can't just let them kill Diana," Andy replied. "We can't let them kill Marina and Troy either. Those two saved our asses, and Diana would come for us if we were captured. She'd do anything to rescue us. We have to do the same for her."

Zoey squeezed his hand. "You're right, and we *will* save her, and if Marina and Troy are still alive, we'll save them too. But we can't just yet. We barely escaped the demigods, so we have to ask for help and steal the Trident before we try to get them back."

"Ask for help?" Andy asked. "What do you mean? Help from who?"

Darko pulled out the small drawstring sack the nymphs who'd saved the group gave them. "We still have the flower the nymphs gave us. I was able to save it while we were fighting the Cyclopes and the demigods and the *astynomia*."

"The nymphs pledged themselves to our cause," Kali continued for the satyr. "While you were passed out, we decided we're going to call on the nymphs and ask if they can reach Olympus in the next several days and gather more people for an army as they go."

"While they're traveling toward us and gathering others, we'll steal the Trident," Zoey added. "With the Helm, the Trident, and an army, we can sneak-attack the gods and rescue our friends, then regroup for later."

Andy grinned and climbed to his feet. "This is perfect! The gods will never see it coming. They think they've already won. Why didn't you wake me up earlier for this? Let's get going. We need to go through the Labyrinth and get into the palace. We don't have any time to waste." The group exchanged nervous glances. "What?" Andy asked. "What's wrong?"

"Before we do any of that," Zoey started, "there's something we have to talk to you about."

"Which is?"

"Remember the pains in your back? The weird wing things that grew out of it?"

"Yes?"

"Well, they're bigger now. After you passed out, they

just kept growing and growing."

Andy's breath caught in his throat. He reached for his back, his fingers brushing something soft—like feathers.

"They kept bleeding too, and you seemed so restless. You were talking in your sleep and rolling around. Once we were far enough away from Hephaestus City we stopped in this cave and tried to patch you up, but it was no use. Prometheus said we needed to let whatever it was run its course, and it turned out he was right. Pretty soon the wings stopped getting bigger—they kinda just stayed the way they were—and your wounds healed themselves, like really fast. You stopped bleeding. That's when we decided it was safe to wake you up. How—how do you feel?"

Andy craned his neck, trying to catch sight of the wings, but could only see white feathers. "I mean, other than the fact that I sprouted some new body parts, I *think* fine? I'm not in near as much pain. Just kind of sore. But how did this happen? Seriously, I don't even know what to say."

"Neither did I," Zoey replied. "But I, uh, talked to Prometheus about all the weird stuff that's been happening with you and me, and he might have an idea of what's going on."

"Which is?" Andy asked, turning to the Titan.

"Zoey told us a little about what happened to you in Aphrodite City," Prometheus said. "How the temple of Anteros seemed to call to you and didn't stop until you got there. How you touched it and got those visions, and when you came back you had pains in your back and didn't need your glasses anymore. Zoey also mentioned that after this happening, when you touched her, she experienced an electric shock, and she's been having strange tingling sensations in her throat ever since. These ringin' a bell?"

"How could they not?" Andy replied. "I mean, I didn't know about all of Zoey's stuff, but the rest of it is possibly the weirdest thing that's ever happened to me, other than being a Chosen One in a war against Greek gods."

"Well, since your wings have grown," the Titan continued, "I've sensed a divine presence growing in you. I've sensed it growing in Zoey since then, too. Not like you're becoming immortal or anything like that—more like the way a descendant of the gods has divine blood and powers and such. Who were the gods you saw in your visions?"

"There was Zeus and a bunch of others in a big dining-hall type place," Andy started. "But for the most part, the visions were centered around Anteros, which makes sense since I touched his statue. There was also a lot of a goddess named Calliope, whom he was in love with."

Prometheus scratched his chin. "Anteros and Calliope faded away a long time ago. They were part of the reason many of the gods decided it was a good idea to destroy the modern world and take back humanity's worship, so they wouldn't suffer the same fate. Calliope was the Goddess of Eloquence. If she lied, she could sometimes make others believe her completely. Her greatest power was convincing those around her to do as she said."

"Which is what I did when I told all those people to get out of the way when we were in Hephaestus City," Zoey said.

Prometheus nodded. "That's right. And Anteros—well, to say the wings Andy has grown are similar to the god's are an understatement. They're identical."

Andy recalled what Anteros's wings had looked like in the visions and tried to imagine them on himself. "Okay, that's weird, but what does all this mean?"

"I can only think of one explanation," the Titan said. "Although Anteros and Calliope faded away, they may not have been completely gone. Because Aphrodite built a temple for Anteros in her city, a part of him could have lingered there, and because he was in love with Calliope, a part of her would have probably lingered within him. I'm guessing that when you touched his statue, whatever was left of him entered your body. Then, when you touched Zoey, whatever was left of Calliope must have entered her body. That would explain the electric shocks, the throat tingling, and now the fact that you've grown wings."

Andy shivered. "So, Anteros and Calliope are possessing me and Zoey? Like a demon or something? But why?"

"They may want to help you in your war against the gods," Prometheus answered. "They might think that inhabiting your bodies and giving you some divine power will be beneficial."

Zoey shook her head. "That doesn't make sense. They faded away because humanity forgot them. Why would they be on our side if we're trying to restore the world to what it once was?"

"That's a fair point," Prometheus said. "Have any other strange things gone on?"

"Not for me," Zoey answered. "I told you everything."

"I had kind of a weird dream," Andy said. "A Titan goddess—I think her name was Asteria—told me the 'truth' about me and Zoey would be coming soon, and that we had to accept it, or it would be detrimental to us."

"Hmmm. Asteria is a goddess of prophecy, so it would make sense that she'd warn you about a big event coming, but I've also known her to meddle with things on occasion," Prometheus said. "If Asteria visited you, then perhaps she's the one who orchestrated this whole ordeal. She could have consulted with another deity, probably a Titan or one of her children, to plant powers inside of you, especially if she thinks you need them."

"If that's the case, then why would they resemble Anteros's and Calliope's powers so closely?" Zoey asked.

Prometheus shrugged. "Probably to throw the gods off her trail. If she was meddling like that, she wouldn't want them to find out and throw her in Tartarus. Honestly though, I can't be sure. However, I am sure about one thing: If you want to save the others, we're going to need to hurry."

"He's right," Kali said. "We've broken the news to Andy. Maybe we can find out more later. Now let's contact the nymphs and ask if they'll be willing to help us save

Diana and the other two who helped us."

Everyone agreed. They walked outside the cave into more forest, the evening crisp and breezy, and quickly built a fire. Darko removed the daylily from its drawstring sack and tossed it into the flames. It burned, its orange petals curling in on themselves and turning crispy black, a smell like vanilla filling the air. Andy held his breath and waited for something to happen.

When the flower became nothing but ash, the fire began shimmering and flickering like sunlight on rippling water. A blurred-out face took form in the flames—then two, then three—and before Andy knew it Eugenia, Harmony, and Narcissa looked out at the group through the fire.

Harmony bounced up and down as if in glee. "I knew we'd see you guys again!"

"Calm yourself, Harmony," Narcissa began, her tone cold and her expression stiff. "I understand you are excited, but we do not yet know why they have contacted us."

Eugenia clasped her hands. "It is good to see you again, Andy and Zoey." The Dryad's jaw dropped when she noticed Andy's wings. "Oh, my. Those are new, aren't they? You will have to elaborate on how you acquired them when we get a chance. Anyway, tell us why you have contacted us today."

"Diana and some of our new friends have been taken by demigods working for Zeus," Zoey said. "They're going to execute Diana on New Mount Olympus, but we don't know about the other two for sure. We're hoping they'll be spared until the execution as well. So, basically we're less than a day away from reaching the Labyrinth and getting into Poseidon's palace to steal the Trident. We're going to try to steal the Trident and reach Olympus before the execution so we can save them, but we can't succeed if we do it alone."

Andy stepped forward. "Which is why we called you. We can't pull off this plan well without a lot of help. Would you be able to rally as many other nymphs as you can within the next few days and come to New Mount Olympus to help us?"

The Dryads' eyes went wide, and they whispered among themselves for a few moments, then turned to the group. "We would be happy to assist you in saving the Daughter of Apollo, and in staging future attacks against the gods," Eugenia said.

"How many people do you think you'll be able to gather for this?" Zoey asked.

"Hundreds, if not thousands," Narcissa answered. "We will begin our journey today."

Andy exchanged hopeful smiles with the rest of the group. "In that case, it looks like it's time for us to head toward the Labyrinth."

CHAPTER FOURTEEN

GHOSTS

Karter stood staring at the trees, unable to sleep. Again.

Consequently, he'd offered to guard the prisoners although it wasn't his turn while the remainder of his party rested for the night. The party only had three people in custody now: Diana and two grandchildren-of-Hephaestus, the ones the Blacksmith of the Gods had appointed to run the forges in his city. The Cyclopes, although three of them were blinded from the battle outside Hephaestus City, still helped carry and guard the prisoners in hopes the gods on Olympus would have mercy and allow them to be healed when they got there. One of the centaurs had been crushed in the fight, but the other stayed with the party and did what he could to aid them as well.

Yesterday night, after the same battle which blinded the Cyclopes and killed one of the *astynomia*, Xander had contacted Zeus and notified the King of the Gods that the Chosen Two of the Prophecy, Prometheus, and the rest of their companions had escaped. Zeus had hardly even blinked at this news. According to his vision, so long as Diana was executed the war would end before it could ever truly begin. However, as an extra precaution, Zeus said he'd be sending the Olympian goddess Artemis and her Huntresses to retrieve the Helm of Darkness and bring Prometheus and the Chosen Two of the Prophecy into custody.

For some reason, Zeus wanted Zoey and Andy alive. Karter wanted to ask why; after all, didn't it make more sense to have them killed? He shook his head. It was no matter. Zeus had a reason for every decision he made, and this was surely no different.

Besides, Karter didn't like to think about Zoey, didn't like to think about the way she had looked at him when she'd realized which side he'd chosen. He didn't like to think about how Spencer and Syrena would feel toward him if they were still here either. What would they have said to him after all they'd done to orchestrate this insane scheme if they were still alive?

He remembered Syrena's screams when Zeus hit her with the green lightning bolt, the way she'd fallen to the ground, her chest a crater of ash, all to bring Zoey and Andy back from the dead. He remembered the way Spencer had shoved the last golden apple at him, insisting Karter take it instead for helping Zoey and Andy survive in Hades. Then the way the Son of Hades had let out a final pained sigh and fallen onto his back. In those moments, Karter had felt as if the world had ended. As if nothing were worth fighting for anymore.

If they were still alive, what would they tell him now? Would Syrena say, "I'm disappointed?" Would Spencer wish him an eternity in Tartarus? The thought of it made him feel as if someone were stabbing his heart, but he knew if anything, he was the one doing the stabbing. After all, he'd betrayed the gods just like they had. To save Spencer no less, to try in some backward way to make up to Syrena for what he'd allowed to happen to her. And now what was Karter doing? Helping the gods again? Why?

Because it is your destiny, he thought. *Written by the Fates long ago. There is nothing anyone can do to change it, and so you accept it. Welcome it.*

Karter brushed the scar on the right side of his face. Destiny or not, it was an odd thing, the fact that he was meant to help his father. Like Zoey had said, Zeus had mutilated his face. And Karter's mother . . .

Karter's eyes filled with hot tears. He didn't like to think about his mother. The last time he'd seen her— Gods, he'd only been six years old. He'd seen her recently in a vision Asteria had given him, but other than that he could barely remember. He didn't like to think about what Zeus's wife, Hera, had done to his mother, didn't like to think about the desperate look in his mother's eyes when she'd told Karter to fly away as fast as he could . . .

Karter shook his head. He was getting lost in his thoughts. Thoughts that didn't matter now. His mother, Syrena, Spencer—they were ghosts of his past, part of his frail human emotions. They were only feelings. Feelings which would fade with time, disappear after an eternity of living as a god. Every Olympian at one time or another had loved and lost, hadn't they? Apollo with Daphne, Artemis with Orion, Aphrodite with Adonis, and countless other instances—and after thousands of years, none of the immortals still missed those people. At least, not as far as Karter knew.

Once Diana was dead, Karter would be made immortal, and in a thousand years he wouldn't remember any of the things haunting him in this moment. Now that he understood he was truly meant to be made a god, he just had to keep reminding himself of the truth.

He looked up at the night sky, at the moon and stars, halfway expecting Asteria to come down and talk to him. This was what she'd intended for him, wasn't it? Becoming a god was his "destined greatness," right? Asteria didn't like Zeus, but maybe Karter living as a god on Olympus could convince them to let their tumultuous past die. Maybe that was why Asteria had taken such an interest in Karter. Perhaps, after all this was over, Asteria could visit Karter without having to do it in secret. Perhaps they could be friends for eternity.

As if in reply to Karter's thoughts, thousands of stars began materializing before him, spinning together in a dance of twinkling light, soon taking the form of Asteria herself.

Asteria frowned, standing before Karter. "What are

you doing, Son of Zeus?"

"Following the path I'm meant to take."

"No," the Titan goddess replied, her expression flaring with anger. "You follow the path you have chosen. A path that can only lead to your destruction."

"My destruction? How can I be destroyed if I'm made an immortal god?"

Asteria stepped toward Karter until her face was only inches from his. She cupped his cheeks with her hands and closed her silver eyes. "Remember, Son of Zeus. Remember who you are, and you will understand."

The night sky swept Karter into the clouds and swirled around him. Finally, his surroundings became nothing more than a blur, taking him back, back, back . . .

Six years ago . . .

Fall, Year 494 AS

Since Karter's punishment, he had not left his room. For two days he lay in bed, the canopy pulled so he remained swathed in darkness, left with nothing but the memory of the gold bolt as it seared his face.

The night of his penalty, his father had made him suffer through the aftermath of the lightning strike until the next morning. Once the sun had risen, the King of the Gods had allowed Apollo to heal him at least somewhat. His father had instructed Apollo to only heal him enough so the wound would not become infected, but also so Karter would be left with a permanent mark.

"I want the wound to scar," Zeus had said to Apollo. *"I want him to be reminded every day when he looks in the mirror that he is to respect the gods and their rulings or suffer the consequences."*

Even if I hadn't been left with my face destroyed, how could I forget? Karter thought. Other than when his mother died, this had to be the worst experience of his life.

A knock sounded at the door. He didn't bother to answer. There had been several knocks at his door since he'd locked himself in here, but he wanted to be left alone.

"Karter?" the familiar voice of a girl called from the hall. "Karter, can we come in? It's Syrena and Spencer."

"Go away," Karter said.

"It's been two days," Syrena continued. "You have to eat and drink. We brought you your favorites."

"I'm not hungry."

There was a pause. Finally, Spencer spoke. "Will you please just let us come in? We want to apologize for what happened. We haven't seen you in two days. We miss you."

Karter sighed. He'd spent the last three years with Spencer and Syrena at his side. He missed them too. "Fine," he said. "Come in."

The door creaked open, and soon Spencer and Syrena pulled aside the canopy and took a seat at the edge of Karter's bed. Syrena held out a glass of ice water with lemon to Karter, while Spencer offered him a plate full of bread, cheese, and grapes. Karter accepted, setting the plate in his lap and lifting the glass to his lips. In only a few gulps the water was gone, cooling his parched throat.

"Your eyes aren't brown anymore," Syrena said. "They're gold. Like the lightning."

Karter ruffled his shaggy black hair, trying to cover his face with it. Syrena grabbed his hand to stop him. "They don't look bad," she said. "They're . . . pretty."

"They draw more attention to the scar," Karter replied, pulling away from her. "Which means they look bad. If they didn't, Violet wouldn't have broken up with me. Those were her exact words, actually. That there was no point in surrounding herself with ugly, unlovable things like scars. And that I'm a shame to the demigods of Olympus. I'm not sure which statement hurts worse."

"Violet is just a vain priss," Spencer cut in. "I never liked her. But you did, so I put up with her. If she's going to stop seeing you just because you have a scar now—well, I'd say she never loved you in the first place then." Spencer's words stung, but Karter knew he needed to hear them. Spencer had a way of telling people the truth without hesitation, even if it meant the truth was painful.

"Spencer is right," Syrena said. "Besides, the scar doesn't look bad. You're still handsome. More importantly, you're far from a shame to the demigods of Olympus. If anyone should be ashamed, it should be me and Spencer. We're the ones who got you into this whole mess. Violet doesn't know what she's missing out on. You're one of the greatest people I know, and anyone would be lucky to be with you."

Karter smiled sadly. "You didn't get me into this mess. I got myself into it."

"But we *did*," Spencer said. "If we hadn't tried to escape—"

"I'd do it again," Karter blurted. "I'd do it again if I had a choice."

"What do you mean?" Spencer asked.

"I mean," Karter began, "that if I had a choice, if I could decide who was going to take a beating, me or you guys, I'd take it every time."

Nine years ago . . .

Spring, Year 491 AS

Karter and Spencer sparred alone in the open courtyard, the tall walls of the Olympian palace on all sides of them shimmering brilliant white under the sun.

As Spencer charged for Karter with a spear, Karter dug his toes into the grass and focused on conjuring lightning as a counter-attack. Karter had grown tired of only using two of his powers—strength and flight—during his and Spencer's sparring sessions and had been trying to conjure lightning for some time now, but with no luck.

His much older and immortal-god brother, Heracles, had visited a few months ago, and had assured him if he was meant to create and control lightning, the power would be coming soon. After all, he was thirteen now, which was the prime age for a demigod's powers to fully emerge.

Hopefully today was the day. He was sick of the disappointed look his father gave him every time he couldn't do it. There hadn't been many children-of-Zeus who could conjure lightning in the course of history, and currently there weren't any alive on Olympus, but his father seemed to have high hopes for him regarding the power.

A flood of pulsing hot energy burst in his chest and snaked through his right arm. He looked down to find sparks of red power popping and hissing in his hand. His heart leapt with joy as the sparks began forming a solid red bolt. Red was the weakest kind of lightning, but it was lightning nonetheless.

He smirked and looked to Spencer, raising the bolt above his head. Finally, he'd done something his father could be proud of him for.

Spencer slowed and dropped his spear. "Karter . . . You . . ."

"Good morning, boys!" the familiar booming voice of a man interrupted from the other end of the courtyard. "There's someone I'd like you to meet."

Karter looked over to see his father standing in one of the palace's arched doorways with a girl he'd never seen before. She must be about ten years old, her dark hair styled in long ringlets, her face soft as sea-foam.

Karter practically jumped up and down in excitement

at the sight of his father, waving his red bolt. Right now, the girl didn't matter. He could meet her later. "Father! Father, look what I've made!"

Annoyance flashed across his father's expression. "Quit with your games, boy, and get over here." Karter paused, furrowing his brow and holding up his hand. The red bolt had disintegrated already. *No*, he thought. *Father must know what I can do.*

Karter looked over at Spencer, who stared at the new girl, his eyes wide with awe, and Karter cringed a little. If he didn't know any better, he'd think Eros, the God of Love, had shot Spencer with a love arrow.

"Come now," Karter's father said, his voice full of irritation. "Come meet our newest Warrior of the Gods. She's traveled a long way to be here: all the way from Poseidon's palace." Spencer started toward Karter's father and the girl. Karter slumped his shoulders and followed suit. It looked as though he'd have to show his father his newest power later.

Once Karter and Spencer made their way across the courtyard to Karter's father and the girl, Karter's father pushed her toward them. "This is Syrena, Daughter of Poseidon," he boomed. "And I have decided she will be the third and final member of your warrior team. Because of this, it is pivotal you welcome her to Olympus and have her train alongside you every day. Considering you're children of the three most powerful gods in our pantheon, I believe if you work well together you could be the best team of demigod warriors we've seen in the last century." He turned around and started back into the palace. "Now, I will leave you to get to know each other, as I have much to attend to."

"Father, wait," Karter cried, grabbing his father's robes.

The god turned around and sighed in exasperation, narrowing his eyes at Karter as though Karter were a nagging Harpy instead of his son. The look made Karter's confidence drop a bit, and he drew back, but he knew once his father saw what he could do, it would make everything better.

"What do you want?" his father asked.

"I made lightning for the first time today," he said. "It's only red, not gold yet, but still. Did you see me do it?"

His father's expression remained that of irritation. "Keep working on your skills, and perhaps someday you will make green lightning—*that* would be truly impressive. Now please, introduce yourselves to Syrena, then get to know her and train with her for the rest of the afternoon until dinner. I have high hopes for the three of you."

Karter watched, numb, as his father walked away.

Sixteen years ago . . .

Summer, Year 484 AS

Karter's mother sang a sweet tune in his ear, the words of the song describing stories of heroes from the old days.

She did that every night—a while after dinner, and right before she tucked him into bed, just like tonight. Her long black hair tickled his arms as she held him close to her chest. He giggled with glee.

It was a hot summer evening in Hera City, making the air inside Karter and his mother's small stone house humid and stuffy. Karter didn't mind, though. He preferred the heat over the chilly days that would come when Persephone, Queen of the Underworld, made her descent into Hades for the fall and winter months. When that happened, his mother would pack the windows with clay, and they'd have to bundle up with layers and layers of clothes to stay warm.

As Karter began to slip into unconsciousness, his mother hoisted him up and started toward his bedroom. She'd tuck him in with a thin blanket, sing a while longer, then stroke his hair, kiss his forehead, and go to bed herself, as was the usual.

There was a loud *bang* at the front of the house, then a cluster of clattering noises, like rocks tumbling down a cliff. Karter's mother gasped, and Karter snapped fully awake.

"What was that?" Karter asked.

Karter's mother set him down and unsheathed the dagger at her hip. "Go to your room, sweetheart. I'll be there in just a moment."

Karter ran to his room and shut the door while his mother went to investigate. He pressed his ear against the wood to hear what was going on, but soon discovered he didn't need to. What transpired next was probably loud enough to wake the whole neighborhood.

There were booming sounds and hissing noises. More loud *bang*s and clatters rang through the air. His mother cried out, "Help! Zeus, please!"

When he heard his mother's cries, Karter knew he couldn't stand by any longer, even if he was only six years old. His mother had told him about heroes from the old days, and especially about the incredible tasks Perseus and Heracles had completed, about the monsters they'd slain. Both had been sons of Zeus, just like Karter was. His mother had even told him the story of Apollo: the one where the god had killed a monstrous serpent to save his own mother, Leto. Did the Fates want him to save his?

Karter threw open the door and burst out of the room to see what was going on, to save his mother just as Apollo had saved Leto in the old days. As a Son of Zeus, he was stronger than the other kids his age and he could fly. Surely that would be enough to destroy whatever villain was attacking his mother, right?

Within seconds he reached the center of the house and stopped dead at what he saw. One of the walls had caved in. Among piles of rubble and furniture his mother lay, bruised and bloodied, her knife cast to the side. Above her was a creature Karter could only imagine existing in his most horrible nightmares. It was a scaly monster, like a dragon, with clusters of sharp claws extending from its feet.

It stood taller than a horse, with so many serpentine heads snaking from its neck Karter couldn't count them all, every pair of eyes glowing red. When the heads caught sight of Karter, they hissed at him. Chills raced up his spine.

"Karter, *fly!*" his mother yelled. "Fly away as fast as you can and find your father. Hera has sent Ladon. This is the work of Hera!"

The scaly monster's heads shrieked, a sound like hundreds of blades dragging across stone. With one quick swipe, it slashed open his mother's throat. She said no more.

"*Mother!*" Karter screamed as blood pooled from his mother's gashed neck onto the floor. "Mother, *get up!*" But she did not move.

This couldn't be happening. No, this had to be a nightmare. His mother had said time and time again Hera could not hurt her, could not hurt him, as Hera had hurt Zeus's mistresses and illegitimate children in the past, all because Karter's father had forbidden the goddess from ever trying. Yet somehow the most terrifying monster Karter had ever seen had come into Hera's city—although it was forbidden for monsters to invade the cities—and had made it all the way to Karter's house, then sliced open his mother's throat right after she'd said this was Hera's doing.

The monster shrieked again. It stomped toward him. Karter swung around and bolted for his room. There was a window there. He'd jump out of it and into the street. Where he'd go next, he had no idea.

"Fly," his mother had told him. *"Fly away as fast as you can and find your father."*

Karter focused on taking flight. Hot power burst in his chest, and he leapt into the air.

CHAPTER FIFTEEN

LABYRINTH

Now . . .

Karter shoved Asteria away. "What in all the gods' names are you trying to do?" The memories had flashed across his mind in an instant, the anguish they caused him stinging like an open wound.

"You want to forget who you are," the Titan goddess said. "You want to become something you are not. I'm trying to help you remember, or else you will destroy yourself."

Karter clenched his jaw. "I don't want to remember, can't you see? I want to forget about Spencer and Syrena, forget about my life on Olympus. I want to forget about my mother."

"No, you don't. Your past is important in shaping who you are and what you value—which I know, deep down, does not include gaining immortality like this. Not in the slightest."

"You're wrong." He balled his fists, fighting the urge to

blast Asteria with gold lightning. "Those things just caused me guilt and pain—endless amounts of it. My mother died because of me. Hera killed her because I was born."

"Hera didn't kill your mother because of you. She didn't even kill your mother for anything your mother did purposefully. Zeus disguised himself before your mother and did not tell her who he really was until it was too late, and when the chance arose, Hera killed her out of jealousy. She would have killed you too had you not been able to escape."

"Syrena was such a good friend to me," Karter continued, ignoring Asteria's reasoning. "And she died because I didn't stick up for her, because I didn't try to save her. And Spencer . . ." A lump formed in his throat. He swallowed it down. "He died because I didn't reach Hades fast enough."

"None of those things are your fault. The universe—"

"You don't understand," Karter said, throwing his hands in the air. "You talk so much about fate and the universe, but you can't see that the universe has already chosen my destiny. I'm meant to execute Diana and become a god, and I prefer it that way. That's what I'm meant to do. That's what I *want* to do."

Asteria stared hard at him for a long time, her eyes round with shock, then narrowed them and began backing away. "I understand, Son of Zeus. I understand now. I won't waste my efforts helping you anymore. Farewell."

Before Karter could reply, Asteria left as she always did, disintegrating into thousands of small glittering stars and floating away.

The grass behind Karter crunched with footsteps, and he swung around to see Violet as she sauntered toward him, her hips swaying.

He ran his hands through his hair and took a deep breath. "Violet. Hello. Why are you, uh, not sleeping?"

"I heard you talking to yourself," Violet said, stopping only inches before him. "It woke me up."

"Oh. I'm sorry."

She smiled and brushed some dirt from his shoulder. "Don't be. I'm glad we can finally have some time to ourselves."

"Uh, what do you mean?" Karter asked, raising a brow.

"I've missed you, love." She wrapped her arms around his neck. "I didn't realize how much I missed you until I didn't have you anymore."

More like until you realized I was going to be made an immortal god, Karter thought. He studied her, studied the pleasing lines of her face and the way her blonde hair fell in messy waves, then finally allowed himself to look into her eyes. *Gods, she's attractive.*

She leaned into him and pressed her lips against his. She tasted sour, like an unripe strawberry, but Karter didn't care. He kissed her back.

He thought he would have fallen in love with her after looking into her eyes, but somehow, he hadn't. How he'd evaded her spell, he had no idea. Perhaps he was immune to it because she'd broken his heart all those years ago, or maybe it was something else.

Either way, it didn't matter. He was sick of feeling rotten about himself, sick of feeling nothing but sorrow, so he kept kissing her until he forgot about everything except how warm her skin felt against his.

* ～ * ～ * ～

By the next evening, Zoey and the rest of the group had traveled far enough northeast that they'd reached a cliff overlooking Poseidon City, miles of forest behind them.

The city was huge, like the rest the group had seen, and sat atop its own cliff which overlooked a beach, ocean waves crashing against the sand. The city's buildings were similar in structure to Aphrodite City's and Hephaestus City's, but their coloring had a blue-green tinge, as if they'd been submerged in the sea for thousands of years and had just recently risen from the water. Zoey could almost imagine the barnacles encrusting the buildings' edges, and the seaweed and coral reefs populating the gardens between them.

Zoey had visited the ocean only once in her life, when her parents were still married. She'd been seven at the time, and her family had taken a vacation to southern California. Instead of booking a flight, they'd driven all the way from Nebraska to Cali in her dad's little Ford Taurus, singing along to classic rock stations the whole way. They rented a pet-friendly house on the beach for a week so even their dog, Daisy, could come with.

She couldn't remember the little details of what they did on that trip, but she could recall swimming in the ocean, visiting an aquarium, and eating lots of good food. However, what stood out the most about the memory was how happy her parents had been—how happy she'd been—at the time.

A part of her wished her mother hadn't turned out to be such an irresponsible and vindictive woman, and that her parents had never split, not only so there would be more memories like the one in southern California to look back on, but also so that she would have never made the mistakes she did and then for years dealt with constant taunting from her peers. How much easier would life have been if at fourteen, she had never needed to scrape up enough money to pay her mother's apartment rent?

But then she thought of how difficult it had been for Andy to let go of the past and assume his role as one of the Chosen Two of the Prophecy, and she decided maybe things were better this way for her. Because of the way things had played out, she could easily bury the past—her greatest mistakes and horrible homelife included—and look to the future.

The future, she thought, biting her lip, her heart skipping with anxiety. *What's going to happen next? Will we be able to steal the Trident, to save Diana, Troy, and Marina?*

It seemed impossible, but then again, so had Greek gods being real and her and Andy traveling into the Underworld to steal the Helm of Darkness, but those things had proved themselves to be true or had come true.

Beside her, Prometheus pointed to the opening of a cave at the bottom of the cliff Poseidon City resided on. "That's the entrance to the Labyrinth."

"Is there something covering it, or is it just open?" Andy asked. The sight of the white feathered wings stemming from his back still startled Zoey every time she looked at him. She'd been just as shocked as him about the possibility of Asteria planting powers inside them, but it made sense when she put the pieces together in her head. Whether it would help or harm them going forward, she had no idea.

"It's open," Prometheus answered.

Andy scrunched his nose and peered at the Labyrinth's entrance. "Why would the gods leave it like that? Aren't they worried about the Minotaur getting out, or someone getting in? Doesn't Poseidon want to protect his portal a little better than that?"

"No one would dare to travel into the Labyrinth," Prometheus said. "They'd get lost or eaten, and even if they managed to reach the portal, they'd die trying to get through it. Besides, the entrance is outside the city, which they aren't allowed to leave. As far as the Minotaur goes, because of the way the Labyrinth has been built, he can't escape either. Anyway, are you guys ready to head in?"

"I think we should wait until after the sun sets to fly down," Zoey replied. "If we do it at night, there's less of a chance of anyone seeing us, since it'll be dark and the citizens will be inside."

"The *astynomia* might still catch us, though," Darko said.

"There's less *astynomia* than citizens, right?" Zoey asked. The satyr nodded. "Okay, then in that case there might still be a chance we're caught, but it's way slimmer if most of the people who live here aren't out, ya know? Plus, it'll be nighttime. So, harder to see."

"Zoey's right," Kali said. "Let's rest a little while, have some dinner, and then when everything's dark head down there."

"You gonna try to fly yourself down, Bird-Boy?" Prometheus asked Andy, grinning. "Or are you gonna keep having the pegasus do it for you?"

Andy cringed. "If you promise to never call me 'Bird-Boy' again, I'll try to fly tonight."

Prometheus clapped Andy on the shoulder. "It's a deal!"

For the next half hour, while Andy attempted flight and the pegasi grazed, the rest of the group prepared for dinner and for the journey into the Labyrinth. Darko hunted several squirrels, which Kali promptly roasted over a fire. Meanwhile, Zoey and Prometheus collected food for their trip. When dinner was ready, Kali called everyone over to eat.

Andy was the last to join them, hanging his head as he made his way over. He hadn't been able to fly. He'd leapt into the air and flapped his wings, but he couldn't coordinate himself enough to stay in the air.

As the sun fell completely, they gorged themselves, and soon their only light was that of the moon and stars.

Prometheus sighed happily, patting his stomach. "Immortals don't have to eat to live, but I sure did get hungry being trapped up in the sky all those years. This stuff isn't as tasty as godly grub, but food in general always tastes better when you haven't had any for almost a century."

"We wouldn't know," Andy said. "Since, uh, we'd starve to death if we couldn't eat for that long."

Zoey climbed to her feet. "Are we ready?"

"I am," Darko replied, hopping to his hooves, while Andy, Kali, and Prometheus stood as well.

"Okay then," Zoey said. "Let's head out."

The group started for the pegasi, and someone grabbed Zoey's arm from behind. She raised an eyebrow, confused, then swung around to see it was Andy. He looked so nervous even his wings seemed to curl in on themselves.

"Zoey—before we go, can I talk to you about something?" he asked. "Like, just you and me?"

Zoey's stomach churned. She already knew what this was about. "Yeah, of course." Andy told everyone else he and Zoey were going to take a few minutes to discuss something privately, then walked farther into the trees. Zoey followed.

Once they'd gotten out of earshot of the others, Andy straightened his shoulders and turned to Zoey.

The words began spilling from his mouth. "Look, Zoey,

this has been on my mind a while. I've thought about telling you a couple of times, but I wimped out before I could, and if something happens to me or you or both of us in Poseidon's palace, I'm going to regret never saying it. So, I'm just gonna come out and say it."

Zoey looked into his eyes, her pulse quickening.

He sucked in a sharp breath. "I care about you, Zoey. I care about you a lot."

"I care about you too," Zoey said.

"No," Andy said. "I mean—yes. I know you care about me. But the way I care about you . . . I mean, when I look at you— I've just always thought you're amazing, okay? I . . ."

"You like me," Zoey answered for him. "As in more than just a friend."

He ran a shaking hand through his hair. "Well, yeah. But it's more than that. I mean— I've never had a girlfriend or even kissed anybody, but the way I feel about you is more than just a crush. It's deeper than that."

Zoey cocked her head. "If you've never had a girlfriend or anything, then how do you know your feelings for me run deeper than a crush? You have nothing to compare them to."

Zoey thought about the last time Andy had tried to explain how he felt toward her, how he'd thought the "rumors" going around the school about her weren't true, and how he'd reacted when she'd asked him, *What if they are true?*

"You barely even know who I am," Zoey said.

Hurt flashed across his face. "What do you mean? Of course I do. You're brave, smart, selfless, beautiful, and . . . well, you're perfect."

She took a step back. "No way. I'm far from perfect. I'm only human."

"Well, yeah, I know that. Both of us are. But what I mean is you're perfect to me."

Zoey turned away from him and crossed her arms to hug her sides. "You wouldn't think so if you knew the truth about me."

"What do you mean? Yes, I would."

Enough is enough, Zoey thought. She couldn't keep hiding her past; she couldn't run from it, no matter how much it hurt. She couldn't lie to Andy as she had last time. The time had come to face the choices she regretted. *Then I can put them behind me.*

She remembered that night so vividly: It'd been summer, and she'd been fourteen. Her mother had told her they were being kicked out of their apartment again. Zoey yelled at her mother for it, screamed that she wanted her dad. Her mother beat her for yelling—the only way her mother seemed to know how to handle problems—then left her alone with her thoughts.

She remembered the idea she'd come up with that night. It sounded horrible. It made her skin crawl. But nothing could be worse than living on the streets again.

She'd gone out every night that week, hidden between

alleyways and shadows, in the rain and in the heat, and she'd offered herself to whatever men she could find. Two took her on the same night, at the same time. They were friends. They did so happily and without a second thought, although she was far too young. She didn't care who they were or why they were willing to take her. All she cared about was that they gave her the money she needed, and then she gave them what they wanted.

As she grew older, she realized she could have died doing what she did, creeping through town at night for one specific purpose. The men could have killed her easily, could have dumped her body in the middle of nowhere. For some reason, they hadn't—and now Zoey wondered, *Why not?* Thoughts like this terrified her. Before the world had ended, they'd kept her up at night.

For years she'd regretted the decision, wished every day she could take it back, especially when Jet told everyone about it. Even though it had kept her and her mother off the streets, it made her feel as though she were less, as if she were tainted. She'd tried to push it down as best she could, but here it was again, staring her straight in the face.

"The rumors are true," Zoey cried, her eyes filling with tears. "I slept with guys for money. I never told anyone except Jet, and after I broke up with him, he told everybody."

"W-what?" Andy asked. The shock in his voice cut Zoey like a knife.

She continued, her voice shaking, her chest tight. "I didn't do it because I wanted to, okay? My mom and I were gonna get kicked out of our apartment again, which we'd only moved into a few months before. We'd lived on the streets before, and I didn't wanna do that again."

"Then why didn't you go get a job or something?"

"We only had a week before they would've kicked us out."

"But there are other ways—I mean, you could have done something else. You could have asked someone for help."

"I didn't have anyone but my mom—my dad and her were divorced. He wouldn't answer my calls. I used to think that—that it was because he abandoned me, but when we were in Deltama Village, Spencer showed me how he died, and I know now he never called me or fought for me because he died in a car crash before he had the chance." The tears began streaming down her cheeks. "I had no other family to contact, and I was so scared. I—I didn't know what else to do."

For a long time, he didn't say anything, and Zoey cried. *I did it*, she thought. *I admitted it. I faced it. I told him. Now he probably hates me, but so be it. This is part of who I am and I can't change it. If he values our friendship the way I do, he will accept me for who I am, all of me.*

The trees beside them rustled, the sounds of chains clanking sounding in the air. "What in all of Tartarus is taking you two so long?" Prometheus asked, stomping toward them.

"We were just finishing up, actually," Andy said.

Zoey wiped her eyes and shot Andy a glare. "That's right."

The Titan raised his eyebrows. "Finishing up, hm? Good to hear, because we really need to hurry and go."

Prometheus started back toward the rest of the group, and Zoey stalked after the Titan. Andy grabbed her arm. She paused, turning to him, hoping he'd say "I understand" or "your past doesn't matter to me."

"Zoey," he said. "I'm sorry . . . I don't . . ."

That was enough for her. She shook him away. "Don't touch me." He didn't try to again. Instead, he followed her and Prometheus and said nothing.

Zoey choked back tears, refusing to cry anymore about this. Why did she care so much about what Andy thought of her past? He was the one who'd confessed his feelings for *her*—not the other way around—and she'd already explained to him why she did the things she had. She'd faced her demons. She'd faced what used to keep her up at night, and if he couldn't accept her for it, then he could consider their friendship over. She'd spent too much of her time in the past dealing with this bullshit from Jet and her classmates, and she wasn't about to let it trickle into the new life she'd been given.

A pang of grief struck her as she remembered Spencer. *If I had told him about my past, he wouldn't have judged me like this*, she thought. *He would have understood.* She'd even almost told Diana, back in Deltama Village, and at this point she knew Diana wouldn't care about Zoey's past either. But, like everyone else from the Before Time, Andy did.

"You're perfect to me," he'd said. At least now he knew the truth, right? At least now he could stop crushing on her, stop idealizing her.

By the time they got back, Darko had already mounted Ajax, Kali Luna. Kali helped Zoey onto Luna's back while Andy hopped onto Ajax, and Prometheus climbed onto Aladdin. They flew down to the beach—careful to stay out of sight—to the entrance of the Labyrinth, the only sound that of waves crashing against the shore.

Up close, the Labyrinth's entrance looked a lot larger than it had when they'd been farther away, its jagged edges climbing at least twenty feet above their heads, the inside pitch-black.

"Can we bring the pegasi in with us?" Andy asked, jumping off Ajax. "If we can't—well, I don't know what we're going to do with them." The rest of the group followed suit, Zoey's feet sinking into watery sand.

"They have to stay out here," Prometheus replied. "There aren't any pegasi in Poseidon's palace, which will draw even more unnecessary attention to us if we're seen, and they can't wait around in the Labyrinth until we get back—it's too dangerous. I'm afraid it's time to say goodbye."

Kali's face fell. She turned to face the pegasi. "I wish you were wrong, but I know you're not. Pegasi are creatures of the air—they're not meant to be trapped in a Labyrinth or at the bottom of the sea." One at a time Kali stroked the pegasi's manes and gave them hugs, talking to them all the while, her voice strained as though she was holding back tears. "Guys—you can't come with us in there. You need to—to fly away. Avoid monsters, and don't get captured. Maybe, if you can find the nymphs who saved us, I'll see you again. If not . . ." She sniffled, and tears trickled down her cheeks. "If not, then thank you. Thank you for everything you've done for me." The pegasi's eyes were glassy, their heads hung low.

Zoey came forward, then wrapped her arms around Aladdin's neck and gave him a squeeze. He nickered and nuzzled her. Andy and Darko hugged Ajax and bid him farewell. Afterward, the three pegasi took to the sky. As they disappeared into the night, Kali wiped tears from her eyes.

Zoey turned toward Kali, her chest aching. Ajax and Aladdin belonged to Kali, and she'd ridden Luna everywhere they'd gone. Kali's heart was probably broken over having to tell them goodbye without knowing if she'd ever be reunited with them.

"We'll see them again," Zoey said, enveloping Kali in an embrace. "I'm sure of it." The chief's daughter buried her face in Zoey's shoulder, hugging her back.

For a long while the group stood outside the Labyrinth, until finally Kali pulled away from Zoey. "We need to go," she said, and the group turned toward the entrance.

"How are we supposed to see in there?" Darko asked.

"It's completely dark."

"Go in and you'll find out," Prometheus replied. The group exchanged curious looks, then tentatively stepped into the Labyrinth, Prometheus close behind.

For a few minutes they walked in complete darkness, the wet sand squelching beneath them. A cool, damp breeze wafted in from the waves, the smell of saltwater permeating the air.

Zoey took another step and blinding light flashed. She gasped, blinking and glancing around, the Labyrinth suddenly illuminated with hues of blue-green.

As her eyes adjusted to the brightness, she realized what was emitting the colored light. Rectangular crystals with pointed ends, thousands of them, were encrusted on the walls and ceiling of the Labyrinth. They jutted every which way like hundreds of rows of crooked teeth glowing the color of the ocean. Where the crystal-covered walls met sandy floor, tiny seashells and strips of seaweed littered the ground.

Ahead of them, the Labyrinth curved, twisted, and turned in different directions, like forks in a road. When Zoey looked back, she saw only darkness.

"Where'd the entrance go?" she asked, a rush of panic coming over her. "Did it close in on us? Are we trapped?"

"No," Prometheus replied. "Darko, the thread." The satyr nodded and pulled the ball of thread he'd stolen from Aphrodite City out of his bag. Prometheus took it and tied the end around one of the bigger crystals near the group, making sure to quadruple-knot it. "If we went back from where we came this instant, we'd get out of here just as easily as we walked in. It's only after we go down one of those paths"—he nodded at the forks ahead—"that we'll lose our way, since all these chambers look the same."

The Titan's explanation gave Zoey some relief, although she still felt a bit jittery, and the group pressed forward.

"How can Poseidon use this place to travel back and forth?" Andy asked. "How does he find his way around?"

Darko shrugged. "He's the one who had it rebuilt. He probably memorized the paths before using it in the first place."

"Even if he did get lost, he could just materialize at the entrance," Prometheus added, unraveling the ball of string along the sand as they walked. "The point of the portal was to cut down on the power it took to transport thousands of miles from the palace, but if he had to use some energy to get himself from the center of the Labyrinth to the entrance, that wouldn't be near as draining."

They walked for a long time, creeping down paths that twisted and turned, meeting dead ends and traveling through other chambers that seemed to go straight for miles. After so long, Zoey, Andy, Darko, and Kali could hardly keep their eyes open, and Prometheus offered to watch for the Minotaur while the group stopped to rest. The sand was damp, cold, and uncomfortable, but Zoey was too exhausted to care. She'd hardly slept since Andy woke from his unconscious state. She curled into a ball next to Kali, making sure to steer clear of Andy, and they slept.

When they finally woke, Zoey couldn't be sure how long they'd been in the Labyrinth, but her stomach growled, her muscles weak and wobbly. They ate some roots and berries Prometheus had collected, replenishing their bodies, then continued their journey.

Several hours of walking passed, and Zoey noticed with each passing step the sand beneath their feet grew drier. The seashells and seaweed littering the ground were scarcer now, the smell of saltwater a distant memory.

As they rounded a corner, they stopped dead, spotting something that sent chills charging through Zoey's body, goose bumps rising on her skin. A yellowed human skeleton, picked completely clean, lay sprawled on the ground here.

"We must be getting close to the center," Prometheus said. "At least, a lot closer than we were before."

"What do you think happened to this guy?" Andy asked. "Do you think he died and decomposed here, or—"

"I think the Minotaur got him," the Titan replied.

The group pressed on, and as they traveled farther, more bones began popping up. What looked like the skeletons of fish, sharks, dolphins, humans, and other creatures Zoey couldn't identify lay fully intact along the sand, as if in warning to anyone who dared come farther.

"What are those things?" Kali asked, pointing at the animal bones.

"They're sea creatures," Andy said. "What I wanna know is how they got in here."

"Poseidon has to feed the Minotaur, I'm sure," Prometheus said. "Animals and people most likely don't wander in here often. He probably brought them for the monster to eat."

Finally, they stepped into a large chamber, the ceiling and walls curved into the shape of a dome. In the center of the chamber, an orb large enough for a pegasus to step through spun around and around, shimmering with watery blue-green shades.

Prometheus tied the end of the string to one of the bigger crystals in the chamber, then pointed at the orb. "That's the portal."

Zoey glanced around nervously. "Where's the Minotaur?"

"He might be prowling around somewhere else and we could miss him altogether," the Titan said. "Let's count ourselves lucky and get through the portal before he comes back."

The rest of the group agreed and stepped toward the spinning orb.

"How do you plan to get us through?" Zoey asked.

"I'm a trickster god," Prometheus began. "If I can disguise each of us as Poseidon well enough, the portal will never know the difference. I'll start with you and Andy, and once you're through the portal I'll transform Darko and Kali, then me, and we'll follow you in. Since these chains have weakened my powers quite a bit, the disguises won't last long without me touching you, so you can't waste any time hesitating to go through the portal. Is everyone ready?"

"As ready as we'll ever be for this, I think," Zoey said, and Andy nodded. The pack holding the Helm was slung over his back. He grasped the handle of the sword at his side with one hand and offered the other to Zoey. She refused it and avoided looking at him.

Prometheus stepped forward and rested his burly hands on Zoey's and Andy's shoulders, then closed his eyes. Zoey took a few deep breaths, preparing herself for the task at hand, waiting for the Titan to transform them.

A guttural roar sounded from behind, so loud it shook the cavern. Zoey's stomach clenched, and she swung around.

A hairy, olive-skinned man dressed in rags who was taller, wider, and more muscular than even Prometheus stood at the cavern's entrance. He had the head of a black-furred bull, with ivory horns over two feet long branching from his skull. His eyes glowed a menacing green, and his teeth were as sharp and long as a saber-tooth tiger's, strings of snot hanging from his wide snout.

Zoey's breath caught in her throat as the Minotaur roared, charging straight for the group.

CHAPTER SIXTEEN

PALACE

Darko seized one of the only two arrows from his quiver and loosed it with his bow. The arrow pierced the creature in the shoulder, and he fell back, bellowing. The group rushed forward, Zoey drawing her axe, her heart racing. Andy unsheathed his sword, Kali brandished her dagger, and Prometheus readied his chains.

The monster advanced for Darko. The satyr loosed his second and last arrow. It pierced the Minotaur in his thigh. The creature roared, spit flying from his lips, but the attack wasn't enough to stop him. He came headfirst at Darko as if to skewer the satyr with his horns. Darko galloped frantically to the side, avoiding the monster by inches. The Minotaur slammed into a wall. Upon impact, the cavern shook. He ripped his head back to face the group and crystals went flying.

Andy ran in front of everyone and waved his sword. "Hey, you ugly freak, come and get me!" The Minotaur huffed and charged. At the last minute, Andy swung his sword, but the creature seemed to have anticipated this. He darted backward before the weapon could slice him, then kicked Andy's blade to the side.

The Minotaur advanced on Andy, ready to impale the boy, but before he could, Prometheus lassoed his chains around the monster's neck, then tugged the creature backward. The Minotaur roared, grappling with the links, and to Zoey's surprise, their metal snapped, the monster free. The Minotaur snarled, bounding for Andy.

"*Andy!*" Zoey screamed, rushing toward them. As mad as she was, if any harm came to him . . .

Andy somersaulted out of the way and seized his blade. The Minotaur rammed into another wall, cramming his horns between crystals and shaking the cavern so much Zoey stumbled to the side.

Kali dashed ahead of Zoey, and in the few moments the Minotaur struggled to free himself from the wall, she jumped onto his back and plunged her dagger into his neck. She twisted the blade and he roared, throwing his head back. Crystals went flying across the cavern, and so did Kali, who smashed into the sandy floor. Darko rushed to her aid.

Zoey bolted toward the creature, axe held high. She focused every bit of strength she had, and when she reached the Minotaur, she swung the weapon at his chest. The blade cut deep. The monster roared. She tried to wrench the axe from his body, but he backhanded her cheek. Pain racked her body as she hit the ground, her head spinning.

Before she could stand, something climbed onto her and pressed her down, the weight of it so heavy she couldn't breathe. *It's the Minotaur,* she thought, panic flooding her senses. *He's going to crush me.*

"Get off her!" Andy shouted.

The sound of a blade gashing through flesh and bone filled Zoey's ears, and the Minotaur bellowed and released her. She caught her breath and rolled over to see Andy as he ripped his sword from the monster's back. Blood seeped from the creature's wounds, but still he stood. For a moment he wavered as though he might collapse, but instead he turned around and slapped Andy's weapon aside. The Minotaur grabbed Andy by the throat and lifted him up off the ground.

Prometheus came running, slamming his body into the Minotaur's side. The collision knocked Andy from the creature's grasp, and Andy tumbled to the ground. Prometheus and the monster hurtled into the sand. Zoey scrambled backward, trying to stay out of their way as they wrestled. Within seconds Prometheus gained the upper hand. He straddled the Minotaur and wrapped what remained of his chains around the creature's neck.

The Minotaur roared, throwing his head back and then thrusting it upward, piercing his horns through Prometheus's chest. Prometheus cried out, his muscles bulging, veins popping out of his arms, but even with the creature's horns stuck straight through him, he didn't give up. With his massive hands, he tightened the chains around the Minotaur's neck and tugged hard. With his legs, he kept the monster bound against the floor.

Soon the Minotaur began gasping for air. He writhed under Prometheus, but Prometheus wouldn't let go. Moments passed, and finally the monster fell limp.

Prometheus pulled himself up and off the horns and collapsed next to the creature. His breaths were shallow, his skin paling. Fluid like molten gold oozed from his injuries and from the corners of his mouth. Zoey rushed to his side, the rest of the group close behind her.

"I'm about . . . to die," Prometheus said, coughing. "Obviously, I'll regenerate—so don't worry about it. But I can't go into Poseidon's palace with you. There isn't enough time."

"Will you find us later on?" Zoey asked.

Prometheus gave her a slow nod. "I'll—try."

"Do you still have enough strength to transform us?" Andy asked. "So we can go through the portal?"

Prometheus reached out. "Take my hands. Zoey and Andy first—then Darko and Kali. I can—get you in. Use the—the submarine to get out."

Zoey nodded and placed her hand in the Titan's. Andy did the same. Prometheus closed his eyes, and soon Zoey felt as if she were heating up from the inside. She felt her skin stretch, heard her bones crack, and when she glanced at Andy next, his wings had disappeared, and he didn't look like himself anymore.

Instead, he was a seven-foot-tall bodybuilder of a man

clothed in white robes, with a silver hair and beard, his skin the same blue-green color as the crystals in the Labyrinth. From the shocked expression he gave her, her appearance must have changed too.

Prometheus let them go. "The disguise is complete. Now go—before it fades off. I'll send the—the other two after you."

"Thank you for everything, Prometheus," Andy said.

"Don't let—my g-granddaughter—down," Prometheus croaked. "Don't let—me down."

A lump formed in Zoey's throat. "We'll do our best."

Andy offered Zoey his hand, and this time she took it. Angry with him or not, she had no idea what awaited them next, and without a guide like they'd had in Hades, they'd be even more vulnerable to the threats coming their way. Right now he needed her, and she needed him.

Together, they stepped toward the orb, and Zoey braced herself. Would the disguise work, or would they die the moment they touched the portal? There was only one way to find out.

She jumped into the portal, pulling Andy with her.

Immediately she felt as if they'd been transported to the bottom of the ocean. They were engulfed by freezing blue-black water, the salty liquid flooding her mouth and nostrils and stinging her eyes. They began whirling around and around and around. She screamed but there was no noise, only bubbles flittering from her lips, her lungs losing oxygen with every passing second. She held tight to Andy's hand, and he squeezed hers, as if trying to reassure her he was still there.

Suddenly she slammed face-first into something hard. She rolled over and groaned, stars dancing in her vision, her head spinning. Oddly enough, the air was dry, and she was dry—other than her hand, which still clung to Andy's and was slippery with sweat. When her vision finally cleared, she let go of Andy, sat up, and looked over at him. He sat up as well. His disguise had already faded away, and she assumed hers had too. *Good thing we left when we did*, she thought. *Or else the portal would have probably killed us.*

She glanced around to find they were in a large empty dome-shaped room, its walls and floor made of pure gold. Behind them, a watery blue orb spun and glowed, acting as the room's only light source. *The other side of the portal*, Zoey thought. *That must be where we came through.*

The orb stopped spinning and made a noise like a sigh. Darko and Kali, complete with Prometheus's disguises, shot from the portal and crashed into the floor. They groaned, glancing up at Zoey and Andy, their appearances already morphing back to normal.

"Are we there yet?" Darko asked, every word spoken echoing off the walls.

Andy climbed to his feet. "Seems like it. Now we just have to steal the Trident and get outta here."

Kali rubbed the back of her head. "Any ideas for where it could be?"

"It's most definitely with Poseidon," Zoey replied. "I

don't think he'd just leave it lying somewhere random."

"Probably not," Darko said.

The group gathered their composure and made their way to the room's only door. Kali opened it, and the group walked into a hallway devoid of anyone else. It sprawled longer than a football field on either side of them and was dimly lit with clusters of glowing crystals similar to the ones in the Labyrinth hanging from the ceiling, its floor made of golden tiles, cold and smooth to the touch. The walls were lined with marble pillars, statues of gods, and dozens more doors—one bigger than all the rest residing on the far-right side of the hall.

"I'm gonna take a wild guess and say that could be a good place to start searching," Andy whispered, pointing at the largest door. "Maybe it's Poseidon's room?"

Zoey began tiptoeing toward it. "Let's find out." The group crept down the hall as quietly as they could. Darko's hooves clapping against the tiles made the most noise, but Zoey didn't think it was enough to alert anyone of their arrival. Once they reached the door, they opened it and slipped inside.

This room was the size of a gym, the tall seafoam-colored walls decorated with tree-sized coral structures and glowing clusters of crystals. From the ceiling hung a chandelier adorned with dangling pearls and seashells. Like the hall outside, the floor's tiles were golden, which matched the canopied bed at the far end of the room.

From behind the bed's canopy, someone was snoring

so loudly and obnoxiously it reminded Zoey of an elephant trumpeting. Something glittered in the corner of her vision, next to the bed, and Zoey peered closer.

Beside the bed and held by a golden stand there stood a bronze three-pronged trident, shiny jewels and pearls encrusted on the handle. Much like the Helm, it emanated ancient power as though it were a god itself. Zoey grinned. It had to be Poseidon's Trident!

Zoey gestured at her companions to catch their attention, then pointed at the Trident. When they spotted it, their eyes grew wide.

"Kali and Darko," Zoey whispered. "You watch the door while Andy and I grab the Trident." They nodded to her plan.

Zoey held her breath as she and Andy tiptoed toward the Trident. If they were in Poseidon's bedroom—and if the Sea God was the person snoring behind the canopy— they needed to be as quiet as possible.

Once they'd crept to the Trident's side, Andy wrapped his hands around the object of power, and Zoey prepared to help him in case he couldn't pick it up by himself. However, to Zoey's surprise, he pulled it from its stand easily despite the fact it was as tall as him.

When they turned around to leave, Zoey caught a glimpse through a slit in the canopy of a silver-haired man with blue skin. He looked identical to the disguises Prometheus had concocted for the group. He was snoring, golden blankets pulled up to his chin.

That's definitely Poseidon, Zoey thought. Beside Poseidon slept a pretty woman with sea-green skin and pin-straight black locks fanned out around her head.

Zoey and Andy snuck back to Darko and Kali. Together, the group slipped out of the room and into the hallway, then gently closed the door behind them.

Darko gestured toward the door at the opposite end of the hall. "Most of these rooms are probably just more bedchambers," he whispered. "The one at the end of the hall—that's our best bet for escape."

They hurried down the hall, toward the door Darko suggested. Suddenly, its knob turned. Zoey and Andy bolted behind a pillar, while Darko and Kali dashed behind a statue.

"Andy, the Helm," Zoey whispered in panic. "Put it on so they can't see you." He nodded and shoved the Trident into Zoey's hand. Thankfully, the object was lighter than she expected, and she didn't drop it. She thought it would weigh a ton, but it weighed no more than the axe at her belt.

Andy hurriedly pulled the Helm from his pack and tugged it over his head. Immediately he disappeared. He grabbed the Trident from Zoey. It vanished with him, and relief flooded her.

The door creaked open. The sound of shoes clacking against tiles echoed through the air. The sounds grew closer, then abruptly stopped.

Zoey's heart pounded. She slowly turned her head.

A beautiful woman standing over six feet tall stared sideways at Zoey with a puzzled look on her face. She wore a cream dress that reached the floor, her skin a sea-green, her irises the color of amethysts. A crown made of pearls and seashells sat atop her head, matching jewelry circling her throat and wrists. Her curly white hair was pinned in an extravagant updo.

Zoey gulped and gave the woman a little wave. "Uh, hi."

The woman crossed her arms, narrowing her eyes into slits. "*Who* are you, and *what* do you think *you're doing* scampering about *my* palace?" She talked dramatically, putting emphasis on tons of her words.

"Your palace?" Zoey squeaked, shrinking back.

"Yes, *my* palace. Haven't you *any idea* who I *am*? Amphitrite, *Goddess* of the Sea and *Wife* of Poseidon?"

An idea crossed Zoey's mind. She focused on what she could say to get Amphitrite to leave them alone. Her throat began to tingle. She put her hand to her heart, feigning shock. "Wait, *you're* Amphitrite? I apologize, I'm just a lowly maid. Pretty new, only worked here a century or so."

Amphitrite's shoulders relaxed. "*Oh*, I see *now*. For a moment you *almost looked* like a *mortal*. But *no*, you *couldn't* be. Your divine essence is *unmistakable*."

"Oh, uh— Yeah, of course," Zoey said, confused and unsure of what the goddess meant. "Anyway, I just finished cleaning Poseidon's bedchamber—and I could've sworn the lady sleeping next to him right now was his wife."

Amphitrite's jaw dropped. She shot the door to Poseidon's room a glare, clenching her fists until her knuckles turned white.

"I've thought she was his wife the whole time I've worked here, actually," Zoey continued, throat still tingling. "Since every time I go in there, I see her. They seem to spend a lot of time together."

Amphitrite didn't say another word to Zoey. Instead, she stomped down the hall toward Poseidon's room, snarling under her breath about "that *floozy* of a Nereid."

Amphitrite threw open the door and stalked in, immediately screaming in her exaggerated way at Poseidon and the woman, but the group didn't waste any time to wait and see what happened next. They sprinted down the hall, then burst through the door and into the next section of the palace. Andy kept the Helm on so he stayed invisible, but Zoey could hear his feet pounding against the floor beside her as they ran.

The chamber they hurried through now had to be a dining hall, because it was even bigger and more open than Poseidon and Amphitrite's bedchamber, with rows of tables and chairs perfect for a feast. Pillars, crystals, and coral structures lined the walls, a chandelier much like the one in Poseidon's room hanging from the ceiling.

They rushed out the other end of the dining room, then careened down more halls that twisted every which way, looking for any sign of water and an exit so they could activate the Pocket-Sized Submarine and escape. As the group flew past several more chambers, Zoey thought she caught a glimpse of some other women lounging about, some working, but the group moved too fast for anyone to notice them.

Finally, the group reached what had to be the throne room, its wide walls lined with crystals, coral, and marble statues. The room's high, arched ceiling stretched to fifty feet tall. A long rug woven from seaweed led down the center of the room to a dais, where two pure-gold thrones adorned with jewels and pearls in swirling patterns sat. At the other side of the room, a massive set of golden doors beckoned the group.

"Is that the entrance?" Kali asked as she pointed at the doors, panting.

Zoey held her side, which ached from all the running. "Has to be," she replied, and the group hastened toward them. Together, they shoved open one of the doors and stumbled outside, then stopped dead at what they saw next.

A flight of marble steps led down into a dark courtyard bigger than a stadium and lit only by clusters of the same glowing crystals they'd seen throughout the palace and in the Labyrinth. There were paths winding in multiple directions, fountains trickling into ponds, and gardens full of flowers. Women with different shades of blue and green skin who were dressed like Amphitrite—Zoey assumed they were goddesses or maybe ocean nymphs of some kind—walked along the paths and congregated around the ponds, laughing and talking without a care in the world.

However, the courtyard itself didn't shock Zoey. It wasn't surprising; it belonged outside a palace. What shocked her was what sprawled for miles beyond.

A dome which looked as if it was made of glass encased the palace and courtyard, as though preserving it inside a giant pocket of air. Outside the dome there was blue-black ocean, with valleys and canyons of rock extending for miles. Inside the mountainous structures, millions more crystals glowed, illuminating houses which looked as if they'd been carved into the rocks. Creatures with the heads and torsos of men, but who had fish tails instead of legs, swam in between the buildings alongside large toothy sharks.

Beside Zoey, Andy asked, "Are those . . . mermaids? Er, mermen?"

"I think they might be the sons of Triton by the Nereids," Darko said. "Amphitrite is technically a Nereid, and I think all these other ladies are too." He gestured at the women in the courtyard. "If I remember correctly, Triton is a child of Poseidon and Amphitrite. The *astynomia* don't learn a lot about him because he's a minor god compared to his father, but instead of legs he has the tail of a fish, and so do all his sons."

"Well, I'm calling them mermen," Andy said.

"What do we do next?" Kali asked. "How are we supposed to get through that?" She pointed at the dome.

"The Trident is one of the most powerful magical items in existence," Zoey began. "And it can cause earthquakes and control the oceans and all that. It's gotta be strong enough to break the glass of the dome. What if we used the Trident to crack it? Water would start filling this place like a bathtub, and we could let the Pocket-Sized Submarine grow and climb into it before the whole place floods."

"I don't think they're going to let us just waltz in and break their dome," Darko said, gesturing at the Nereids in the courtyard.

"Do you have a better plan?" Zoey asked.

The satyr shook his head. "Not really."

"Sounds like that's what we're doing, then," Andy said, still invisible. "Let's go." They started down the marble stairs.

Rumbles like cracks of thunder sounded in the air, and the ground began to tremble. The Nereids in the courtyard shrieked. Zoey yelped, stumbling, trying not to lose her footing. Ahead there was a *thud*, and Andy reappeared. He tumbled down the stairs, the Helm flying off his head.

"Andy!" Zoey cried.

He landed at the bottom of the flight, the Trident still in hand, then turned and gave Zoey a quick thumbs-up. "I'm okay," he said.

The Helm stopped rolling ten feet ahead of him, bouncing up and down as the ground shook. A collective gasp sounded through the courtyard. The Nereids had stopped walking and talking and laughing, now staring at Andy and the rest of the group in shock.

From somewhere inside the palace, a man bellowed. It

was a sound so loud and angry and ancient it sounded as though it could swallow entire continents.

"*Where is my Trident?*"

CHAPTER SEVENTEEN

CETUS

Zoey's stomach clenched.

She glanced over her shoulder to find no one was behind them, but the man's voice echoed across the courtyard. Zoey, Darko, and Kali leapt down the last several stairs.

"We have to hurry," Zoey said.

The Nereids in the courtyard drew knives from their skirts and stalked toward the group, their delicate features twisting from shock to fury. There had to be at least fifteen of them.

"It's the traitors who put Hades and Persephone in Tartarus," one said, her voice far too sweet for the horrible expression on her face and the sharp blade in her hand. "Get the Helm and the Trident back and kill these intruders."

Darko clopped ahead and grabbed the Helm before the Nereids could, while Andy scrambled to his feet and charged for them, brandishing the Trident. "Stay back! I know how to use this!"

He slammed the base of the Trident down, and to

Zoey's surprise, the force shook the ground beneath the Nereids like an earthquake, sending them screeching and falling backward. Andy glanced over his shoulder at the rest of the group, his lips in the shape of an O as though he hadn't meant to do that.

"*Where is my Trident?*" Poseidon boomed again from inside the palace. It seemed as if his voice was getting closer.

Zoey seized the Pocket-Sized Submarine from her robes. "Andy, break a hole in the dome. We have to activate the submarine and get out of here!"

The group dashed pell-mell to the left side of the courtyard, toward the closest wall of the glass dome, darting around clusters of glowing crystals, the earth beneath them trembling still. The Nereids climbed to their feet and stumbled after.

Within minutes the group reached the glass. A brown-haired merman swam down to stare at them curiously, but when Andy reared back the Trident as though he were about to bat a home run, the merman's expression morphed into one of terror and he splashed away.

With a yell, Andy slammed the Trident's prongs against the glass. The dome cracked in all directions from the point where Andy hit it, until stopping twenty feet above their heads.

Frigid ocean water began spilling into the courtyard and over Zoey's bare feet. The water felt like icicles stabbing her skin, but she refused to waver. She threw the Pocket-Sized Submarine into the liquid and hurried backward. "Give it space to grow," she told the others, and they backed away with her, the water pooling around their calves.

Behind them, the Nereids snarled in rage. The group swung around to see the nymphs racing toward them, blades ready. Andy ran forward and splashed the base of the Trident through the water and against the ground, sending shudders so powerful through the earth and liquid the nymphs went toppling back.

The glass dome made a sound like a groan, and Zoey turned to see it fracturing farther and farther in all directions, the ocean shooting violently through its cracks. The Pocket-Sized Submarine was unfolding itself like bronze paper. With each passing second it grew larger, taking form, tipping back and forth as the water continued to spill into the courtyard.

"*Where is my Trident?*" Poseidon roared from inside the palace, this time louder than any other. A monstrous *boom* sounded, and the golden entryway doors flew off their hinges and down the staircase, then crashed into a fountain.

Poseidon came bounding down the stairs, Amphitrite at his side. His white robes billowed behind him, each step shaking the courtyard. Even from this far away, the god possessed a commanding presence, ancient power more potent than that of the Helm's and the Trident's emanating from him now that he was awake and upset.

The Nereids ran toward him when they saw him. "We tried to stop them, good Lord of the Seas, we tried," they cried over and over. "It's the traitors, the traitors who stole the Helm of Darkness from King Hades. They have taken your Trident."

Poseidon waved a hand dismissively at the Nereids as he reached the bottom of the steps, then turned to the group and glowered. "How dare you steal from the gods," he boomed. "You will pay with your lives for this. I do not care if my brother wanted to keep you alive before. Doing so is pure idiocy. This ends now."

Zoey walked backward toward the Pocket-Sized Submarine, the icy liquid tugging at her waist, her legs numb. By this time, it was the size of a small car and was shaped like an elongated oval with a flat top and bottom, three circular windows on each side and one in the front and rear. What appeared to be rotors attached to its back and underside unfolded themselves, a door on the side closest to Zoey popping open. Inside, a few lightbulbs flickered on to reveal compartments, spinning gears and cogs, and five seats: two in the front, three in the back.

The glass dome groaned again, fracturing even more, a waterfall of ocean tumbling down.

"Get in!" Zoey shouted, saltwater pelting her in the face. She coughed and spluttered. "Get into the submarine!"

The group wasted no time. Kali clambered in first, then kneeled at the door and pulled Zoey and Darko out of the water and into the sub. They scrambled toward the back, cold water dripping off them and onto the smooth metallic floor. Outside, Andy shoved the Trident into the sub. He began climbing in, but Kali grabbed him under the arms and heaved him up before he could finish.

"Do we have everything?" Kali asked, putting her hand on the door once Andy was safely inside. "The Helm, the Trident?"

Zoey quickly glanced around. The Helm was secure under Darko's arm, and the Trident lay beside Andy. "Yes," she said. Kali slammed the door shut and sealed it. From the rear window, Zoey could see Poseidon as he charged toward them. He waved his arms, parting the water as he advanced.

The dome groaned, this time louder than any other, and Zoey watched through the front and side windows as cracks spread farther and farther across the glass until a colossal chunk broke away and plummeted into the water beside them. Angry ocean whirled up and around the submarine, sending them spinning. The force tossed them against the walls. They screamed. When the sub finally slowed to a stop, Zoey's stomach still churning, all that was visible outside was blue-black water and the blurred outline of glowing crystals, glass fragments swirling around.

Andy clambered to the front of the submarine. He jumped into the driver's seat, a nautical-styled steering wheel in front of it. There was a dashboard of buttons and levers beside the wheel and two pedals under his feet.

"You think you know how to drive this thing?" Zoey asked.

"I don't," Andy said, pounding the buttons. A pair of

headlights flashed on, illuminating Poseidon's palace before them. It was completely submerged in water now. "But I have a driver's license, and I used to play a lot of video games. I'll figure it out."

Zoey scrambled past Darko and Kali and into the seat next to Andy. She looked over the dashboard, panic brewing in her chest. "And how exactly does playing a lot of video games help you drive a magical submarine?"

"Like this," Andy said, pulling the lever closest to the wheel all the way down and pressing on one of the pedals. The submarine sped forward. Andy grabbed the steering wheel and spun it to the right. The submarine flung around. He slammed his foot on the pedal, and they shot through the water straight ahead.

Zoey peered into the blue-black abyss, catching glimpses of broken glass, mermen, sharks, and rocks as they flashed in all directions. "I think we lost Poseidon."

"Uh, we didn't, actually," Darko said at the rear end of the sub, his tone laced with fear. "He's right behind us." Zoey looked back to see the sea god, his face contorted with rage, as he darted through the water like a fish.

"Does this thing go any faster?" Zoey cried. Andy pressed his foot down harder on the pedal, and the submarine sped up.

"Is he gone?" Andy asked a few minutes later. "I think this is the fastest it goes."

Zoey looked back again. She guessed they had to be going over a hundred miles per hour, zigzagging through the canyons and valleys, but within moments Poseidon was visible in the rear window. "He's catching up," Zoey said.

"We don't have any other options left," Andy said, tensing. "We have to fight."

"Do you think we're ready?" Zoey asked, then took a deep breath, trying to calm her racing heart as the realization hit her. It didn't matter if they were ready. Whether they were or not, Poseidon wasn't going to let them go.

Andy tugged the wheel back, and the sub tipped upward. They raced toward the surface, Poseidon swimming behind. "Eventually we're going to have to battle a whole pantheon of gods if we wanna save Diana and the twins. If we wanna save the world. Besides, we have the Helm, the Trident, and ourselves." Zoey swallowed hard. She understood what Andy meant.

While they traveled, Kali opened the compartments on the upper sides of the sub. Sheathed weapons—spears, swords, daggers, and a bow and quivers of arrows—fell out from them. "Lucky for us, Marina and Troy must have been paranoid," she said.

After about ten minutes, the submarine broke the surface. Up here the sun was hidden behind gray clouds, rain drizzling down. Kali grabbed the spear she'd found, while Darko slung a quiver of arrows over his back and readied his bow, Andy picking up the Trident.

Zoey made sure her dagger and axe were secure at her belt, then pulled the Helm over her head, chills passing through her as she disappeared. She was terrified, more terrified even than when she'd been at the edge of Tartarus. They'd never battled a god as powerful as Poseidon. In fact, the only god they'd ever fought was Persephone, and they wouldn't have been able to survive the encounter without Karter's help. Zoey didn't know what to expect. She had no idea if they could win this.

Andy opened a door on the roof of the sub and climbed out. Darko went next, then Kali, then Zoey. When Zoey stepped onto the top of the sub, she readied her axe. The group situated themselves back-to-back then, staring out at thousands of miles of ocean, preparing for a showdown with the God of the Sea.

They waited.

And waited.

And waited.

But nothing happened.

Darko lowered his bow. "Where is he? He was right behind us."

As if in reply to Darko's question, something burst from the water hundreds of feet away. Waves crashed toward the submarine and tipped it back and forth, nearly sending the group toppling into the ocean. Zoey yelped, dropping her axe into the water as they stumbled to their knees, holding onto each other so they wouldn't fall.

A shadow passed over them, and Zoey looked up to see what it was. Any shred of hope she may have had for victory dissolved the instant she laid eyes on it.

Before them rose the largest creature she'd ever seen. It

looked like a snake with pointy fins extending all the way down its back, its eyes yellow, its scales silver. Its head alone was the size of a bus, a long tail thrashing behind it for as far as she could see. Bloody fish guts were stuck between its sharp teeth, each one long enough to shish-kebab everyone standing on the submarine.

Atop the creature's head kneeled Poseidon, another young man Zoey hadn't seen yet sitting next to the god. He had a shock of curly white hair, skin the same shade as Poseidon's, and a navy-colored fish tail instead of legs, a large twisting seashell in hand. *That must be Triton*, Zoey thought. *Son of Poseidon and Amphitrite.*

Zoey stood up straight, trying not to succumb to her fear. Was her father watching over her? What about Spencer? If they were, could they protect her now? Give her strength?

She knew one thing: if this was the end, at least she'd go down fighting for humanity alongside people she cared about.

"Greetings, traitors," Poseidon said, his booming voice reverberating through the air. "Allow me to make this simple for you. Hand over the objects of power you have stolen, and I will ensure your deaths are swift and painless. If not, you will suffer greatly and die slowly and horribly."

No one said anything, but Andy brandished the Trident at Poseidon. Zoey shot the boy a wide-eyed look; his expression was determined, but it twitched as if fear was threatening to overcome him at any moment.

Poseidon sneered, and the sea-serpent monster inched closer to the group. "Your attempt to remain brave is commendable, and if you're as idiotic as you look, you might even think you have a chance to survive. However, against me, my son Triton, and the Trojan Cetus"—he gestured at the sea monster—"a creature so strong only Heracles has been able to defeat it, I can assure you that you have no chance. Stand down."

Andy spread his feet and crouched down. His wings unfolded and extended far above his head, and he leapt into the air and flapped them furiously. He flew without wavering—higher and higher—until he was eye level with the Sea God. The Trojan Cetus hissed.

Poseidon drew back a little, staring at Andy as if he'd seen the boy before and was trying to place from where. "It cannot be. This—this is impossible. You faded away centuries ago. Anteros?"

Now it was Andy's turn to look confused. "Wait, what? I'm not Anteros."

"You are not," Triton piped up. His voice was softer than his father's, more boyish. "And yet, you must be. I met you before. You do not look exactly as you did—you look like a mortal now—but your divine essence is unmistakable."

Zoey remembered what Amphitrite had said to her in the hall earlier: *For a moment you almost looked like a mortal. But no, you couldn't be. Your divine essence is unmistakable.*

Then she thought of the question she'd asked the Fates the first time she met them: *"Why are our threads of life so special? You said they turned white and started to glow, but what does that mean?"*

"We cannot say," they'd said. *"In time, you will discover it for yourself."*

The realization hit Zoey like a truck.

She ripped the Helm off her head. "Andy, that's it!" she yelled. He looked down at her. "No god is trying to give us powers. We had powers all along, but they only started to come back after you touched the statue and then me. Somehow, we must be gods, but in mortal form. *We* are Anteros and Calliope—that's why you were so drawn to the statue and why when we died in the Storm, our life threads turned white and started to glow."

Poseidon turned to Zoey. "Calliope? But how . . . If both of you faded away, then why would you try to usurp the gods for humanity? They are the very reason you . . ." He trailed off, then shook his head. "It is no matter. This does not change the fact that you are both traitors. It does not change the prophecy foretold, nor the fact that you conspired against the gods. You must be killed."

Poseidon dove off one side of the Trojan Cetus, the side closest to Andy, waving his arms in circular motions as he came down. The water beneath him swirled up toward him. He did a flip, the spinning water swishing into a tsunami wave. The wave paused, suspended midair. Poseidon landed on the liquid as if it were solid. Upon impact it rippled within itself but kept its shape.

The Lord of the Seas looked to Triton and the Trojan Cetus. "My son, I task you with retrieving the Helm of Darkness while I take back my Trident. And Cetus"—the sea monster turned to Poseidon—"you may have the mortal girl and the satyr aiding Anteros and Calliope. Only after the Trident and the Helm are safe with me may you take them as well."

The Trojan Cetus nodded, licking its teeth with a forked tongue the color of ash. Poseidon faced Andy and raised his arms. The tsunami wave shot up at lightning speed, lifting the god with it, straight for Andy.

Triton leapt off the sea monster and splashed into the water, then swam toward Zoey like a shark stalking its prey. *Crap!* she thought, tugging the Helm over her head and disappearing. She ripped the dagger from her belt. *Why'd I take this off in the first place?*

Darko loosed an arrow at the god. It pierced him where neck met shoulder. He stopped, screaming in pain, golden blood trickling into the water.

The assault only bought them seconds. Triton raised the large twisting seashell to his lips and blew into it. A sound like a car horn trumpeted across the sky, and a *crack* of thunder split the clouds above. The ocean pushed the submarine back and forth, the rain beginning to teem.

Darko and Kali were pitched off the sub. Zoey cried out, slipping off the edge. Freezing saltwater swarmed her. It stung her eyes and filled her nose and mouth.

Someone took hold of her arm, the arm without a hand, and pulled her up. She blinked and spluttered and gasped. Her vision was blurry, drenched curls stuck to her face, but she could tell it was Triton. With one hand the god held her, and with the other, he seized the Helm off her head, taking it for himself.

Triton shoved Zoey deep underneath the surface. She paddled, swimming up, but he kicked her down with his tail. *The knife*, she remembered, bubbles flying from her lips as air escaped her lungs. *I still have the knife.*

Triton brought his tail down at her again, as if to push her farther beneath. She clenched her hand around the dagger, mustering every bit of strength she had, and slashed his tail with the blade. He squirmed and she wrenched it out, then thrashed again blindly. She felt the dagger rip through something rigid and textured, as though it was tearing through Triton's scales and the flesh beneath.

His tail kicked frantically. Golden liquid clouded the water. Zoey paddled out of the way and toward the surface.

She flung her head out of the water and gulped several deep breaths. She did her best to rub the liquid out of her eyes so she could see, the ocean churning. Twenty feet to the right, Kali tugged a spear from the center of Triton's back, Darko splashing nearby. The god went still and floated belly-up.

The waters calmed the moment Triton "died," the rain lessening into a drizzle, but Zoey's stomach fell. In all the chaos of fighting him, she'd forgotten he'd taken the Helm of Darkness from her. What if Triton dropped it and it was sinking to the bottom of the ocean right now? "Darko," she called. "Kali! The Helm . . ." Darko lifted his arm to reveal he had the Helm in hand, and Zoey breathed a sigh of relief.

A shadow came over them, a hiss sounding from the left. Zoey turned to see the Trojan Cetus slithering through the water toward her, raising its head high above the surface, its forked tongue flicking across its teeth.

In that moment, Zoey froze. She felt as if time itself stood still. Fighting Triton had been difficult enough—she'd almost drowned doing it—and she hadn't even been the one to kill him in the end. That was Kali's doing. All she had for a weapon was this knife, and she was missing her dominant hand. Not to mention she was in the middle of the ocean sitting before a gigantic ancient sea monster. She didn't stand a chance—not any at all.

Why should she try? She'd tried to get the Helm from Persephone in Tartarus, and it had ended in losing her hand. She'd tried to save Karter in Hephaestus City, and it had ended in getting everyone captured. Why would this be any different?

The monster reared back as if ready to strike, and Zoey caught a glimpse of Andy in the distance, fluttering through the sky, Trident in hand. Poseidon rode the tsunami wave, wielding ropes of water and lashing Andy with them, over and over. Andy used the Trident to block the assaults, but he seemed to be growing tired. He wavered. It looked as if he might finally fall.

"You leave her alone!" Kali yelled, and Zoey looked up. A spear soared for the sea monster. The weapon bounced off the creature's head, not a scratch made. The Trojan Cetus turned its attention to Kali, hissing all the while.

Andy is fighting a god by himself, Zoey thought. *And Kali made a last-ditch effort to get the monster's attention off you. And you can't even try to fight this thing?*

It was then that time started again. Suddenly the fact that Zoey had barely been able to survive the fight with Triton didn't matter. The fact that she'd not been the one to kill him didn't matter; the fact that all she had was a knife for a weapon didn't matter. Her missing dominant hand didn't matter.

Fate had chosen her to overcome all odds. She'd fallen in the face of adversity, and now she chose to rise again.

Zoey loosened her grip on the dagger and let it sink. A crazy idea crossed her mind, a thought so insane it might not work. But that didn't matter. She had to try.

She focused on the Trojan Cetus, focused on talking it out of serving Poseidon, focused on talking it out of eating her and her friends.

Her throat began to tingle.

"Trojan Cetus," she said. Her voice sounded commanding and powerful, like how she would imagine a great goddess to speak. The monster turned to her. She thought she saw a flicker of surprise in its yellow gaze.

"Has Poseidon really diminished you to this?" she

asked. "Has he really lessened your worth so much that all he would ask of you is to kill *us*? Doesn't he see how weak and insignificant we are? We're only mortal and unarmed, powerless against you, the great Trojan Cetus."

The monster leaned in, as if it were dying to hear what she had to say next.

"Killing us won't bring glory to your name, at least not the glory it deserves," Zoey continued. "Killing us will only keep you as a pawn of Poseidon, of the gods. Do you want to stay a pawn forever, or would you prefer to be the master of your own destiny?" She paused for dramatic effect. "If you choose the latter, then I ask you to side with us against the gods. If you do, if you defeat Poseidon today in the name of humanity, your name will go down in history as the greatest creature to have ever lived."

The Trojan Cetus dipped beneath the surface and slithered toward her. *No, this can't be*, she thought, her confidence sucked away in an instant. *It didn't work and now this thing is going to eat me and kill my friends and—*

Rough scales rubbed against her feet, her legs, and she went up, up, up, out of the water, until she was suspended fifty feet in the air. She sat on her hand and knees atop the head of the Trojan Cetus, dripping with saltwater and trembling in fear and perhaps, now that she realized what was happening, excitement.

Still paddling in the water below, Darko and Kali gawked at her in awe. She gave them a small smile, then turned toward Andy and Poseidon in the distance. The

Sea God conjured another tsunami wave and shoved it at Andy. The boy tried to flap away but was sucked into the barrel.

"Andy!" Zoey cried.

When the wave died down, Andy was gone.

Zoey grabbed the sea monster's slippery fin as best she could despite being soaked herself. "Trojan Cetus," she said. The tingling in her throat began to spread through her, growing until her whole body seemed to thrum with power. "You will bring glory to your name today. You will take charge of your own destiny, no longer a pawn of the gods. Defeat Poseidon, retrieve the Trident, and save the winged boy!"

The Trojan Cetus launched itself through the water toward Poseidon. Zoey held on tight, wind and rain whipping her in the face.

In seconds they reached Poseidon. He'd already allowed his tsunami wave to diminish. It looked as if he was about to dive into the water, to go after his Trident no doubt. When he saw Zoey and the Trojan Cetus approaching, his expression twisted in rage.

"What is the meaning of this, Cetus?" he boomed. "Kill her! Kill Calliope!"

The sea monster hissed, rearing back as if to strike. Poseidon waved his hands, drawing up a wall of ocean between himself and the sea monster and thrusting it forward. The water-wall collided into Zoey and the Trojan Cetus. The creature didn't budge, but Zoey cried out and went tumbling down its back, scraping her knees and elbows all the way down until she crashed through the surface, her skin stinging at the impact. She began sinking down.

Saltwater bit into her scratches, her body aching, but she swam back up. She didn't get this far to let Poseidon win.

"—spell should be worn off now," she heard Poseidon say as the water cleared from her ears, his tone full of irritation. She swung around to see the sea monster hovering over the god, jaws wide open, tongue licking its teeth. "Have you forgotten that you serve me, Cetus? Let me remind you the gods allowed you to live again because of me, because I advocated for your recreation. You are a creature of the sea, and thus belong to *me*, and so you will do as I say, not what some treacherous Harpy tells you to do. Now go and kill the traitors!"

The creature paused for a moment, as if recognizing who Poseidon was and realizing what it was doing.

"Now, Trojan Cetus," Zoey commanded, energy humming through her. "Bring glory to your name! Defeat the Lord of the Seas!"

The Trojan Cetus hissed and lunged for Poseidon. Poseidon screamed as the sea monster plucked him up with its teeth in one quick motion and flung him down its throat.

Poseidon was gone for now, but Zoey's senses flooded with panic. She looked around frantically, trying to see through the water surrounding, but Andy was nowhere, only vast strokes of deep liquid blue.

"Trojan Cetus," Zoey said, her voice tremoring. What if Andy was gone forever? "Please save the boy. Please save the boy with the white feathered wings." The sea monster dove out of sight.

A few moments later, the Trojan Cetus rose again, this time next to Zoey and just barely out of the water. Andy lay on its head, eyes closed, cheeks pale, completely still.

Zoey gasped and pulled herself up onto the creature, scrambling to Andy's side. "Andy," she said, shaking him. "Andy, wake up."

He didn't respond. She pressed her fingers against his neck. A pulse throbbed ever so faintly. However, his chest wasn't rising and falling. It didn't seem like he was breathing. Was there water trapped in his lungs? In his air passageways? How could she fix it?

She lifted him into a sitting position. She had no idea what she was doing, but she had to do something, anything to save him. He couldn't die. Not like this.

Water spilled from his mouth and nose. He began hacking, more liquid flying out, and she swallowed back tears. He was okay. It was okay. Everything was okay.

When he finally stopped coughing and caught his breath, he turned to her, confusion in his eyes. Beneath the storm clouds, they looked even more gray than usual. "What happened?"

"Poseidon and Triton are dead for now," Zoey said. "Kali, Darko, and I took care of Triton. And I, uh, convinced our new friend here it was in his best interest to help us instead of the gods, and he ate Poseidon in one swallow. Didn't even chew. I don't know how long it will take for Poseidon to regenerate now, but I'm guessing we at least have time to escape."

Andy looked down, sucking in a sharp breath when he saw he sat atop the Trojan Cetus. "Uh, okay, that's badass. And the Trident?"

Zoey had nearly forgotten about the Trident, but now that she'd used her powers to get the sea monster on their side, she had no doubt it would help them.

"Trojan Cetus?" she said, her throat tingling. "Would you finish your mission today by bringing the Trident to me, so Poseidon can never use it to control you or any other sea creature again?"

The Trojan Cetus rose a bit more out of the water, revealing the Trident as it lay farther down its back. Andy grinned, making his way toward it and grabbing it. "Uh, thanks, man. For, you know, helping out and not eating us and stuff."

Zoey and Andy hopped off the sea monster and splashed into the water. As it stared at them now, completely calm and not out to eat anyone, it almost seemed cute—at least, in a weird, monster-y way. If Zoey had been able to get it on their side without the use of magic, she would have considered bringing it with them, at least until they got to land, but she wasn't sure how long her magic would last, and if the creature would realize she'd convinced it to betray its master.

"I promise to repay you for what you've done today," Zoey said, unsure of how to say goodbye. "Your name will go down in history. You know, as a hero."

The sea monster slipped beneath the surface and disappeared.

CHAPTER EIGHTEEN

JOURNEY

"Uh, where're Darko and Kali?" Andy asked.

As if it weren't confusing enough to wake up after getting totally owned by Poseidon and have Zoey tell him she'd single-handedly taken care of the god and his crazy pet sea monster with her new mystical voice-powers, when Andy looked around, Darko, Kali, and their Not-So-Pocket-Sized-Submarine were nowhere in sight, miles of ocean before them.

"Oh no," Zoey said beside him. She pointed farther out. "They were right over there when I last saw them. They wouldn't have just left. What if the Trojan Cetus—"

Before she could finish her sentence, something shiny and bronze rose from the water several yards away. Andy grinned.

Their submarine's top door popped open, and Darko and Kali poked their heads out.

"Ahoy there, mateys," Andy said in his best pirate voice. When he'd first seen the nautical-styled steering wheel in the submarine he'd wanted to say something silly like that, but they'd been running for their lives, so it wasn't exactly the right time.

Zoey giggled, while Darko and Kali raised eyebrows at Andy. "Is that some kind of secret code, or did you hit your head when Poseidon smashed you with that wave?" Kali asked, her tone laced with sarcasm. Now it was Darko's turn to laugh.

Andy chuckled and rolled his eyes. "Wow, I knew there'd be a warm welcoming committee when I got back from the biggest battle of my life, but I didn't realize it was going to be this awesome. Thanks, Kali."

"You're welcome," Kali replied sweetly.

Andy and Zoey swam to the sub. Darko and Kali helped pull them inside, and soon they were safe, secure, and soaked.

Kali shut the door and sealed it. "What now?"

"Well, we need to get to land," Darko said. "That's west of us. Then we have to start in the direction of New Mount Olympus to meet up with the nymphs."

"Let's start with 'west,'" Andy said, setting the Trident on the floor. "I can figure out which way we need to go by looking at the sun when it starts to set. Then, after we get together with the nymphs, we can save Diana and the others."

"You make it sound so easy when you say it like that," Zoey said. "But you know it's going to be a more complicated journey than that, right?" She gave him a dazzling smile, her blue eyes shining.

He recalled the talk he and Zoey had before going into the Labyrinth. How he'd told her about his feelings for her, and in turn how she'd told him the truth about her past—then the way he'd reacted.

He wanted to tell her he was sorry, that he wasn't being fair to her when he'd reacted that way. He wanted to tell her none of those things mattered, because in the end it didn't change who she was. And it didn't change the fact that he loved her. Yes, he loved her.

An image of Anteros and Calliope dancing in the garden flashed across his mind. Was he really Anteros, and Zoey Calliope, like Zoey had suggested? How did that work, anyway? And if it was true, was that why he had feelings for Zoey? Was it some sort of freaky past-life phenomenon, and why he'd always been drawn to her?

He smiled back at Zoey, pushing thoughts like those away. There was time to figure out his questions later. Besides, even if there was some god inside him or he was a god or whatever the hell was going on, it didn't change the way he felt about her, and it didn't change the fact that he needed to apologize to her for what happened before. He couldn't do it now, not in front of Darko and Kali, but he'd do it soon.

When the time is right, he thought. *I'll tell her I'm sorry.*

Soon the sun began to set, and Andy steered them west.

* ~ * ~ * ~

Zeus stood atop the sprawling balcony outside his bed-chamber, overlooking the Garden of Olympus as night fell.

There were only a few days left until the Daughter of Apollo would arrive; he knew this from the visions he had received recently. From there, Karter would execute her.

"My son," Zeus whispered, a sneer on his lips. "You have always been an important pawn of the game. *My* game."

The King of the Gods chuckled, satisfied. Soon the war would be over, the Dreaded Prophecy diminished to nothing, just as destiny had always intended for the Greek pantheon. Finally, they would never have to worry about being forgotten and fading away again.

Of course, a few complications had arisen. Something always did. First there was the fact that Apollo had betrayed Zeus: his own son, and a fellow Olympian! Yes, it was time Apollo be cast into Tartarus. The deed could not be postponed any longer. Zeus would have to appoint someone else to take over Apollo's duties, but it would not be hard to do. Any god or goddess would gladly volunteer for the opportunity to take Apollo's title.

Not only that, but Hephaestus's insufferable twin grandchildren, Troy and Marina, had been captured alongside the Daughter of Apollo. Apparently, they were guilty of aiding the enemy. After Zeus had allowed them to live in such a privileged manner after the lies their mother spat, this was how they chose to repay him? They would die for it. In fact, they would be struck with green lightning as soon as they arrived on Olympus.

But the complications did not stop there. Prometheus—the cockroach—and the Chosen Two of the Prophecy—may they burn in Tartarus for all eternity—had escaped capture. Zeus had already decided Prometheus would pay for his insolence with a punishment far more severe than the last, and the Chosen Two would suffer so greatly they would beg for Zeus to stop their hearts.

Oh, Zeus wished he could kill those wretched, mortal nuisances. He wished more than anything he could drain the life from them, watch their faces twist with horror and anguish—but he could not. The visions had brought him more knowledge than just how the war would end with the Daughter of Apollo's execution. He could not risk the development of a second prophecy after all the trouble this one had caused him.

Purple light flashed from behind, illuminating Zeus's surroundings. The god swung around to find another one of his Olympian sons, Hermes, stepping through a shimmering oval-shaped portal and onto the balcony. The Messenger of the Gods usually held a cunning expression, his mouth turned in a crooked smile and his eyes glittering with mischief. However, tonight his face was drawn into a frown of concern. His black hair—always slicked back with cosmetic oils—was tousled and uncombed.

"What is it?" Zeus asked, immediately aware that something else must have gone wrong. If Karter and the rest of Zeus's demigod warriors had lost the Daughter of

Apollo, Zeus swore on the River Styx they would regret ever being born.

"It's Poseidon," Hermes said, almost frantically. "There was an attack on his palace. The Trident was stolen."

"By the mortals from the Before?"

"Yes—Triton and Amphitrite saw them. We still haven't found Poseidon, but—"

Zeus held up a hand to silence Hermes, electricity crackling along his fingertips. This was a dilemma, yes, but it would not take long to resolve. Even without the Helm of Darkness and Poseidon's Trident, the gods were unstoppable. They still had the Master Lightning Bolt, which dwarfed all other magical items with its power. Besides, Zeus had seen in his visions that the death of the Daughter of Apollo would bring a new era of peace to the gods. This was a minor inconvenience, nothing more. Zeus was sure of it.

"There is no need to worry," the King of the Gods said. "No need at all. Those two have only gotten this far through fantastical strokes of luck, which end now. I already sent Artemis and her Huntresses to search for those filthy insects, and have you ever known Artemis to lose a hunt?"

To be continued in the final installment of the War on the Gods trilogy . . .

THE MASTER LIGHTNING BOLT

A. P. Mobley is a young-adult fantasy author with an undying love for Greek mythology and epic, magical tales. She grew up in Wyoming and currently lives there, working part-time as a substitute teacher and studying to earn her degree in English. She considers herself a huge nerd, loves chocolate a little too much, and can be found snuggling with one of her pets into late hours of the night.

Follow her on Twitter and Instagram:
@author_apmobley.

If you liked *Poseidon's Trident*, make sure to leave it a review on Amazon and Goodreads! Reviews help authors, and if you'd like to see more stories from A. P. Mobley, reviewing her books is the best way to support her.

ACKNOWLEDGMENTS

There are several people who had a hand in the production of this book that I want to thank.

First, my editor, Nikki Mentges at NAM Editorial. You help me so much in improving my work, and I learn something every time we work together. I hope that as time goes on, I will only continue learning from you.

Next, my illustrator, Gabrielle Ragusi. You make the most incredible art and I can't imagine anyone else working on the illustrations for this project.

Third, my formatters, Megan and Josh at Cloud Kitten Publishing. You guys work so hard and are just beyond stellar in everything you do.

Last, Jenna Moreci, one of my favorite authors and biggest inspirations. Even though this book is technically my third published work, I still found myself watching your YouTube videos to make it the best I could.